Prophe
for Every Season

Twelve Months
of Prophetic Power

(Volume 1)

– –

Breakthrough prayers to maximise
and navigate your seasons in life.

– –

Dr Sola Fola-Alade

Prophetic Prayers for Every Season
(Volume 1)

ISBN: 978-1-7392730-4-0

Published by:
Empowerment Initiatives Ltd
(also trading as Vision Media Communication)
Email: registrar@empowermentuniversity.com

Printed in the United Kingdom

Dedication

This book is dedicated to the army of praying people God is raising at this time who will wield their spiritual swords intelligently in prayer warfare to take back individuals, families, and territories for God's glory.

"Blessing I will bless you, and multiplying I will multiply your descendants as the stars of the heaven and as the sand which is on the seashore; and your descendants shall possess the gate of their enemies"

- Genesis 22:17

Dr Sola Fola-Alade

August 2024

Contents

Introduction

Every season of life comes with its unique challenges, opportunities, and spiritual battles.

Just as the natural world cycles through winter, spring, summer, and autumn, our lives also experience seasons of planting, growth, harvest, and rest. These seasons are not random; they are divinely orchestrated to shape us, to build our faith, and to draw us closer to God's purpose for our lives.

"Prophetic Prayers for Every Season: Twelve Months of Prophetic Power" is a guide designed to help you navigate these spiritual seasons with precision and authority. This book is not just a collection of prayers; it is a spiritual tool equipped with prophetic declarations that align your heart and mind with God's will for each specific season of your life. Whether you find yourself in a season of breakthrough, waiting, warfare, or celebration, these prayers are crafted to empower you to maximise the potential of each moment.

The foundation of this book lies in the belief that prayer is a powerful, divine weapon. When wielded correctly, it can change atmospheres, to unlock doors that have been long shut, and to propel you into the fullness of God's plan. The prayers contained within this book are not mere words; they are prophetic declarations - designed to be spoken aloud, with authority, and with the expectation that Heaven will respond.

The Bible tells us in Ecclesiastes 3:1:

> *"To everything, there is a season, and a time for every purpose under heaven."*

Just as every season in the natural has its appropriate actions - planting in spring, harvesting in autumn - so too does every spiritual season have its appropriate prayers and declarations. Recognising the season you are in and praying accordingly is a key to walking in victory and purpose.

This book is divided into twelve sections, each corresponding to a month of the year, with a specific theme for that season. Each section contains four weeks of prayers, structured to guide you through the month, helping you to stay in tune with God's timing and purpose for your life. As you pray through each week, you will find that your spiritual sensitivity increases, your faith is strengthened, and your capacity to hear God's voice is sharpened.

I encourage you to approach this book with an open heart, ready to engage with God on a deeper level. These prayers are not just to be read; they are to be declared with conviction, believing that as you speak, the very words you utter are being enforced by the armies of Heaven.

In the journey of life, there are seasons that will stretch you, seasons that will break you, and seasons that will build you. But through it all, God is with you, guiding you with His hand and speaking to you through His Word.

As you journey through these twelve months of prophetic prayers, may you find the strength to face every challenge, the wisdom to discern every opportunity, and the faith to walk boldly into the future that God has prepared for you.

Let this book be your companion, your guide, and your spiritual weapon as you navigate the seasons of life. Each prayer is a step closer to aligning with God's perfect will for your life.

May you experience breakthrough, deliverance, and divine favour as you embark on this journey of prophetic prayer.

SECTION 1

Preparation

Prayers to Maximise Seasons

Father Lord, help me to be sensitive to the leading of the Holy Spirit, to understand that which you want me to prioritise in this season.

> "But Martha was distracted by all the preparations that had to be made. She came to him and asked, "Lord, don't you care that my sister has left me to do the work by myself? Tell her to help me!" "Martha, Martha," the Lord answered, "you are worried and upset about many things, but few things are needed—or indeed only one. Mary has chosen what is better, and it will not be taken away from her.""
> - *Luke 10:40-42*

Heavenly Father, help me to awaken from sleep and rise to fulfil purpose.

"This is why it is said: "Wake up, sleeper, rise from the dead, and Christ will shine on you."
- *Ephesians 5:14*

I pray for the wisdom to prepare and position myself for seasons of opportunities.

"Be very careful, then, how you live—not as unwise but as wise." - *Ephesians 5:15*

Dear Lord, help me to take advantage of each opportunity and use it with wisdom and diligence.

"Making the most of every opportunity, because the days are evil." - *Ephesians 5:16*

Father Lord, help me to understand the purpose for the various positions I occupy and give me the grace to work diligently where I am so that I can be promoted.

"When Esther's words were reported to Mordecai, he sent back this answer: "Do not think that because you are in the king's house you alone of all the Jews will escape. For if you remain silent at this time, relief and deliverance for the Jews will arise from another place, but you and your father's family will perish. And who knows but that you have come to your royal position for such a time as this?" - *Esther 4:14*

I pray for grace to heed your prophetic direction so that your promises may be fulfilled in my life on time and in season.

"Therefore, wash yourself and anoint yourself, put on your best garment and go down to the threshing floor; but do not make yourself known to the man until he has finished eating and drinking. Then it shall be, when he lies down, that you shall notice the place where he lies; and you shall go in, uncover his feet, and lie down; and he will tell you what you should do." And she said to her, "All that you say to me I will do." - *Ruth 3:3-5*

Heavenly Father, I pray that you will silence every voice speaking against my progress and destiny fulfilment in this season.

"And the angel answered and said to him, "I am Gabriel, who stands in the presence of God, and was sent to speak to you and bring you these glad tidings. But behold, you will be mute and not able to speak until the day these things take place, because you did not believe my words which will be fulfilled in their own time." - *Luke 1:19-20*

"Death and life are in the power of the tongue, and those who love it will eat its fruit." - *Proverbs 18:21*

Prayers for Preparation for Emergence

Heavenly Father, I pray that you will help me to believe in your word and that which is spoken through your prophets so that I will prosper.

> "So, they rose early in the morning and went out into the Wilderness of Tekoa; and as they went out, Jehoshaphat stood and said, "Hear me, O Judah and you inhabitants of Jerusalem: Believe in the Lord your God, and you shall be established; believe His prophets, and you shall prosper." - *2 Chronicles 20:20*

Father Lord, I pray that you will help me to continually seek you and grow in my understanding of you so I will continue to prosper.

"Uzziah was sixteen years old when he became king, and he reigned fifty-two years in Jerusalem. His mother's name was Jecholiah of Jerusalem. And he did what was right in the sight of the Lord, according to all that his father Amaziah had done. He sought God in the days of Zechariah, who had understanding in the visions of God; and as long as he sought the Lord, God made him prosper." - *2 Chronicles 26:3-5*

I pray that I will be a person that can carry the burden of others and stand in the gap for them to stop destruction in their lives and in the land.

"So, I sought for a man among them who would make a wall, and stand in the gap before Me on behalf of the land, that I should not destroy it; but I found no one." - *Ezekiel 22:30*

I pray that I will be a person of significance and weight.

"Also, He said to them, "Is a lamp brought to be put under a basket or under a bed? Is it not to be set on a lampstand? For there is nothing hidden which will not be revealed, nor has anything been kept secret but that it should come to light. If anyone has ears to hear, let him hear." - *Mark 4:21-23*

Heavenly Father, help me to continually set my watch in prayer to see what you will say to me.

"I will stand at my watch and station myself on the ramparts; I will look to see what he will say to me, and what answer I am to give to this complaint." - *Habakkuk 2:1-3*

Heavenly Father, help me to take heed of what you say to me and apply your word in my life so that I may receive more revelations.

"Consider carefully what you hear" he continued. "With the measure you use, it will be measured to you—and even more. Whoever has will be given more; whoever does not have, even what they have will be taken from them." - *Mark 4:23-25*

Dear Lord, I pray that you will help me to adequately incubate your word and prophecies over my life with prayer so that I may carry it to full term, become your word and reveal your glory.

"For the creation waits in eager expectation for the children of God to be revealed." - *Romans 8:19*

"Shall I bring to the time of birth, and not cause delivery?" says the Lord.

"Shall I who cause delivery shut up the womb?" says your God." - *Isaiah 66:9*

Prayers for Preparation for an Upgrade

I pray that I will move from glory to glory, receive a spiritual upgrade and have a change of garment in this season.

> "But you shall receive power when the Holy Spirit has come upon you; and you shall be witnesses to Me in Jerusalem, and in all Judea and Samaria, and to the end of the earth." - *Acts 1:8*

Father Lord, help me to upgrade in prophetic precision and potency.

"Then the Lord came down in the pillar of cloud and stood in the door of the tabernacle and called Aaron and Miriam. And they both went forward. Then He said, "Hear now My words: If there is a prophet among you, I, the Lord, make Myself known to him in a vision; I speak to him in a dream. Not so with My servant Moses; he is faithful in all My house." - *Numbers 12:5-7*

Heavenly Father, give me the grace to fast more to see an increase in revelation, authority and a new level of power.

"Then Jesus answered and said, "O faithless and perverse generation, how long shall I be with you? How long shall I bear with you? Bring him here to Me." And Jesus rebuked the demon, and it came out of him; and the child was cured from that very hour. Then the disciples came to Jesus privately and said, "Why could we not cast it out?" So, Jesus said to them, "Because of your unbelief; for assuredly, I say to you, if you have faith as a mustard seed, you will say to this mountain, 'Move from here to there,' and it will move; and nothing will be impossible for you." - *Matthew 17:17-20*

Father Lord, I pray that you will make me into someone you can partner with to carry greatness.

"And having come in, the angel said to her, "Rejoice, highly favoured one, the Lord is with you; blessed are you among women!" But when she saw him, she was troubled at his saying, and considered what manner of greeting this was. Then the angel said to her, "Do not be afraid, Mary, for you have found favour with God. And behold, you will conceive in your womb and bring forth a Son and shall call His name Jesus. He will be great and will be called the Son of the Highest; and the Lord God will give Him the throne of His father David." - *Luke 1:28-32*

I pray that I will be connected with the right people that will help to grow that which God has spoken over me.

"Now Mary arose in those days and went into the hill country with haste, to a city of Judah, and entered the house of Zacharias and greeted Elizabeth." - *Luke 1:39-40*

I pray that I will walk with the wise so I will be wise, I will not be a companion of fools.

"He who walks with wise men will be wise, but the companion of fools will be destroyed." - *Proverbs 13:20*

I pray that I will increase in prophetic precision and potency, such that I will be able to make decrees that will change the course of my life and that of my family and land.

"And Elijah the Tishbite, of the inhabitants of Gilead, said to Ahab, "As the Lord God of Israel lives, before whom I stand, there shall not be dew nor rain these years, except at my word." - *1 Kings 17:1*

Prayers to Develop Capacity for More

Heavenly Father, I pray that as I build the capacity to make the most of unusual opportunities, that you will open the windows of heaven and pour out a great blessing for me.

> "Bring all the tithes into the storehouse, that there may be food in My house, and try Me now in this," Says the Lord of hosts "If I will not open for you the windows of heaven and pour out for you such blessing that there will not be room enough to receive it." - *Malachi 3:10*

Dear Lord, help me to develop my skills and competence so I will be a person that is sought after.

"Let our master now command your servants, who are before you, to seek out a man who is a skilful player on the harp. And it shall be that he will play it with his hand when the distressing spirit from God is upon you, and you shall be well." So, Saul said to his servants, "Provide me now a man who can play well, and bring him to me." Then one of the servants answered and said, "Look, I have seen a son of Jesse the Bethlehemite, who is skilful in playing, a mighty man of valour, a man of war, prudent in speech, and a handsome person; and the Lord is with him." - *1 Samuel 16:16-18*

I pray that I will grow my leadership and management agility so I will be set over kingdoms (industries) and distinguish myself above others in my field.

"It pleased Darius to set over the kingdom one hundred and twenty satraps, to be over the whole kingdom; and over these, three governors, of whom Daniel was one, that the satraps might give account to them, so that the king would suffer no loss. Then this Daniel distinguished himself above the governors and satraps, because an excellent spirit was in him; and the king gave thought to setting him over the whole realm." - *Daniel 6:1-3*

Father Lord, give me the wisdom required to increase my productive capacity and impact.

"But these are the ones sown on good ground, those who hear the word, accept it, and bear fruit: some thirtyfold, some sixty, and some a hundred."
- *Mark 4:20*

I pray that I will build the right character so I will not manage opportunities irresponsibly.

"When I was a child, I spoke as a child, I understood as a child, I thought as a child; but when I became a man, I put away childish things."
- *1 Corinthians 13:11*

"That we should no longer be children, tossed to and fro and carried about with every wind of doctrine, by the trickery of men, in the cunning craftiness of deceitful plotting." - *Ephesians 4:14*

Heavenly Father, help me to be disciplined and focused so I can become that which you want me to be.

"The labour of fools wearies them, for they do not even know how to go to the city! Woe to you, O land, when your king is a child, And your princes feast in the morning! Blessed are you, O land, when your king is the son of nobles, and your princes feast at the proper time—for strength and not for drunkenness! Because of laziness the building decays, and through idleness of hands the house leaks." - *Ecclesiastes 10:15-18*

Father Lord, please help me to be able to control my emotions so I do not give place to the enemy.

"Be angry, and do not sin": Do not let the sun go down on your wrath, nor give place to the devil."
- *Ephesians 4:26-27*

SECTION 2

Relationships

Prayers on Singleness

Heavenly Father, please give me a divine vision for my marriage.

> "Can two walk together, unless they are agreed?" - *Amos 3:3*

Father Lord, open my eyes and help me to choose the right life partner to go through life with.

> "Therefore, a man shall leave his father and mother and be joined to his wife, and they shall become one flesh." - *Genesis 2:24*

Heavenly Father, grant me the wisdom and discernment to choose a partner that I will be equally yoked with.

"Do not be unequally yoked together with unbelievers. For what fellowship has righteousness with lawlessness? And what communion has light with darkness?" - *2 Corinthians 6:14*

"You shall not plough with an ox and a donkey together." - *Deuteronomy 22:10*

Heavenly Father, grant me seeing eyes and listening ears to recognise who you have destined me to be with. May we see ourselves the way you see us.

"Then the rib which the Lord God had taken from man He made into a woman, and He brought her to the man. And Adam said: "This is now bone of my bones and flesh of my flesh; She shall be called Woman, because she was taken out of Man." - *Genesis 2:22-23*

"But the Lord said to Samuel, "Do not look at his appearance or at his physical stature, because I have refused him. For the Lord does not see as man sees; for man looks at the outward appearance, but the Lord looks at the heart." - *1 Samuel 16:7*

Father Lord, may I never act before your time and choose a partner before you have fully made them.

"And the temple, when it was being built, was built with stone finished at the quarry, so that no hammer or chisel or any iron tool was heard in the temple while it was being built." - *1 Kings 6:7*

I pray that my spouse will be an asset and not a liability and I will be an asset to my spouse.

"And the Lord God said, "It is not good that man should be alone; I will make him a helper comparable to him." - *Genesis 2:18*

"As iron sharpens iron, so a man sharpens the countenance of his friend." - *Proverbs 27:17*

Heavenly Father, help me to maximise my season of singleness, I will focus on the things that please you, and serve you without distractions.

"But I want you to be without care. He who is unmarried cares for the things of the Lord—how he may please the Lord. But he who is married cares about the things of the world—how he may please his wife. There is a difference between a wife and a virgin. The unmarried woman cares about the things of the Lord, that she may be holy both in body and in spirit. But she who is married cares about the things of the world—how she may please her husband." - *1 Corinthians 7:32-34*

Prayers on Being Joined with Your Spouse

Heavenly Father, I pray that you will transform me into the helper you have made comparable to my spouse.

> "And the Lord God said, "It is not good that man should be alone; I will make him a helper comparable to him." - *Genesis 2:18*

I pray that as I become one flesh with the spouse you have created me to be with, shame and secrecy will have no place in our marriage.

"Therefore a man shall leave his father and mother and be joined to his wife, and they shall become one flesh. And they were both naked, the man and his wife, and were not ashamed." - *Genesis 2:24-25*

I decree and declare that the power of agreement will be evident in my marriage, relationships and life, in Jesus' name.

"Assuredly, I say to you, whatever you bind on earth will be bound in heaven, and whatever you loose on earth will be loosed in heaven. "Again I say to you that if two of you agree on earth concerning anything that they ask, it will be done for them by My Father in heaven." - *Matthew 18:18-19*

Heavenly Father, I pray that I will be committed to my husband/wife. I have chosen them before you God and I will remain faithful to my choice.

"Husbands, likewise, dwell with them with understanding, giving honour to the wife, as to the weaker vessel, and as being heirs together of the grace of life, that your prayers may not be hindered." - *1 Peter 3:7*

"So then, they are no longer two but one flesh. Therefore what God has joined together, let not man separate." - *Matthew 19:6*

Heavenly Father, I pray against temptation in my marriage. May I always satisfy the needs of my spouse, so they do not look elsewhere.

"Come, let us take our fill of love until morning; Let us delight ourselves with love." - *Proverbs 7:18*

I pray that nothing will come between me and my spouse. We will always be one.

"Therefore, what God has joined together, let not man separate." - *Mark 10:9*

Heavenly Father, I pray that no one will ever take my martial position.

"The king loved Esther more than all the other women, and she obtained grace and favour in his sight more than all the virgins; so, he set the royal crown upon her head and made her queen instead of Vashti." - *Esther 2:17*

Prayers to Become the Woman or Man Your Spouse Desires

Heavenly Father, may I always be pleasing and desirable to my spouse.

> "But he who is married cares about the things of the world—how he may please his wife. There is a difference between a wife and a virgin. The unmarried woman cares about the things of the Lord, that she may be holy both in body and in spirit. But she who is married cares about the things of the world—how she may please her husband."
> - *1 Corinthians 7:33-34*

Father Lord, teach me how to please and honour my spouse so I can bring out the King/Queen in them.

> "'Then let the young woman who pleases the king be queen instead of Vashti.' This thing pleased the king, and he did so." - *Esther 2:4*

Heavenly Father, guide my speech and behaviour so I will never disrespect my spouse.

> "But Queen Vashti refused to come at the king's command brought by his eunuchs; therefore, the king was furious, and his anger burned within him." - *Esther 1:12*

I pray that I will always win my spouse's heart and influence them positively.

> "Now when the turn came for Esther the daughter of Abihail the uncle of Mordecai, who had taken her as his daughter, to go in to the king, she requested nothing but what Hegai the king's eunuch, the custodian of the women, advised. And Esther obtained favour in the sight of all who saw her." - *Esther 2:15*

Dear Lord, grant me the gift of submission under my husband's mission, and may he also be submitted to you.

"Wives, submit to your own husbands, as to the Lord. For the husband is head of the wife, as also Christ is head of the church; and He is the Saviour of the body. Therefore, just as the church is subject to Christ, so let the wives be to their own husbands in everything." - *Ephesians 5:22-24*

I pray that I will always be a voice of encouragement and source of prayer to my spouse.

"Two are better than one, because they have a good reward for their labour. For if they fall, one will lift up his companion. But woe to him who is alone when he falls, for he has no one to help him up."
- *Ecclesiastes 4:9-10*

Father Lord, may I create a warm and godly environment in my home that my spouse and children will look forward to returning to.

"That Christ may dwell in your hearts through faith; that you, being rooted and grounded in love."
- Ephesians 3:17

"I have spread my bed with tapestry, coloured coverings of Egyptian linen. I have perfumed my bed with myrrh, aloes, and cinnamon. Come, let us take our fill of love until morning; let us delight ourselves with love." - *Proverbs 7:16-18*

Prayers for Increased Sensitivity to Your Spouse

Heavenly Father, make me receptive to my spouse's emotions and feelings.

> "For we do not have a High Priest who cannot sympathise with our weaknesses, but was in all points tempted as we are, yet without sin. Let us therefore come boldly to the throne of grace, that we may obtain mercy and find grace to help in time of need." - *Hebrews 4:15-16*

Father Lord, heal my heart so I do not respond to my spouse from my own place of hurt

"Search me, O God, and know my heart; Try me, and know my anxieties; and see if there is any wicked way in me and lead me in the way everlasting." - *Psalms 139:23-24*

I pray that I will be quick to listen, slow to speak and slow to get angry.

"So then, my beloved brethren, let every man be swift to hear, slow to speak, slow to wrath; for the wrath of man does not produce the righteousness of God." - *James 1:19-20*

I pray that my spouse and I will have honest and open communication, that we will hear, listen and understanding one another

"Husbands, likewise, dwell with them with understanding, giving honour to the wife, as to the weaker vessel, and as being heirs together of the grace of life, that your prayers may not be hindered." - *1 Peter 3:7*

Heavenly Father, I pray that you will increase my emotional intelligence.

"There is one who speaks like the piercings of a sword, but the tongue of the wise promotes health." - *Proverbs 12:18*

> "Keep your heart with all diligence, for out of it spring the issues of life." - *Proverbs 4:23*

Father Lord, remove any barriers to listening to and understanding my spouse.

> "Teach me, and I will hold my tongue; cause me to understand wherein I have erred." - *Job 6:24*

"Finally, all of you be of one mind, having compassion for one another; love as brothers, be tender-hearted, be courteous." - *1 Peter 3:8*

Dear Lord, make me empathetic and compassionate like you so I can better serve my spouse.

> "Brethren, if a man is overtaken in any trespass, you who are spiritual restore such a one in a spirit of gentleness, considering yourself lest you also be tempted. Bear one another's burdens, and so fulfil the law of Christ." - *Galatians 6:1-2*

SECTION 3

Power

Prayers for Understanding How God Speaks to You

Father Lord, help me to hear and follow the whispers of the Holy Spirit.

> "When he has brought out all his own, he goes on ahead of them, and his sheep follow him because they know his voice." - *John 10:4*

Heavenly Father, help me to keep watch so that I may discern what You will say to me in this season of my life. Help me to hear Your voice, that I may grasp Your vision.

"I will stand at my watch and station myself on the ramparts; I will look to see what he will say to me, and what answer I am to give to this complaint."
- Habakkuk 2:1

Father Lord, I pray that I will understand the various ways that you will use to speak to me.

"For God does speak—now one way, now another—though no one perceives it. In a dream, in a vision of the night, when deep sleep falls on people as they slumber in their beds, He may speak in their ears and terrify them with warnings." *- Job 33:14-16*

Dear Lord, I pray that You will send me the right mentors to help me better understand how You speak to me.

"And he ran to Eli and said, "Here I am; you called me." But Eli said, "I did not call; go back and lie down." So he went and lay down. Again the Lord called, "Samuel!" And Samuel got up and went to Eli and said, "Here I am; you called me. "My son," Eli said, "I did not call; go back and lie down. "Now Samuel did not yet know the Lord: The word of the Lord had not yet been revealed to him. A third time the Lord called, "Samuel!" And Samuel got up and went to Eli and said, "Here I am; you called me. "Then Eli realised that the Lord was calling the boy."
- 1 Samuel 3:5-8

I pray that I may perceive and understand the promptings and cautions of the Spirit.

"Much time had been lost, and sailing had already become dangerous because by now it was after the Day of Atonement. So Paul warned them, "Men, I can see that our voyage is going to be disastrous and bring great loss to ship and cargo, and to our own lives also." But the centurion, instead of listening to what Paul said, followed the advice of the pilot and of the owner of the ship." - *Acts 27-9-10*

Heavenly Father, help me to be perceptive to understand the instructions you give me through dreams.

"During the night Paul had a vision of a man of Macedonia standing and begging him, "Come over to Macedonia and help us." - *Acts 16:9*

Father Lord, help me to understand and be sensitive to the season I am in.

"So, the child grew and became strong in spirit, and was in the deserts till the day of his manifestation to Israel." - *Luke 1:80*

discerned." - *1 Corinthians 2:14*

I pray that I may strengthen myself in the Spirit before assuming public platforms.

"And the child grew and became strong in spirit; and he lived in the wilderness until he appeared publicly to Israel." - *Luke 1:80*

I pray for increased spiritual authority to dislodge any gatekeepers opposing my progress.

"Now Joshua the son of Nun sent out two men from Acacia Grove to spy secretly, saying, "Go, view the land, especially Jericho. "So they went and came to the house of a harlot named Rahab, and lodged there." - *Joshua 2:1*

"Now a certain woman named Lydia heard us. She was a seller of purple from the city of Thyatira, who worshipped God. The Lord opened her heart to heed the things spoken by Paul." - *Acts 16:14*

Prayers to Resist the Enemy

Heavenly Father, give me the grace to be persistent in knocking on the door you have opened for me. Every power that has resisted me until now will begin to bow.

"Then he said to me, "Do not fear, Daniel, for from the first day that you set your heart to understand, and to humble yourself before your God, your words were heard; and I have come because of your words. But the prince of the kingdom of Persia withstood me twenty-one days; and behold, Michael, one of the chief princes, came to help me, for I had been left alone there with the kings of Persia. Now I have come to make you understand what will happen to your people in the latter days, for the vision refers to many days yet to come."
- *Daniel 10:12-14*

Father Lord, the gate of my dream life is protected. The enemy will not be able to penetrate and manipulate my dreams.

"Then he dreamed, and behold, a ladder was set up on the earth, and its top reached to heaven; and there the angels of God were ascending and descending on it. And behold, the Lord stood above it and said: "I am the Lord God of Abraham your father and the God of Isaac; the land on which you lie I will give to you and your descendants." - *Genesis 28:12-14*

I pray against every horn of the enemy that has been raised to scatter my life and destiny. May God raise His craftsmen to terrify them.

"Then I raised my eyes and looked, and there were four horns. And I said to the angel who talked with me, "What are these?" So, he answered me, "These are the horns that have scattered Judah, Israel, and Jerusalem." Then the Lord showed me four craftsmen." - *Zechariah 1:18-20*

I pray that any hidden viper in my life will be revealed.

"Paul gathered a pile of brushwood and, as he put it on the fire, a viper, driven out by the heat, fastened itself on his hand." - *Acts 28:3*

Heavenly Father, help me to be vigilant and sober so I will not give room for the enemy in my life.

"Be sober, be vigilant; because your adversary the devil walks about like a roaring lion, seeking whom he may devour." - *1 Peter 5:8*

"Now when the devil had ended every temptation, he departed from Him until an opportune time." - *Luke 4:13*

Dear Lord, give me the grace to submit to you and resist the devil so he will flee from me.

"Therefore submit to God. Resist the devil and he will flee from you." - *James 4:7*

I decree and declare that an open door will be set before my family and I such that no one can shut, in the name of Jesus.

"I know your works. See, I have set before you an open door, and no one can shut it; for you have a little strength, have kept My word, and have not denied My name." - *Revelations 3:8*

Prayers to Defeat the Invisible Enemy

Father Lord, I pray that you will give me spiritual authority such that when new doors and opportunities are opened onto me, I will be able to defeat the invisible enemy.

> "For a great and effective door has opened to me, and there are many adversaries." - *1 Corinthians 16:9*

Heavenly Father, I pray that as your spirit dwells in me to bring about liberation, I will be set free from every invisible enemy.

"Now the Lord is the Spirit; and where the Spirit of the Lord is, there is liberty." - *2 Corinthians 3:17*

I decree and declare that when the invisible enemy comes against me, he shall stumble and fall.

"When the wicked came against me, to eat up my flesh, my enemies and foes, they stumbled and fell." - *Psalm 27:2*

I pray that I will be wise to recognise and defeat any invisible enemy in my life.

"Behold, I send you out as sheep in the midst of wolves. Therefore be wise as serpents and harmless as doves." - *Matthew 10:16*

By the grace of God, my family and I will not be handed over to the invisible enemy, we will be kept safe in Jesus' name.

"And have not shut me up into the hand of the enemy; You have set my feet in a wide place." - *Psalm 31:18*

I decree and declare that neither life nor death, nor angels, nor demons nor powers will be able to separate me from Christ.

"For I am persuaded that neither death nor life, nor angels nor principalities nor powers, nor things present nor things to come, nor height nor depth, nor any other created thing, shall be able to separate us from the love of God which is in Christ Jesus our Lord." - *Romans 8:38-39*

I pray that I will be strong in the Lord and in his power and put on the whole armour of God to defeat the invisible enemy against my life and destiny.

"Finally, my brethren, be strong in the Lord and in the power of His might. Put on the whole armour of God, that you may be able to stand against the wiles of the devil. For we do not wrestle against flesh and blood, but against principalities, against powers, against the rulers of the darkness of this age, against spiritual hosts of wickedness in the heavenly places. Therefore take up the whole armour of God, that you may be able to withstand in the evil day, and having done all, to stand." - *Ephesians 6:10-13*

SECTION 4

Faith

Prayers for Standing in Faith

Dear Lord, I pray that you will touch my heart and replace every doubt concerning your will for my life with faith fuelled by Your word.

> "But let him ask in faith, with no doubting, for the one who doubts is like a wave of the sea that is driven and tossed by the wind. For that person must not suppose that he will receive anything from the Lord; he is a double-minded man, unstable in all his ways." - *James 1:6-8*

Heavenly Father, please give me the type of faith that values the gift of my salvation over material things.

> "But seek first the kingdom of God and his righteousness, and all these things will be added to you." - *Matthew 6:33*

I pray for grace to grow in Your word so that I will always be found standing in faith.

> "For though by this time you ought to be teachers, you need someone to teach you again the basic principles of the oracles of God. You need milk, not solid food, for everyone who lives on milk is unskilled in the word of righteousness, since he is a child. But solid food is for the mature, for those who have their powers of discernment trained by constant practice to distinguish good from evil." - *Hebrews 5:12-14*

Father Lord, help me to hold steadfast to my faith, I will not give heed to deceiving spirits or doctrines in my life and destiny.

> "Now the Spirit expressly says that in latter times some will depart from the faith, giving heed to deceiving spirits and doctrines of demons." - *1 Timothy 4:1*

I pray that I will stand firm in you so that I will not be deceived by false prophets.

> "So that we may no longer be children, tossed to and fro by the waves and carried about by every wind of doctrine, by human cunning, by craftiness in deceitful schemes." - *Ephesians 4:14*

Heavenly Father, give me the grace to stand firm in my faith until I have finished the race.

> "I have fought the good fight, I have finished the race, I have kept the faith." - *2 Timothy 4-7*

Dear Lord, I ask that you will give me the grace to stand firm and planted in You like a tree by streams of water, that I may continually draw from Your Word. Increase my faith as I meditate on Your Word, day and night.

> "Have I not commanded you? Be strong and courageous. Do not be afraid; do not be discouraged, for the Lord your God will be with you wherever you go." - *Joshua 1:9*

Prayers to Strengthen Your Faith

Heavenly Father, I pray that my faith will be strengthened as I continue to hear your word.

> "So then faith comes by hearing, and hearing by the word of God." - *Romans 10:17*

Father Lord, please help me to walk in the counsel of the godly and not in the way of the wicked. Strengthen my faith to choose righteousness daily.

> "Therefore, since we have been justified by faith, we have peace with God through our Lord Jesus Christ. Through him we have also obtained access by faith into this grace in which we stand, and we rejoice in hope of the glory of God." - *Romans 5:1-2*

I pray for the faith to constantly delight in you Lord. Through trial and tribulations, may I have the faith to derive joy from seeking your kingdom first above anything else

"Delight yourself also in the Lord, and He shall give you the desires of your heart." - *Psalm 37:4*

Dear Lord, grant me the faith and discernment of the Shunammite woman, that I will be able to recognise and honour Your presence in my life and in the lives of others.

"Now it happened one day that Elisha went to Shunem, where there was a notable woman, and she persuaded him to eat some food. So it was, as often as he passed by, he would turn in there to eat some food. And she said to her husband, "Look now, I know that this is a holy man of God, who passes by us regularly. Please, let us make a small upper room on the wall; and let us put a bed for him there, and a table and a chair and a lampstand; so it will be, whenever he comes to us, he can turn in there." - *2 Kings 4:8-10*

I pray that, regardless of what I go through, I will practise relentless faith as I continue to run the race God has called me to.

"Therefore, since we are surrounded by such a great cloud of witnesses, let us throw off everything that hinders and the sin that so easily entangles. And let us run with perseverance the race marked out for us, fixing our eyes on Jesus, the pioneer and perfecter of faith. For the joy set before him he endured the cross, scorning its shame, and sat down at the right hand of the throne of God." - *Hebrews 12:1-2*

Father Lord, help me move on from old victories and experiences so I can see the new opportunities you are bringing my way so that my faith will be strengthened.

"See, I am doing a new thing! Now it springs up; do you not perceive it? I am making a way in the wilderness and streams in the wasteland."
- *Isaiah 43:19*

Heavenly Father, help me to recognise the peace I have in You amid tribulation, so that my faith will be strengthened.

"These things I have spoken to you, that in Me you may have peace. In the world you will have tribulation; but be of good cheer, I have overcome the world." - *John 16:33*

Prayers for Faith to Turn Your Expectations into Manifestation

Father Lord, increase my faith to trust in every promise You have spoken over my life, even when the fulfilment seems distant.

"Yet he did not waver through unbelief regarding the promise of God but was strengthened in his faith and gave glory to God, being fully persuaded that God had power to do what he had promised."
- *Romans 4:20-21*

Heavenly Father, strengthen my faith to hold onto the things I hope for, even when I cannot see them. Help me to trust in the evidence of Your unseen work.

> "Then Jesus told him, 'Because you have seen me, you have believed; blessed are those who have not seen and yet have believed." - *John 20:29*

I pray that I will take action towards the things God has spoken in your word concerning me.

> "Therefore, everyone who hears these words of mine and puts them into practice is like a wise man who built his house on the rock." - *Matthew 7:24*

Dear Lord, grant me the faith to patiently wait on Your timing. Teach me to trust that Your timing is perfect and give me peace as I wait for the fulfilment of Your promises.

> "But those who hope in the Lord will renew their strength. They will soar on wings like eagles; they will run and not grow weary; they will walk and not be faint." - *Isaiah 40:31*

I pray for the grace to wait patiently for the promises God has spoken to me to be fulfilled.

> "That you do not become sluggish, but imitate those who through faith and patience inherit the promises." - *Hebrews 6:12*

Heavenly Father, as I read Your word, please give me the grace, by faith to perceive and see the things which are yet to come

"Open my eyes that I may see wonderful things in your law." - *Psalm 119:18*

Father Lord, give me the ability to wage war over every prophecy you have spoken concerning my life.

"This charge I commit to you, son Timothy, according to the prophecies previously made concerning you, that by them you may wage the good warfare." - *1 Timothy 1:18*

Prayers for Faith to Overcome Battles

Dear Lord, when I face challenges and crises, give me the faith to believe that I have won every battle through Christ Jesus. Help me to trust that You are in control, no matter the circumstances.

> "For the Lord your God is he who goes with you to fight for you against your enemies, to give you the victory." - *Deuteronomy 20:4*

> "But thanks be to God, who gives us the victory through our Lord Jesus Christ." - *1 Corinthians 15:57*

Heavenly Father, grant me the faith to believe in the fulfilment of Your promises in my life, even when they seem impossible.

"With men this is impossible, but with God all things are possible." - *Matthew 19:26*

"Against all hope, Abraham in hope believed and so became the father of many nations, just as it had been said to him, "So shall your offspring be." Without weakening in his faith, he faced the fact that his body was as good as dead—since he was about a hundred years old—and that Sarah's womb was also dead. Yet he did not waver through unbelief regarding the promise of God, but was strengthened in his faith and gave glory to God." - *Romans 4:18-20*

I pray that when situations seem hopeless, my faith will be strengthened to believe in Your power to restore and resurrect what seems lost, just as You restored life to the Shunammite woman's son.

"When Elisha reached the house, there was the boy lying dead on his couch. He went in, shut the door on the two of them and prayed to the Lord. Then he got on the bed and lay on the boy, mouth to mouth, eyes to eyes, hands to hands. As he stretched himself out on him, the boy's body grew warm. Elisha turned away and walked back and forth in the room and then got on the bed and stretched out on him once more. The boy sneezed seven times and opened his eyes. Elisha summoned Gehazi and said, "Call the Shunammite." And he did. When she came, he said, "Take your son." - *2 Kings 4: 32-26*

I pray for the grace to bounce back from every difficult situation in the name of Jesus.

"The righteous person may have many troubles, but the Lord delivers him from them all." - *Psalm 34:19*

"But those who hope in the Lord will renew their strength. They will soar on wings like eagles; they will run and not grow weary; they will walk and not faint." - *Isaiah 40:31*

I pray that by faith, I will break free from the spirit of fear hindering the answers to my prayers and causing sorrow in my life.

"But the angel said to him, "Do not be afraid, Zacharias, for your prayer is heard; and your wife Elizabeth will bear you a son, and you shall call his name John. And you will have joy and gladness, and many will rejoice at his birth." - *Luke 1:13-14*

I pray that my faith will not fail during the day of small beginnings, so that I will have the strength to face every battle before me and emerge victorious.

"Though your beginning was small, yet your latter end would increase abundantly." - *Job 8:7*

"For who has despised the day of small things? For these seven rejoice to see the plumb line in the hand of Zerubbabel. They are the eyes of the Lord, which scan to and fro throughout the whole earth." - *Zechariah 4:10*

Father Lord, help me to consistently confess the truth of Your word over every difficult situation in my life.

"Let us hold fast the confession of our hope without wavering, for He who promised is faithful." - *Hebrews 10:23*

SECTION 5

Victory

Prayers for the Battle for Your Blessing

Dear Lord, give me the power, strength and courage to cut down and drive out whosoever and whatsoever is occupying my lot.

> "And Joshua spoke to the house of Joseph to Ephraim and Manasseh saying, you are a great people and have great power; you shall not have only one lot, but the mountain country shall be yours. Although it is wooded, you shall cut it down, and its farthest extent shall be yours; for you shall drive out the Canaanites, though they have iron chariots and are strong." - *Joshua 17:17-18*

I pray that I will have the strategy to gain victory over every battle of life.

> "For which of you, intending to build a tower, does not sit down first and count the cost, whether he has enough to finish it lest, after he has laid the foundation, and is not able to finish, all who see it begin to mock him, saying, 'This man began to build and was not able to finish'? Or what king, going to make war against another king, does not sit down first and consider whether he is able with ten thousand to meet him who comes against him with twenty thousand? Or else, while the other is still a great way off, he sends a delegation and asks conditions of peace. So likewise, whoever of you does not forsake all that he has cannot be My disciple." - *Luke 14:28-33*

Father Lord, equip and prepare me for any battle of life. I will not fight any battle I am not prepared for.

> "I will not drive them out from before you in one year, lest the land become desolate, and the beasts of the field become too numerous for you. Little by little I will drive them out from before you, until you have increased, and you inherit the land." - *Exodus 23:29-30*

I pray that I will receive the grace to acquire the necessary knowledge so that I am strong enough to face all battles and not run away.

"A wise man is strong, yes, a man of knowledge increases strength." - *Proverbs 24:5*

Dear Lord, I receive the wisdom to study every battle I am facing to know the necessary steps to take to gain victory, in Jesus' name.

"That which has been is what will be, that which is done is what will be done, And there is nothing new under the sun. Is there anything of which it may be said, "See, this is new"? It has already been in ancient times before us." - *Ecclesiastes 1:9-10*

Heavenly Father, in every battle I face, I will not grow weary or lose heart but will fight to the end and see victory.

"And let us not grow weary while doing good, for in due season we shall reap if we do not lose heart." - *Galatians 6:9*

I pray that in the face of every battle, I will not faint, and I will be strong till the victory is won.

"If you faint in the day of adversity, your strength is small." - *Proverbs 24:10*

Prayers to Navigate the Politics of Your Next Level

Father Lord, give me the grace to manage and maintain the promotion and opportunities you have given to me so I may live a life full of victory.

> "Then the king promoted Shadrach, Meshach, and Abed-Nego in the province of Babylon." - *Daniel 3:30*

I pray there shall be no error or fault found in me. Anyone looking for a charge against me will find none.

> "So, the governors and satraps sought to find some charge against Daniel concerning the kingdom; but

they could find no charge or fault, because he was faithful; nor was there any error or fault found in him. Then these men said, "we shall not find any charge against this Daniel unless we find it against him concerning the law of his God." - *Daniel 6:4-5*

Dear Lord, I pray that you will put the solutions of kings and nations in my hands that will bring victory in all areas of my life.

"Now it came to pass in the morning that his spirit was troubled, and he sent and called for all the magicians of Egypt and all its wise men. And Pharaoh told them his dreams, but there was no one who could interpret them for Pharaoh." - *Genesis 41:8*

I pray that I will be brought before kings quickly for good and your name, Lord, will be glorified.

"Then Arioch quickly brought Daniel before the king, and said thus to him, "I have found a man of the captives of Judah, who will make known to the king the interpretation." - *Daniel 2:25*

I pray that because of the excellent spirit in me, I will be chosen among many.

"It pleased Darius to set over the kingdom one hundred and twenty satraps, to be over the whole kingdom; and over these, three governors, of whom

Daniel was one, that the satraps might give account to them, so that the king would suffer no loss. Then this Daniel distinguished himself above the governors and satraps, because an excellent spirit was in him; and the king gave thought to setting him over the whole realm." - *Daniel 6:1-3*

I pray for the grace to give honour, to pray and to intercede for those who are in authority that I may live a peaceful and victorious life.

"Therefore, I exhort first of all that supplications, prayers, intercessions, and giving of thanks be made for all men, for kings and all who are in authority, that we may lead a quiet and peaceable life in all godliness and reverence." – *1 Timothy 2:1-2*

Heavenly Father, help me to work in unity with those around me, in my family, at my workplace, in church and in my friendship groups.

"Pride goes before destruction, And a haughty spirit before a fall. Better to be of a humble spirit with the lowly, than to divide the spoil with the proud."
- *Proverbs 16:18-19*

"Where there is no wood, the fire goes out; And where there is no talebearer, strife ceases."
- *Proverbs 26:20*

Prayers for Winning the Battle Against Temptation

I pray that I will know my temptation triggers that I may gain victory over them.

> "Now in the process of time the daughter of Shua, Judah's wife, died; and Judah was comforted, and went up to his sheep shearers at Timnah, he and his friend Hirah the Adullamite." - *Genesis 38:12*

Father Lord, give me victory over all temptation. I pray your presence will not depart from me.

"And she said, "The Philistines are upon you, Samson!" So, he awoke from his sleep, and said, "I will go out as before, at other times, and shake myself free!" But he did not know that the Lord had departed from him." - *Judges 16:20*

I pray that I will not exchange what belongs to me, my authority and my position for a simple pleasure.

"For all these riches which God has taken from our father are really ours and our children's; now then, whatever God has said to you, do it." - *Genesis 31:16*

Heavenly Father, help me to learn the patterns for the things that tempt me. I will not love what has been sent to overpower and destroy me.

"Afterward it happened that he loved a woman in the Valley of Sorek, whose name was Delilah. And the lords of the Philistines came up to her and said to her, "Entice him, and find out where his great strength lies, and by what means we may overpower him, that we may bind him to afflict him; and every one of us will give you eleven hundred pieces of silver." - *Judges 16:4-5*

I pray that I will recognise and be sensitive to where and when I am most tempted.

"Let no one say when he is tempted, "I am tempted by God;" for God cannot be tempted by evil, nor does He Himself tempt anyone." - *James 1:13*

I break any hold of sin and temptation over my life. I will not be held bound, in Jesus' name.

"Then the Philistines took him, and put out his eyes, and brought him down to Gaza. They bound him with bronze fetters, and he became a grinder in the prison." - *Judges 16:21*

Heavenly Father, help me to submit myself to accountability. To confess any sin and temptation that comes my way.

"And the prayer of faith will save the sick, and the Lord will raise him up. And if he has committed sins, he will be forgiven. Confess your trespasses to one another, and pray for one another, that you may be healed. The effective, fervent prayer of a righteous man avails much." - *James 5:15-16*

Prayers for Victory over Deception

Father Lord, help me to test every spirit. I will not be deceived by the spirit of this age.

> "So, the great dragon was cast out, that serpent of old, called the Devil and Satan, who deceives the whole world; he was cast to the earth, and his angels were cast out with him." - *Revelation 12:9*

Heavenly Father, I ask for an increase in discernment that I may be able to discern every deceiving spirit that wants to appear as light.

> "And this I pray, that your love may abound still more and more in knowledge and all discernment,

that you may approve the things that are excellent, that you may be sincere and without offence till the day of Christ, being filled with the fruits of righteousness which are by Jesus Christ, to the glory and praise of God." - *Philippians 1:9-11*

I pray I will not be deceived or tempted by what I desire, in Jesus' name.

"And when He had fasted forty days and forty nights, afterward He was hungry. Now when the tempter came to Him, he said, "If You are the Son of God, command that these stones become bread." - *Matthew 4:2-3*

"So, Jacob went near to Isaac his father, and he felt him and said, "The voice is Jacob's voice, but the hands are the hands of Esau." And he did not recognize him, because his hands were hairy like his brother Esau's hands; so, he blessed him. Then he said, "Are you really my son Esau?" He said, "I am."" - *Genesis 27:22-25*

I pray that I will not make life changing and altering decisions during the night season.

"Now it came to pass in the evening, that he took Leah his daughter and brought her to Jacob; and he went in to her. And Laban gave his maid Zilpah to his daughter Leah as a maid. So it came to pass in the morning, that behold, it was Leah. And he said to Laban, "What is this you have done to me? Was it not for Rachel that I served you? Why then have you deceived me?"" - *Genesis 29:23-25*

I pray that I will not be tempted nor compelled to make important decisions in a hurry but will instead enquire from God before acting.

"And these wineskins which we filled were new, and see, they are torn; and these our garments and our sandals have become old because of the very long journey." Then the men of Israel took some of their provisions; but they did not ask counsel of the Lord. So, Joshua made peace with them, and made a covenant with them to let them live; and the rulers of the congregation swore to them. And it happened at the end of three days, after they had made a covenant with them, that they heard that they were their neighbours who dwelt near them."
- *Joshua 9:13-16*

I pray that isolation will not make me gravitate towards a counterfeit camouflaging as the real thing.

"Now Absalom would rise early and stand beside the way to the gate. So it was, whenever anyone who had a lawsuit came to the king for a decision, that Absalom would call to him and say, "What city are you from?" And he would say, "Your servant is

from such and such a tribe of Israel." And so it was, whenever anyone came near to bow down to him, that he would put out his hand and take him and kiss him. In this manner Absalom acted toward all Israel who came to the king for judgement. So, Absalom stole the hearts of the men of Israel."
- 2 Samuel 15:2, 5-6

Dear Lord, help me to be sober and vigilant, fair-minded and to seek your Word daily so I will not be deceived.

"These were more fair-minded than those in Thessalonica, in that they received the word with all readiness, and searched the Scriptures daily to find out whether these things were so." *- Acts 17:11*

SECTION 6

Results

Prayers for Being on Time

Heavenly Father, give me great insight to key into your divine timing. May I know what you are doing per season and be a ready vessel for your Kingdom.

> "Then an angel of the Lord appeared to him, standing on the right side of the altar of incense. And when Zacharias saw him, he was troubled, and fear fell upon him. But the angel said to him, "Do not be afraid, Zacharias, for your prayer is heard; and your wife Elizabeth will bear you a son, and you shall call his name John. And you will have joy and gladness, and many will rejoice at his birth. For he will be great in the sight of the Lord, and shall drink neither wine nor strong drink. He will also be filled with the Holy Spirit, even from his mother's womb." - *Luke 1:11-15*

Father Lord, grant me the wisdom, knowledge and understanding to know what I should be doing now and the grace to do it diligently.

"Of the sons of Issachar who had understanding of the times, to know what Israel ought to do, their chiefs were two hundred; and all their brethren were at their command." - *1 Chronicles 12:32*

Heavenly Father, help me to fill my life with your Word, so when it is time to show your glory, you can use me.

"Jesus said to them, "Fill the waterpots with water." And they filled them up to the brim. And He said to them, "Draw some out now, and take it to the master of the feast." And they took it." - *John 2:7-8*

Heavenly Father, may I not be known before your divine timing for my life. Help me to trust in your timing and be prepared for it.

"For no one does anything in secret while he himself seeks to be known openly. If You do these things, show Yourself to the world." For even His brothers did not believe in Him. Then Jesus said to them, "My time has not yet come, but your time is always ready." - John 7:4-6

"So, the child grew and became strong in spirit, and was in the deserts till the day of his manifestation to Israel." - *Luke 1:80*

I pray that God will reveal to me what I should be doing by this time and who I should be. May He grant me speed and grace to make up for lost time.

"For though by this time you ought to be teachers, you need someone to teach you again the first principles of the oracles of God; and you have come to need milk and not solid food." - *Hebrews 5:12*

"So, I will restore to you the years that the swarming locust has eaten, the crawling locust, The consuming locust, And the chewing locust, my great army which I sent among you. You shall eat in plenty and be satisfied, and praise the name of the Lord your God, who has dealt wondrously with you; And My people shall never be put to shame."
- *Joel 2:25-26*

Dear Lord, grant me the wisdom to know when to plant and when to harvest.

"To everything there is a season, A time for every purpose under heaven: A time to be born, and a time to die; A time to plant, and a time to pluck what is planted." - *Ecclesiastes 3:1-2*

I decree and declare that my harvest season has come.

> "But when the grain ripens, immediately he puts in the sickle, because the harvest has come."
> - *Mark 4:29*

Prayers to Become the Best Version of Yourself

Heavenly Father, help me live up to the expectation of what it means for me to be a son of God.

> "For the earnest expectation of the creation eagerly waits for the revealing of the sons of God."
> - *Romans 8:19*

Father Lord, give me the patience required to cultivate all my giftings to the optimum level.

> "Then Jesus said to those Jews who believed Him, "If you abide in My word, you are My disciples indeed." - *John 8:31*

"Blessed is he who reads and those who hear the words of this prophecy and keep those things which are written in it; for the time is near." - *Revelation 1:3*

I pray that I will grow from a mustard seed into a large tree. I will not be small; I will fulfil my God-given potential.

"It is like a mustard seed which, when it is sown on the ground, is smaller than all the seeds on earth; but when it is sown, it grows up and becomes greater than all herbs, and shoots out large branches, so that the birds of the air may nest under its shade." - *Mark 4:31-32*

I pray that I will live up to my God-given potential, and I will emerge into all God has destined for me to be.

"For since the creation of the world His invisible attributes are clearly seen, being understood by the things that are made, even His eternal power and Godhead, so that they are without excuse."
- *Romans 1:20*

Dear Lord, help me go through the process of emergence, give me the humility required to die to myself so I can fully become who you have called me to be.

"So, the child grew and became strong in spirit and was in the deserts till the day of his manifestation to Israel." - *Luke 1:80*

I pray that I will be a living proof of God's glory, full of grace and truth.

"And the Word became flesh and dwelt among us, and we beheld His glory, the glory as of the only begotten of the Father, full of grace and truth."
- *John 1:14*

I decree and declare that all the words God has spoken over me will come to pass.

"In the beginning was the Word, and the Word was with God, and the Word was God. He was in the beginning with God. All things were made through Him, and without Him nothing was made that was made. In Him was life, and the life was the light of men." - *John 1:1-4*

Prayers to Emerge into Your Season of Abundance

Father Lord, open the eyes of my understanding so I can know you deeper and reflect your truth to the world.

> "Arise, shine; For your light has come! And the glory of the Lord is risen upon you. For behold, the darkness shall cover the earth, and deep darkness the people; But the Lord will arise over you, And His glory will be seen upon you." - *Isaiah 60:1-2*

Heavenly Father, help me to be a light in my generation and may my light never be hidden or dampened.

"You are the light of the world. A city that is set on a hill cannot be hidden. Nor do they light a lamp and put it under a basket, but on a lampstand, and it gives light to all who are in the house. Let your light so shine before men, that they may see your good works and glorify your Father in heaven."
- *Matthew 5:14-16*

Dear Lord, grant me deeper revelation of your Word, so that the light I carry, and the level of my emergence, shall increase to glorify you here on earth as in heaven.

"Also, I heard the voice of the Lord, saying: "Whom shall I send, and who will go for Us?" Then I said, "Here am I! Send me." - *Isaiah 6:8*

"The earth was without form, and void; and darkness was on the face of the deep. And the Spirit of God was hovering over the face of the waters. Then God said, "Let there be light"; and there was light. And God saw the light, that it was good; and God divided the light from the darkness."
- *Genesis 1:2-4*

I decree and declare that I will not miss my season of results and opportunities.

"He who keeps his command will experience nothing harmful; And a wise man's heart discerns both time and judgement." - *Ecclesiastes 8:5*

"A little sleep, a little slumber, A little folding of the hands to rest; So, shall your poverty come like a prowler, And your need like an armed man."
- Proverbs 24:33-34

Father Lord, make me a problem solver, so that people can come to your light through me.

"The Gentiles shall come to your light, And kings to the brightness of your rising." *- Isaiah 60:3*

"Now it came to pass in the morning that his spirit was troubled, and he sent and called for all the magicians of Egypt and all its wise men. And Pharaoh told them his dreams, but there was no one who could interpret them for Pharaoh. Then Pharaoh sent and called Joseph, and they brought him quickly out of the dungeon; and he shaved, changed his clothing, and came to Pharaoh."
- Genesis 41:8,14

I pray that I will stand before kings, but Lord before I do, grant me the wisdom to discern and understand so I may be effective.

"Do you see a man who excels in his work? He will stand before kings; He will not stand before unknown men." *- Proverbs 22:29*

I decree and declare the spirit of excellence and favour over me.

> "Therefore, your gates shall be open continually; They shall not be shut day or night, that men may bring to you the wealth of the Gentiles, And their kings in procession." - *Isaiah 60:11*

Prayers to Make Room for Results

Father Lord, help me to see farther and go further in life with destiny that I may grow faster.

"By this My Father is glorified, that you bear much fruit; so, you will be My disciples." – *John 15:8*

Heavenly Father, help me to see and give me the grace to call forth every seed potential you have placed on the inside of me.

"Then God said, "Let the earth bring forth grass, the herb that yields seed, and the fruit tree that yields fruit according to its kind, whose seed is in itself, on the earth;" and it was so. And the earth brought forth

grass, the herb that yields seed according to its kind, and the tree that yields fruit, whose seed is according to its kind. And God saw that it was good."
- *Genesis 1:11*

I pray that I will be placed in the right nurturing environments that will enable me to bear good fruits.

"Listen! Behold, a sower went out to sow. And it happened, as he sowed, that some seed fell by the wayside; and the birds of the air came and devoured it. Some fell on stony ground, where it did not have much earth; and immediately it sprang up because it had no depth of earth. But when the sun was up it was scorched, and because it had no root it withered away. And some seed fell among thorns; and the thorns grew up and choked it, and it yielded no crop." – *Mark 4:3-7*

I pray that my eyes will be opened to see what God is doing and be in alignment with His will on earth so that I may bear good fruits.

"Then Jesus answered and said to them, "Most assuredly, I say to you, the Son can do nothing of Himself, but what He sees the Father do; for whatever He does, the Son also does in like manner."
- *John 5:19*

Dear Lord, I pray that my ears will be inclined to you so I may know what to do per time.

"And Jacob called his sons and said, "Gather together, that I may tell you what shall befall you in the last days: "Gather together and hear, you sons of Jacob, and listen to Israel your father." - *Genesis 49:1-2*

Father Lord, bring stability into my life and destiny that I may produce good and profitable results.

"Reuben, you are my firstborn, My might and the beginning of my strength, The excellency of dignity and the excellency of power. Unstable as water, you shall not excel, because you went up to your father's bed; Then you defiled it - He went up to my couch." - *Genesis 49:3-4*

I pray that God will bless me in all that I lay my hands to do and there will be increase in my life.

"He said, "Bring it near to me, and I will eat of my son's game, so that my soul may bless you." So, he brought it near to him, and he ate; and he brought him wine, and he drank. Then his father Isaac said to him, "Come near now and kiss me, my son." And he came near and kissed him; and he smelled the smell of his clothing, and blessed him and said: "Surely, the smell of my son Is like the smell of a field Which the Lord has blessed." - *Genesis 27:25-27*

SECTION 7

Advancement

Prayers for Advancing into Your Season of Productivity

I pray that I will not have activity without productivity, but rather advance into my promised land.

"The Lord our God spoke to us in Horeb, saying: 'You have dwelt long enough at this mountain. Turn and take your journey, and go to the mountains of the Amorites, to all the neighbouring places in the plain, in the mountains and in the lowland, in the South and on the seacoast, to the land of the Canaanites and to Lebanon, as far as the great river, the River Euphrates." - *Deuteronomy 1:6-7*

I decree and declare I will be fruitful. Dear Lord, help me to manifest and give birth to all that You have placed on the inside of me, that your glory will be displayed for all to see.

> "Then God blessed them, and God said to them, "Be fruitful and multiply; fill the earth and subdue it; have dominion over the fish of the sea, over the birds of the air, and over every living thing that moves on the earth." - *Genesis 1:28*

Heavenly Father, give me the ability to produce good fruits at the expected season. Grant me favourable conditions that will enable me to bear good fruits.

> "Blessed is the man who walks not in the counsel of the ungodly, nor stands in the path of sinners, nor sits in the seat of the scornful; But his delight is in the law of the Lord, and in His law he meditates day and night. He shall be like a tree Planted by the rivers of water, that brings forth its fruit in its season, whose leaf also shall not wither; And whatever he does shall prosper." - *Psalm 1:1-3*

Father Lord, enable me to move from a consumer mentality to a producer mentality.

> "Then the manna ceased on the day after they had eaten the produce of the land; and the children of Israel no longer had manna, but they ate the food of the land of Canaan that year." - *Joshua 5:12*

I pray that I will make good use of the talents God has given me. I receive the reward that comes with being productive.

"And to one he gave five talents, to another two, and to another one, to each according to his own ability; and immediately he went on a journey. Then he who had received the five talents went and traded with them and made another five talents."
- *Matthew 25:15-16*

I pray that I will not be a waster of the resources God has placed on the inside of me. I will bear fruits and not be cut down.

"And if it bears fruit, well. But if not, after that you can cut it down." - *Luke 13:9*

Dear Lord, give me the grace to be disciplined and diligent that I may not be poor, but have much to eat.

"Much food is in the fallow ground of the poor, and for lack of justice there is waste. He who spares his rod hates his son, but he who loves him disciplines him promptly." - *Proverbs 13:23-24*

"The lazy man does not roast what he took in hunting, but diligence is man's precious possession."
- *Proverbs 12:27*

Prayers for Advancement in Your Field

I pray that I will be submitted to the season of preparation, so that I will be prepared for the field God called me to function within.

> "The Lord God planted a garden eastward in Eden, and there He put the man whom He had formed." - *Genesis 2:8*

Father Lord, reveal any area where I am not prepared that is causing you to withhold your best for my life, due to my lack of preparation.

"Before any plant of the field was in the earth and before any herb of the field had grown. For the Lord God had not caused it to rain on the earth, and there was no man to till the ground." - *Genesis 2:5*

I pray that I will develop the competencies and skills required for my next level so that I can advance in my field.

"Now therefore, let Pharaoh select a discerning and wise man, and set him over the land of Egypt. Let Pharaoh do this, and let him appoint officers over the land, to collect one-fifth of the produce of the land of Egypt in the seven plentiful years." - *Genesis 41:33-34*

I pray for grace to maximise my capacity and take on more responsibility. I will advance in my chosen field in Jesus' name.

"He also chose David His servant and took him from the sheepfolds; From following the ewes that had young He brought him, to shepherd Jacob His people, And Israel His inheritance. So, he shepherded them according to the integrity of his heart and guided them by the skilfulness of his hands." - *Psalms 78:70-72*

Father Lord, I pray I will develop the right conduct and protocol for the place you are preparing me for.

"Then Pharaoh sent and called Joseph, and they brought him quickly out of the dungeon; and he shaved, changed his clothing, and came to Pharaoh."
- *Genesis 41:14*

Heavenly Father, help me to develop my character for the place you have for me, that I may always showcase a godly character.

"Joseph said to them, "Do not be afraid, for am I in the place of God? But as for you, you meant evil against me; but God meant it for good, in order to bring it about as it is this day, to save many people alive." - *Genesis 50:19-20*

I pray that even if there are limited roles and opportunities in my field, I will find provision in Jesus' name.

"And my God shall supply all your need according to His riches in glory by Christ Jesus."
- *Philippians 4:19*

Prayers for Birthing Your God Given Dreams

Father Lord, help me to turn my God given dreams and potentials into tangible products.

> "But I make known to you, brethren, that the gospel which was preached by me is not according to man. For I neither received it from man, nor was I taught it, but it came through the revelation of Jesus Christ."
> - *Galatians 1:11-12*

Heavenly Father, reveal to me your pattern for my life and destiny. Help me to build according to the revealed pattern.

"And let them make Me a sanctuary, that I may dwell among them. According to all that I show you, that is, the pattern of the tabernacle and the pattern of all its furnishings, just so you shall make it."
- *Exodus 25:8-9*

Dear Lord, help me to build according to your revealed pattern, that your glory will be seen to honour and to validate.

"Thus, Moses did; according to all that the Lord had commanded him, so he did. And he raised up the court all around the tabernacle and the altar and hung up the screen of the court gate. So, Moses finished the work. The Cloud and the Glory Then the cloud covered the tabernacle of meeting, and the glory of the Lord filled the tabernacle."
- *Exodus 40:16, 33-35*

I pray I will not build nor labour in vain. Father Lord, build the land of my life.

"Unless the Lord builds the house, they labour in vain who build it; unless the Lord guards the city, the watchman stays awake in vain." - *Psalms 127:1*

I pray that I will build on the right foundation and that the work of my hands will endure.

"Each one's work will become clear; for the Day will declare it, because it will be revealed by fire; and the fire will test each one's work, of what sort it is. If anyone's work which he has built on it endures, he will receive a reward. If anyone's work is burned, he will suffer loss; but he himself will be saved, yet so as through fire." - *1 Corinthians 3:13-15*

Father Lord, I pray the treasures you have given me will not be taken away and replaced with counterfeits.

"So, Shishak king of Egypt came up against Jerusalem, and took away the treasures of the house of the Lord and the treasures of the king's house; he took everything. He also carried away the gold shields which Solomon had made. Then King Rehoboam made bronze shields in their place and committed them to the hands of the captains of the guard, who guarded the doorway of the king's house." - *2 Chronicles 12:9-10*

Heavenly Father, I ask that you give me wisdom and prosperity in all areas of life.

"And when the queen of Sheba had seen all the wisdom of Solomon, the house that he had built, the food on his table, the seating of his servants, the service of his waiters and their apparel, his cupbearers, and his entryway by which he went up to the house of the Lord, there was no more spirit in

her. Then she said to the king: "It was a true report which I heard in my own land about your words and your wisdom. However, I did not believe the words until I came and saw with my own eyes; and indeed the half was not told me. Your wisdom and prosperity exceed the fame of which I heard."
- 1 Kings 10:4-7

Prayers for Making Progress

Dear Lord, when you come to take account of the resources you have deposited within me, there will be progress. The land of my life will be a fertile ground.

"For the kingdom of heaven is like a man travelling to a far country, who called his own servants and delivered his goods to them." - *Matthew 25:14*

I pray that in every level of life and at every stage, I will always be in right standing with God.

"Examine yourselves as to whether you are in the faith. Test yourselves. Do you not know yourselves, that Jesus Christ is in you? Unless indeed you are disqualified." - *2 Corinthians 13:5*

Father Lord, help me to always walk in your ways and standard set for my life and destiny.

"In the year that King Uzziah died, I saw the Lord sitting on a throne, high and lifted up, and the train of His robe filled the temple. Above it stood seraphim; each one had six wings: with two he covered his face, with two he covered his feet, and with two he flew. And one cried to another and said: "Holy, holy, holy is the Lord of hosts; The whole earth is full of His glory!" - *Isaiah 6:1-3*

Father Lord, I pray that I will not please man and displease you. I will be approved and commended by you.

"I know your works, your labour, your patience, and that you cannot bear those who are evil. And you have tested those who say they are apostles and are not and have found them liars; and you have persevered and have patience and have laboured for My name's sake and have not become weary." - *Revelations 2:2-3*

Heavenly Father, prune anything in me that is not of you, that is limiting my progress in you.

"Nevertheless, I have this against you, that you have left your first love." - *Revelations 2:4*

Father Lord, take centre place in my life and my family. Help me to recognise and know when you are knocking at the door of my life.

"Behold, I stand at the door and knock. If anyone hears My voice and opens the door, I will come in to him and dine with him, and he with Me."
- *Revelations 3:20*

I pray that my ears will be open to hear what God is saying and turn from anything that does not give Him glory. My place and position in God will not be taken away.

"Remember therefore from where you have fallen; repent and do the first works, or else I will come to you quickly and remove your lampstand from its place—unless you repent. But this you have, that you hate the deeds of the Nicolaitans, which I also hate. "He who has an ear, let him hear what the Spirit says to the churches. To him who overcomes I will give to eat from the tree of life, which is in the midst of the Paradise of God." - *Revelations 2:5-7*

SECTION 8

Restoration

Prayers for Healing and Strength

I pray against financial, relational, spiritual, physical and emotional depletion in my life in the name of Jesus.

> "The Lord will guide you always; he will satisfy your needs in a sun-scorched land and will strengthen your frame. You will be like a well-watered garden, like a spring whose waters never fail." - *Isaiah 58:11*

Dear Lord, please take away disappointments and despondency. Restore the joy of my salvation, in the name of Jesus.

> "Restore to me the joy of your salvation and grant me a willing spirit, to sustain me." - *Psalm 51:12*

Heavenly Father, search my heart and heal me from every stain of betrayal, heartbreak and disappointment.

> "But I will restore you to health and heal your wounds,' declares the Lord, 'because you are called an outcast, Zion for whom no one cares."
> - *Jeremiah 30:17*

Father Lord, heal my heart from any traumatic experience that is causing me to lose my faith in you. Restore my faith in you, O Lord.

> "But she said to them, "Do not call me Naomi; call me Mara, for the Almighty has dealt very bitterly with me. I went out full, and the Lord has brought me home again empty. Why do you call me Naomi, since the Lord has testified against me, and the Almighty has afflicted me?" - *Ruth 1:20-21*

I pray that I will not take any past hurts and pain into my new season. I am fully restored in Jesus Name.

> "Forget the former things; do not dwell on the past. See, I am doing a new thing! Now it springs up; do you not perceive it? I am making a way in the wilderness and streams in the wasteland."
> - *Isaiah 43:18-19*

Father Lord, please turn my sorrow into dancing and help me to move from bitter to better by your divine grace.

"This being so, I myself always strive to have a conscience without offence toward God and men." - *Acts 24:16*

I cast away every shadow of shame. I decree and declare that I have been set free into boldness and confidence.

"Now Dinah the daughter of Leah, whom she had borne to Jacob, went out to see the daughters of the land. And when Shechem, the son of Hamor the Hivite, prince of the country, saw her, he took her and lay with her, and violated her." - *Genesis 34:1-2*

"Instead of your shame you will receive a double portion, and instead of disgrace you will rejoice in your inheritance. And so you will inherit a double portion in your land, and everlasting joy will be yours." - *Isaiah 61:7*

Prayers for a Season of Recovery

I pray that God will bring about a season of recovery and restoration in my life such that I will be established, strengthened and settled.

> "But may the God of all grace, who called us to His eternal glory by Christ Jesus, after you have suffered a while, perfect, establish, strengthen, and settle you." - *1 Peter 5:10*

I decree and declare that this is my season of recovery, there will be no more losses in my life, it's my time of gain in Jesus' name.

> "To everything there is a season, a time for every purpose under heaven; a time to gain, and a time to

lose; a time to keep." - *Ecclesiastes 3:1;6*

Father Lord, thank you for writing a new story with my life. It is my season of replenishment and recovery in Jesus Name.

"He restores my soul; He leads me in the paths of righteousness For His name's sake." - *Psalms 23:3*

Dear Lord, help me to fully heal and recover from any traumatic experiences and unresolved conflict that is trying to dislocate me from God's will.

"He heals the broken-hearted and binds up their wounds." - *Psalm 147:3*

I pray that as I cry out to God, He will hear me and bring about recovery in my life.

"O Lord my God, I cried out to You, and You healed me. O Lord, You brought my soul up from the grave; you have kept me alive, that I should not go down to the pit." - *Psalm 30:2-3*

I decree and declare that the siege is broken in my life. God is turning things around such that my life will look like a dream.

"Now there were four leprous men at the entrance of the gate; and they said to one another, "Why are we sitting here until we die? If we say, 'We will enter the city,' the famine is in the city, and we shall die there. And if we sit here, we die also. Now therefore, come, let us surrender to the army of the Syrians. If they keep us alive, we shall live; and if they kill us, we shall only die." And they rose at twilight to go to the camp of the Syrians; and when they had come to the outskirts of the Syrian camp, to their surprise no one was there." - *2 Kings 7:3-5*

"When the Lord brought back the captivity of Zion, we were like those who dream." - *Psalm 126:1*

I decree and declare an end to robbery and plundering in my life, I am being ushered into my season of recovering in Jesus' name.

"But this is a people robbed and plundered; all of them are snared in holes, and they are hidden in prison houses; they are for prey, and no one delivers; for plunder, and no one says, "Restore!""
- *Isaiah 42:22*

Prayers for Replenishment

Father Lord, please help me recognise the areas in my life that have been depleted - financially, emotionally or spiritually.

"And my God will meet all your needs according to the riches of his glory in Christ Jesus."
- *Philippians 4:19*

Heavenly Father, grant me the spiritual wisdom needed to stay nourished by your word, and the community you have placed me in, so that I will not be depleted.

"Let the message of Christ dwell among you richly, as you teach and admonish one another with all wisdom through psalms, hymns, and songs from the Spirit, singing to God with gratitude in your hearts." - *Colossians 3:16*

I pray that I will recognise any activity that is overwhelming me or causing me to burn out.

"Martha, Martha,' the Lord answered, 'you are worried and upset about many things, but few things are needed—or indeed only one. Mary has chosen what is better, and it will not be taken away from her." - *Luke 10:41-42*

Dear Lord, help me not to be distracted by the cares of this world and cause me instead to seek your kingdom first above all else.

"Since then, you have been raised with Christ, set your hearts on things above, where Christ is, seated at the right hand of God. Set your minds on things above, not on earthly things." - *Colossians 3:2*

Heavenly Father, help me to walk step by step with you daily, so that I will always be replenished by your spirit in Jesus' name.

"Whether you turn to the right or to the left, your ears will hear a voice behind you, saying, "This is the way; walk in it." - *Isaiah 30:21*

Heavenly Father, please give me the wisdom to manage my finances so that I will not be financially depleted, but I will always have more than enough.

> "You have sown much, and bring in little; You eat, but do not have enough; You drink, but you are not filled with drink; You clothe yourselves, but no one is warm; And he who earns wages, earns wages to put into a bag with holes." – *Haggai 1:6*

Father Lord, give me a large heart that can easily forgive those who have wronged me, so that I can be replenished from any hate or bitterness.

> "Then Peter came to Jesus and asked, 'Lord, how many times shall I forgive my brother or sister who sins against me? Up to seven times? Jesus answered, 'I tell you, not seven times, but seventy-seven times."
> - *Matthew 18:21-22*

SECTION 9

Growth

Prayers to Create the Right Conditions for Your Emergence

I pray that I will guard Your word so that Satan will not take away that which You have sown in my heart, in Jesus' name.

> "And these are the ones by the wayside where the word is sown. When they hear, Satan comes immediately and takes away the word that was sown in their hearts." - *Mark 4:15*

Heavenly Father, I ask that You will help me to be a person that not only receives Your word with gladness but follows through to apply it.

"These likewise are the ones sown on stony ground who, when they hear the word, immediately receive it with gladness; and they have no root in themselves, and so endure only for a time. Afterward, when tribulation or persecution arises for the word's sake, immediately they stumble."
- *Mark 4:16-17*

Father Lord, I pray that you will help me to not be preoccupied by the cares of the world and deceitfulness of riches which can choke your word in my life.

"And the cares of this world, the deceitfulness of riches, and the desires for other things entering in choke the word, and it becomes unfruitful."
- *Mark 4:18-19*

Heavenly Father, I pray that you will direct me to be planted in the right atmosphere to nurture my seed.

"He shall be like a tree planted by the rivers of water, that brings forth its fruit in its season, whose leaf also shall not wither; and whatever he does shall prosper." - *Psalm 1:3*

I pray, Lord, that I will create the right conditions for my growth by being mindful of the things and people I am listening to.

"While He was still speaking, someone came from the ruler of the synagogue's house, saying to him, "Your daughter is dead. Do not trouble the Teacher." - *Luke 8:49*

Dear Lord, help me to have the right mindset to face the challenges ahead of me. I pray that I will not be a person that makes excuses, but one that makes progress, in Jesus' name.

"Sir," the invalid replied, "I have no one to help me into the pool when the water is stirred. While I am trying to get in, someone else goes down ahead of me." Then Jesus said to him, "Get up! Pick up your mat and walk." - *John 5:7-8*

Father Lord, I pray that from today I will stop making any excuses that are limiting my progress and destiny.

"But the men who had gone up with him said, "We are not able to go up against the people, for they are stronger than we."" - *Numbers 13:31*

Prayers to Emerge into Your Season of Greatness

Dear Lord, I pray that as I follow You, You will make me a great nation, bless me and make my name great.

> "Now the Lord had said to Abram: "Get out of your country, from your family and from your father's house, to a land that I will show you. I will make you a great nation; I will bless you and make your name great; and you shall be a blessing." - *Genesis 12:1-2*

Father, I pray that You will build something out of nothing in my life, as I continue to submit to Your will.

"And Moses said: "By this you shall know that the Lord has sent me to do all these works, for I have not done them of my own will."" - *Numbers 16:28*

I decree and declare that this is my season of fruitfulness! In this year, I will eat the fruit and increase of the land, in Jesus' name.

"When you come into the land, and have planted all kinds of trees for food, then you shall count their fruit as uncircumcised. Three years it shall be as uncircumcised to you. It shall not be eaten. But in the fourth year all its fruit shall be holy, a praise to the Lord. And in the fifth year you may eat its fruit, that it may yield to you its increase: I am the Lord your God." - *Leviticus 19:23-25*

I pray that as I am planted by the river of water, I will bear fruit every month.

"Along the bank of the river, on this side and that, will grow all kinds of trees used for food; their leaves will not wither, and their fruit will not fail. They will bear fruit every month, because their water flows from the sanctuary. Their fruit will be for food, and their leaves for medicine." - *Ezekiel 47:12*

"And he showed me a pure river of water of life, clear as crystal, proceeding from the throne of God and of the Lamb. In the middle of its street, and on either side of the river, was the tree of life, which bore twelve fruits, each tree yielding its fruit every month. The leaves of the tree were for the healing of the nations. And there shall be no more curse, but the throne of God and of the Lamb shall be in it, and His servants shall serve Him." - *Revelations 22:1-3*

I pray that as I continue to grow, the exceeding greatness of God's glory will be revealed powerfully through me.

"And you said: 'Surely the Lord our God has shown us His glory and His greatness, and we have heard His voice from the midst of the fire. We have seen this day that God speaks with man; yet he still lives." - Deuteronomy 5:24

I decree and declare that this is my season of greatness, in the mighty name of Jesus.

"You shall increase my greatness, and comfort me on every side." - *Psalm 71:21*

Father Lord, I pray that I will be humble and not exalt myself, so that you will exalt me.

"But he who is greatest among you shall be your servant. And whoever exalts himself will be humbled, and he who humbles himself will be exalted." - *Matthew 23:11-12*

Prayers for Diligence Through the Process

Dear Lord, I pray that you will help me to not behave in a way that will cause me to be rejected by you.

> "Now the Lord said to Samuel, "How long will you mourn for Saul, seeing I have rejected him from reigning over Israel? Fill your horn with oil and go; I am sending you to Jesse the Bethlehemite. For I have provided myself a king among his sons."
> - *1 Samuel 16:1*

Father Lord, I pray that I will not be prematurely exposed. Lord, help me to be ready and fully prepared for the

platforms you have created for me during the time of my lifting.

> "Woe to you, O land, when your king is a child, and your princes feast in the morning." - *Ecclesiastes 10:16*

Heavenly Father, I pray that as I wait for my own platform, you will help me to be a good follower of those before me. I will not be sluggish in serving others, in Jesus' name.

> "That you do not become sluggish, but imitate those who through faith and patience inherit the promises." - *Hebrews 6:12*

I pray that I will be diligent in studying to present myself approved by God and that I will be able to rightly divide the word of truth.

> "Be diligent to present yourself approved to God, a worker who does not need to be ashamed, rightly dividing the word of truth." - *2 Timothy 2:15*

Dear God, I pray that you will help me to grow in my discipleship, for your name's sake.

> "Now so it was that after three days they found Him in the temple, sitting in the midst of the teachers, both listening to them and asking them questions." - *Luke 2:46*

I pray for revelation and grace to live my life in a way that imitates Christ.

"Imitate me, just as I also imitate Christ."
- 1 Corinthians 11:1

I pray that I will be rewarded as I diligently seek God, in Jesus' name.

"But without faith it is impossible to please Him, for he who comes to God must believe that He is, and that He is a rewarder of those who diligently seek Him." - *Hebrews 11:6*

Prayers to Become a Valuable Person

Father Lord, I pray that you will make me a valuable person, such that Gentiles will come to my light and kings to the brightness of my rising.

> "The Gentiles shall come to your light, And kings to the brightness of your rising." - *Isaiah 60:3*

Heavenly Father, help me to invest my time in prayer and solitude with You such that my value increases, transforming me into a person in high demand that is sought after by others.

"Now in the morning, having risen a long while before daylight, He went out and departed to a solitary place; and there He prayed." - *Mark 1:35*

I pray that God will help me to guide my children to keep His ways and do righteousness and justice, so that they will be people that He can rely on and entrust with His work.

"And the Lord said, "Shall I hide from Abraham what I am doing, since Abraham shall surely become a great and mighty nation, and all the nations of the earth shall be blessed in him? For I have known him, in order that he may command his children and his household after him, that they keep the way of the Lord, to do righteousness and justice, that the Lord may bring to Abraham what He has spoken to him." - *Genesis 18:17-19*

I pray that me and my children will be people of high value in our spheres of influence, industry and nation, in Jesus' name.

"And may he be to you a restorer of life and a nourisher of your old age; for your daughter-in-law, who loves you, who is better to you than seven sons, has borne him." - *Ruth 4:15*

"But the people answered, "You shall not go out! For if we flee away, they will not care about us; nor if half of us die, will they care about us. But you are worth ten thousand of us now. For you are now more help to us in the city." - *2 Samuel 18:3*

Dear Lord, I pray that you will help me to be a person that is not just concerned about what You will *give* me, but how You will *make* me, in Jesus' name.

"And the younger of them said to his father, 'Father, give me the portion of goods that falls to me.' So, he divided to them his livelihood." - *Luke 15:12*

"And I am no longer worthy to be called your son. Make me like one of your hired servants." - *Luke 15:19*

Father Lord, I pray that as I continue to serve faithfully where I'm currently placed, my value will increase.

"Let your light so shine before men, that they may see your good works and glorify your Father in heaven." - *Matthew 5:16*

Heavenly Father, please help me to be tired of the status quo and my place of ease, so that I can grow and increase in value.

"Moab has been at ease from his youth; He has settled on his dregs, and has not been emptied from vessel to vessel, nor has he gone into captivity. Therefore, his taste remained in him, and his scent has not changed." - *Jeremiah 48:11*

SECTION 10

Breakthrough

Prayers to Break Negative Cycles

I decree and declare that I have dwelt long enough on the mountain of pain and negative cycles; I am breaking forth in this season, in Jesus' Name.

> "The Lord our God said to us at Horeb, "You have stayed long enough at this mountain. Break camp and advance into the hill country of the Amorites; go to all the neighbouring peoples in the Arabah, in the mountains, in the western foothills, in the Negev and along the coast, to the land of the Canaanites and to Lebanon, as far as the great river, the Euphrates." - *Deuteronomy 1:6*

Heavenly Father, I pray that you will reveal to me the cause of every evil cycle in my life.

"My people are destroyed from lack of knowledge. "Because you have rejected knowledge, I also reject you as my priests; because you have ignored the law of your God, I also will ignore your children."
- *Hosea 4:6*

Dear Lord, I pray that you will help me to foresee evil and hide myself.

"The prudent see danger and take refuge, but the simple keep going and pay the penalty."
- *Proverbs 22:3*

I decree and declare an end to every negative cycle passed down from generations, in Jesus' name.

"So it was, whenever Israel had sown, Midianites would come up; also, Amalekites and the people of the East would come up against them. Then they would encamp against them and destroy the produce of the earth as far as Gaza, and leave no sustenance for Israel, neither sheep nor ox nor donkey." - *Judges 6:3-4*

Father Lord, I pray that you will help me not to cover my transgressions but to confess and renounce them so I can find mercy and continue to prosper.

"Whoever conceals their sins does not prosper, but the one who confesses and renounces them finds mercy. Blessed is the one who always trembles before God, but whoever hardens their heart falls into trouble." - *Proverbs 28:13-14*

Dear Lord, I pray that by your power, I will break free from any negative cycles caused by deception.

Then Jacob said to Laban, "Give me my wife, for my days are fulfilled, that I may go in to her." And Laban gathered together all the men of the place and made a feast. Now it came to pass in the evening, that he took Leah his daughter and brought her to Jacob; and he went in to her. And Laban gave his maid Zilpah to his daughter Leah as a maid. So it came to pass in the morning, that behold, it was Leah. And he said to Laban, "what is this you have done to me? Was it not for Rachel that I served you? Why then have you deceived me?"
- *Genesis 29:23-25*

I decree and declare that I will not endure curses but will instead enjoy blessings, because the negative cycles are ending in my life, my cities shall again spread out through prosperity.

"Again proclaim, saying, 'Thus says the Lord of hosts: "My cities shall again spread out through prosperity; the Lord will again comfort Zion, and will again choose Jerusalem." - *Zachariah 1:17*

character, I will be vindicated in Jesus' name.

"With it we bless our God and Father, and with it we curse men, who have been made in the similitude of God. Out of the same mouth proceed blessing and cursing. My brethren, these things ought not to be so." - James 3:9-10

Father Lord, I ask that you will help me to deal with and break free from any division and strife in my family.

"Moreover, Absalom would say, "Oh, that I were made judge in the land, and everyone who has any suit or cause would come to me; then I would give him justice." And so it was, whenever anyone came near to bow down to him, that he would put out his hand and take him and kiss him. In this manner Absalom acted toward all Israel who came to the king for judgement. So, Absalom stole the hearts of the men of Israel." - *2 Samuel 15:4-6*

I pray for liberation from the spirit of mistrust or suspicion brought about by any offence.

"And then many will be offended, will betray one another, and will hate one another." - *Matthew 24:10*

Prayers to Shut the Door to the Enemy

I pray the enemy will not have an open door to break into my life and family.

> "And they called to Lot and said to him, "Where are the men who came to you tonight? Bring them out to us that we may know them carnally." - *Genesis 19:5*

Dear Lord, anything that is in me that is a door for the enemy to enter my life and my destiny, I remove them in the name of Jesus, I shut those doors now.

> "If she is a wall, we will build upon her A battlement

of silver; And if she is a door, we will enclose her with boards of cedar." - *Song of Songs 8:9*

I pray that the enemy will not find an opportune way into my life and Family. Any way in me that's not of you oh Lord, I pray you will uproot it.

"Therefore, putting away lying, "Let each one of you speak truth with his neighbour," for we are members of one another. "Be angry, and do not sin": do not let the sun go down on your wrath, nor give place to the devil. Let him who stole steal no longer, but rather let him labour, working with his hands what is good, that he may have something to give him who has need." - *Ephesians 4:25-28*

Father Lord, may the enemy not find an opportune time to destroy my life or any member of my family, in Jesus' name.

"Now when the devil had ended every temptation, he departed from Him until an opportune time." - *Luke 4:13*

"Then an opportune day came when Herod on his birthday gave a feast for his nobles, the high officers, and the chief men of Galilee." - *Mark 6:21*

Heavenly Father, help me to guard my eyes so I will not lust after what does not bring you glory.

"Then it happened one evening that David arose from his bed and walked on the roof of the king's house. And from the roof he saw a woman bathing, and the woman was very beautiful to behold. So, David sent and inquired about the woman. And someone said, "Is this not Bathsheba, the daughter of Eliam, the wife of Uriah the Hittite?" Then David sent messengers, and took her; and she came to him, and he lay with her, for she was cleansed from her impurity; and she returned to her house. And the woman conceived; so she sent and told David, and said, "I am with child." - *2 Samuel 11:2-5*

I pray that the gate of my ear is shut to the enemy, the music I listen to and the conversations in engage will bring you glory.

"Now the serpent was more cunning than any beast of the field which the Lord God had made. And he said to the woman, "Has God indeed said, 'You shall not eat of every tree of the garden'?" And the woman said to the serpent, "We may eat the fruit of the trees of the garden; but of the fruit of the tree, which is in the midst of the garden, God has said, 'You shall not eat it, nor shall you touch it, lest you die.' Then the serpent said to the woman, "You will not surely die." - *Genesis 3:1-4*

Dear Lord, in my home, in my workplace and city, I will be a door for God's purposes and agenda to be fulfilled. The

enemy will not be able to enter my life to use me for his evil agenda.

"When an unclean spirit goes out of a man, he goes through dry places, seeking rest, and finds none. Then he says, 'I will return to my house from which I came.' And when he comes, he finds it empty, swept, and put in order. Then he goes and takes with him seven other spirits more wicked than himself, and they enter and dwell there; and the last state of that man is worse than the first. So shall it also be with this wicked generation." - *Matthew 12:43-45*

"Now after the piece of bread, Satan entered him. Then Jesus said to him, "What you do, do quickly."" - *John 13:27*

Prayers to Enforce Your Breakthrough

Heavenly Father, for where I've been forgotten by my helpers, I pray that there will be a remembrance, in Jesus' name.

> "But remember me when it is well with you, and please show kindness to me; make mention of me to Pharaoh and get me out of this house. Then he restored the chief butler to his butlership again, and he placed the cup in Pharaoh's hand. But he hanged the chief baker, as Joseph had interpreted to them. Yet the chief butler did not remember Joseph but forgot him." - *Genesis 40:14, 21-23*

Father Lord, I pray that for every door you've set before me, that no one will be able to shut it in the name of Jesus, because I have kept your word and have not denied your name.

"I know your works. See, I have set before you an open door, and no one can shut it; for you have a little strength, have kept My word, and have not denied My name." - *Revelations 3:8*

I pray that God's favour will open every door that has been shut against me and any members of my Family.

"But You, O Lord, shall endure forever, And the remembrance of Your name to all generations."
- *Psalm 102:12*

Dear Lord, I pray that you will remove anything that is hindering me from obtaining the key to knowledge that I need to open the door to my next level of breakthrough.

"Woe to you lawyers! For you have taken away the key to knowledge. You did not enter in yourselves, and those who were entering in you hindered."
- *Luke 11:52*

Heavenly Father, help me to pass every test you are taking me through. I pray that I will not fail or miss the purpose of the test.

"And you shall remember that the Lord your God led you all the way these forty years in the wilderness, to humble you and test you, to know what was in your heart, whether you would keep His commandments or not. So He humbled you, allowed you to hunger, and fed you with manna which you did not know nor did your fathers know, that He might make you know that man shall not live by bread alone; but man lives by every word that proceeds from the mouth of the Lord."
- Deuteronomy 8:2-3

I pray that I will not be entrapped by the enemy. I break every entrapment in the name of Jesus.

"For why should you, my son, be enraptured by an immoral woman, and be embraced in the arms of a seductress? For the ways of man are before the eyes of the Lord, And He ponders all his paths. His own iniquities entrap the wicked man, and he is caught in the cords of his sin. He shall die for lack of instruction, and in the greatness of his folly he shall go astray." *- Proverbs 5:20-23*

I decree and declare that no curse over my life or that of my family will alight, in the mighty name of Jesus.

"Like a fluttering sparrow or a darting swallow, an undeserved curse does not come to rest."
- Proverbs 26:2

SECTION 11

Enlargement

Prayers to Break out of Limitation and Mediocrity

I pray against anything limiting my shining; nothing will militate against my rising and I will break out of mediocrity in Jesus' name.

> "But the path of the just is like the shining sun, that shines ever brighter unto the perfect day. The way of the wicked is like darkness; they do not know what makes them stumble." - *Proverbs 4:18-19*

I pray that everything covering my destiny will be removed in Jesus' name. My lamp will not be put under a basket.

"Nor do they light a lamp and put it under a basket, but on a lampstand, and it gives light to all who are in the house." - *Matthew 5:15*

"Now the Angel of the Lord came and sat under the terebinth tree, which was in Ophrah, which belonged to Joash the Abiezrite, while his son Gideon threshed wheat in the winepress, in order to hide it from the Midianites." - *Judges 6:11*

I decree and declare that I will manifest God's glory, my light will no longer be hidden.

"The city had no need of the sun or of the moon to shine in it, for the glory of God illuminated it. The Lamb is its light." - *Revelations 21:23*

I break the hold of the curse of blindness causing any limitation in my life.

"The Lord will strike you with madness and blindness and confusion of heart. And you shall grope at noonday, as a blind man gropes in darkness; you shall not prosper in your ways; you shall be only oppressed and plundered continually, and no one shall save you." - *Deuteronomy 28:28-29*

"Having their understanding darkened, being alienated from the life of God, because of the ignorance that is in them, because of the blindness of their heart." - *Ephesians 4:18*

I pray against the curse of blindness that wants to cause me to be forgotten to bring about delay in my life.

"Then the chief butler spoke to Pharaoh, saying: "I remember my faults this day. When Pharaoh was angry with his servants, and put me in custody in the house of the captain of the guard, both me and the chief baker." - *Genesis 41:9-10*

I pray that I will break free from every spirit of fear causing procrastination or indecision in my life to delay my destiny.

"But the men who had gone up with him said, "We are not able to go up against the people, for they are stronger than we." And they gave the children of Israel a bad report of the land which they had spied out, saying, "The land through which we have gone as spies is a land that devours its inhabitants, and all the people whom we saw in it are men of great stature. There we saw the giants (the descendants of Anak came from the giants); and we were like grasshoppers in our own sight, and so we were in their sight." - *Numbers 13:31-33*

I pray against any operation of a curse causing a distorted self-image in my life. I will see myself as God sees me in Jesus' name, so I can walk in the fullness of all He has for me.

"And the Angel of the Lord appeared to him, and said to him, "The Lord is with you, you mighty man of valour!" Gideon said to Him, "O my lord, if the Lord is with us, why then has all this happened to us? And where are all His miracles which our fathers told us about, saying, 'Did not the Lord bring us up from Egypt?' But now the Lord has forsaken us and delivered us into the hands of the Midianites." Then the Lord turned to him and said, "Go in this might of yours, and you shall save Israel from the hand of the Midianites. Have I not sent you?" So he said to Him, "O my Lord, how can I save Israel? Indeed my clan is the weakest in Manasseh, and I am the least in my father's house." - *Judges 6:12 & 13-15*

"There we saw the giants (the descendants of Anak came from the giants); and we were like grasshoppers in our own sight, and so we were in their sight." - *Numbers 13:33*

Prayers for Multiplication of Your Resources

Father Lord, I pray that you will multiply the resources in my hands, in Jesus' name.

> "Now may He who supplies seed to the sower, and bread for food, supply and multiply the seed you have sown and increase the fruits of your righteousness, while you are enriched in everything for all liberality, which causes thanksgiving through us to God." - *2 Corinthians 9:10-11*

Heavenly Father, I pray that you will help me to have a multiplication mindset as You desire.

"Then God blessed them, and God said to them, "Be fruitful and multiply; fill the earth and subdue it; have dominion over the fish of the sea, over the birds of the air, and over every living thing that moves on the earth." - *Genesis 1:28*

I pray, oh Lord, that I will be a person that is not just seedful, but fruitful.

"Then God said, 'Let the earth bring forth grass, the herb that yields seed, and the fruit tree that yields fruit according to its kind, whose seed is in itself, on the earth.' And it was so." - *Genesis 1:11*

Dear Lord, I pray that you will help me to unlock the potential that you have blessed me with to its fullest extent.

"Now may He who supplies seed to the sower, and bread for food, supply and multiply the seed you have sown and increase the fruits of your righteousness, while you are enriched in everything for all liberality, which causes thanksgiving through us to God." - *2 Corinthians 9:10-11*

Father Lord, help me to be faithful in what you have entrusted into my hand so that it may be multiplied.

"And to one he gave five talents, to another two, and to another one, to each according to his own ability;

and immediately he went on a journey. Then he who had received the five talents went and traded with them and made another five talents. And likewise he who had received two gained two more also."
- *Matthew 25:15-17*

"So take the talent from him and give it to him who has ten talents." - *Matthew 25:28*

I pray that God will reveal secrets to me of how I can multiply my resources and impact, in Jesus' name.

"So Elisha said to her, "What shall I do for you? Tell me, what do you have in the house?" And she said, "Your maidservant has nothing in the house but a jar of oil." Then he said, "Go, borrow vessels from everywhere, from all your neighbours - empty vessels; do not gather just a few. And when you have come in, you shall shut the door behind you and your sons; then pour it into all those vessels, and set aside the full ones." So she went from him and shut the door behind her and her sons, who brought the vessels to her; and she poured it out. Now it came to pass, when the vessels were full, that she said to her son, "Bring me another vessel." And he said to her, "There is not another vessel." So the oil ceased."
- *2 Kings 4:2-6*

Heavenly Father, help me to be an available vessel for you to use, empty out the things filling my life that's stopping

me from giving myself fully to you.

"Then he said, "Go, borrow vessels from everywhere, from all your neighbours - empty vessels; do not gather just a few." - *2 Kings 4:3*

Prayers for Enlargement of Your Financial Capacity

Heavenly Father, I pray that you will help me to have the right attitude to money so I can multiply and not squander it.

> "There is desirable treasure, and oil in the dwelling of the wise, but a foolish man squanders it."
> - *Proverbs 21:20*

Dear Lord, I pray that you will help me to stop wastage through foolish spending so that my financial capacity will be enlarged.

> "Much food is in the fallow ground of the poor, and for lack of justice there is waste." - *Proverbs 13:23*

I pray that I will be set free from the spirit and stronghold of debt. I will have the means to pay what I owe, in Jesus' name.

> "The rich rules over the poor, and the borrower is servant to the lender." - *Proverbs 22:7*

> "Indeed the wages of the labourers who mowed your fields, which you kept back by fraud, cry out; and the cries of the reapers have reached the ears of the Lord of Sabaoth. You have lived on the earth in pleasure and luxury; you have fattened your hearts as in a day of slaughter. You have condemned, you have murdered the just; he does not resist you."
> - *James 5:4-6*

Heavenly Father, I pray that I will never be dishonest with money, in Jesus' name.

> "Wealth gained by dishonesty will be diminished, but he who gathers by labour will increase."
> - *Proverbs 13:11*

Heavenly Father, I pray that you will help me not to be greedy with money.

"He who is greedy for gain troubles his own house, but he who hates bribes will live." - *Proverbs 15:27*

I pray against the curse of blindness that wants to deceive me into making wrong financial decisions.

"Now it came to pass in the evening, that he took Leah his daughter and brought her to Jacob; and he went in to her. And Laban gave his maid Zilpah to his daughter Leah as a maid." - *Genesis 29:23-24*

Father Lord, I pray that as I remain faithful over what is in my hands you will enlarge my financial capacity.

"His lord said to him, 'Well done, good and faithful servant; you were faithful over a few things, I will make you ruler over many things. Enter into the joy of your lord." - *Matthew 25:21*

Prayers to Invoke Financial Wealth

Father Lord, I pray that you will give me the power to get wealth and activate the covenant of Abraham over my life.

> "And you shall remember the Lord your God, for it is He who gives you power to get wealth, that He may establish His covenant which He swore to your fathers, as it is this day." - *Deuteronomy 8:18*

I pray that as I am faithful with little, I will be furnished with authority over much, in Jesus' name.

> "And he said to him, "Well done, good servant; because you were faithful in a very little, have authority over ten cities." - *Luke 19:17*

Dear Lord, I pray that I will shift from a slave mentality to an owner mentality.

"Then Joseph said to the people, "Indeed I have bought you and your land this day for Pharaoh. Look, here is seed for you, and you shall sow the land." - *Genesis 47:23*

I decree and declare that I will enter a new dimension of supernatural wealth, in Jesus' mighty name.

"So it shall be, when the Lord your God brings you into the land of which He swore to your fathers, to Abraham, Isaac, and Jacob, to give you large and beautiful cities which you did not build, houses full of all good things, which you did not fill, hewn-out wells which you did not dig, vineyards and olive trees which you did not plant - when you have eaten and are full..." - *Deuteronomy 6:10-11*

Heavenly Father, please help me to discern and maximise my season of supernatural favour and wealth.

"Now the children of Israel had done according to the word of Moses, and they had asked from the Egyptians articles of silver, articles of gold, and clothing. And the Lord had given the people favour in the sight of the Egyptians, so that they granted them what they requested. Thus they plundered the Egyptians." - *Exodus 12:35-36*

Dear Lord, I pray that you will enlarge my financial capacity, such that I will be able to store up wealth for my family and future generations.

> "There are four things which are little on the earth, but they are exceedingly wise: the ants are a people not strong, yet they prepare their food in the summer." - *Proverbs 30:24-25*

Heavenly Father, open my eyes to understand your power at work in me to inherit the wealth of nations.

> "Then you shall see and become radiant, and your heart shall swell with joy; because the abundance of the sea shall be turned to you, the wealth of the Gentiles shall come to you." - *Isaiah 60:5*

SECTION 12

Celebration

Prayers on Thanksgiving to Provoke Miracles

I pray that through my praise, everything that represents bitter waters in my life and destiny will be turned to sweet waters.

> "Let the peoples praise You, O God; let all the peoples praise You." - *Psalm 67:5*

I pray that I will live a life full of praise so that my life and that of my family will not be full of pain.

> "Then He took the five loaves and the two fish, and looking up to heaven, He blessed and broke them,

and gave them to the disciples to set before the multitude." - *Luke 9:16*

Dear Lord, as my family and I praise you continually, let the earth yield her increase and bless us.

"Then the earth shall yield her increase; God, our own God, shall bless us." - *Psalm 67:6*

Heavenly Father, in every situation, I bow down before you in praise. I will not be afraid nor dismayed.

"And Jehoshaphat bowed his head with his face to the ground, and all Judah and the inhabitants of Jerusalem bowed before the Lord, worshipping the Lord." - *2 Chronicles 20:18*

Father Lord, I and my family will continually lift our voices loud and high in praises before you and we shall be established.

"Then the Levites of the children of the Kohathites and of the children of the Korahites stood up to praise the Lord God of Israel with voices loud and high. So they rose early in the morning and went out into the Wilderness of Tekoa; and as they went out, Jehoshaphat stood and said, "Hear me, O Judah and you inhabitants of Jerusalem: believe in the Lord your God, and you shall be established; believe His prophets, and you shall prosper." - *2 Chronicles 20:19-20*

I pray that I and my family will receive beauty for ashes, oil of joy for mourning and a garment of praise for the spirit of heaviness.

"To console those who mourn in Zion, to give them beauty for ashes, the oil of joy for mourning, the garment of praise for the spirit of heaviness; that they may be called trees of righteousness, the planting of the Lord, that He may be glorified." - *Isaiah 61:3*

I pray that things of praise will not end in my life and family. Our praises will bring forth fruitfulness in all areas of our lives.

"Sing, O barren, you who have not borne! Break forth into singing, and cry aloud, you who have not laboured with child! For more are the children of the desolate than the children of the married woman," says the Lord. "Enlarge the place of your tent, and let them stretch out the curtains of your dwellings; do not spare; lengthen your cords, and strengthen your stakes." - *Isaiah 54:1-2*

Prayers for Your Shining

I pray for the wisdom that will cause my life and destiny to shine forever.

> "Those who are wise shall shine like the brightness of the firmament, and those who turn many to righteousness like the stars forever and ever."
> - *Daniel 12:3*

I pray that as the star of Jesus was not hidden but shined and announced him, my star will not be hidden.

> "Saying, "Where is He who has been born King of the Jews? For we have seen His star in the East and have come to worship Him." - *Matthew 2:2*

I pray that whoever has seen my star potential and is troubled as a result will be put to shame.

"When Herod the king heard this, he was troubled, and all Jerusalem with him." - *Matthew 2:3*

Father Lord, scatter every gathering and conspiracy of the enemy over my life because of my star, in Jesus' name.

"And when he had gathered all the chief priests and scribes of the people together, he inquired of them where the Christ was to be born." - *Matthew 2:4*

Heavenly Father, destroy those who seek to destroy my life and my star. With my ear I will hear of their destruction.

"Now when they had departed, behold, an angel of the Lord appeared to Joseph in a dream, saying, "Arise, take the young Child and His mother, flee to Egypt, and stay there until I bring you word; for Herod will seek the young Child to destroy Him." Now when Herod was dead, behold, an angel of the Lord appeared in a dream to Joseph in Egypt, saying, "Arise, take the young Child and His mother, and go to the land of Israel, for those who sought the young Child's life are dead." Then he arose, took the young Child and His mother, and came into the land of Israel." - *Matthew 2:13, 19-21*

I pray against anyone that wants to manipulate my star and overpower me; my star will be untouchable because you have blessed me.

"Then God came to Balaam and said, "Who are these men with you?" So Balaam said to God, "Balak the son of Zippor, king of Moab, has sent to me, saying, 'Look, a people has come out of Egypt, and they cover the face of the earth. Come now, curse them for me; perhaps I shall be able to overpower them and drive them out.'" And God said to Balaam, "You shall not go with them; you shall not curse the people, for they are blessed." - *Numbers 22:9-12*

I decree and declare that creation will arise to help me in the actualisation of my star.

"Then he dreamed still another dream and told it to his brothers, and said, "look, I have dreamed another dream. And this time, the sun, the moon, and the eleven stars bowed down to me." - *Genesis 37:9*

Prayers for An Attitude of Gratitude

I pray that in everything I will give thanks and maintain an attitude of gratitude.

"Pray without ceasing, in everything give thanks; for this is the will of God in Christ Jesus for you."
- *1 Thessalonians 5:17-18*

Father Lord, give me a deep and ongoing appreciation of your goodness in my life despite all the uncertainty and ongoing turmoil.

"Giving thanks always for all things to God the Father in the name of our Lord Jesus Christ."
- *Ephesians 5:20*

Heavenly Father, transform my perspective. Instead of looking at what I have lost, help me to see what you are doing in my life and family.

> "Blessed be the Lord, who daily loads us with benefits, the God of our salvation! Selah."
> - *Psalm 68:19*

Dear Lord, give me the grace to be grateful for what you have done in the past and for it to serve as a reminder of what you will do even though I may not currently see it.

> "Abram passed through the land to the place of Shechem, as far as the terebinth tree of Moreh. And the Canaanites were then in the land. Then the Lord appeared to Abram and said, "To your descendants I will give this land." And there he built an altar to the Lord, who had appeared to him."
> - *Genesis 12:6-7*

Heavenly Father, help me to be grateful for who you are and who you are in my life. Also, help me to be grateful for the privilege of knowing you and all that you have available to me.

> "One thing I have desired of the Lord, that will I seek: that I may dwell in the house of the Lord all the days of my life, to behold the beauty of the Lord, and to inquire in His temple. For in the time of trouble He shall hide me in His pavilion; in the secret place

of His tabernacle He shall hide me; he shall set me high upon a rock." - *Psalm 27:4-5*

I pray that I will be grateful for the promise of the brighter future God has for me and my family.

"Thus says the Lord: "Refrain your voice from weeping, and your eyes from tears; For your work shall be rewarded, says the Lord, and they shall come back from the land of the enemy. There is hope in your future, says the Lord, that your children shall come back to their own border." - *Jeremiah 31:16-17*

I pray that my testimony will always be "Thus far the Lord has helped me" no matter what the circumstances look like.

"Then Samuel took a stone and set it up between Mizpah and Shen, and called its name Ebenezer, saying, "Thus far the Lord has helped us."
- *1 Samuel 7:12*

Prayers to Stop Disappointments, Complaints and Lamentations in Your Life

I pray the enemy will not be able to use disappointment to push me away from your presence and blind me to see what God is doing in my life.

> "Yet at the scent of water it will bud and bring forth branches like a plant." - *Job 14:9*

Dear Lord, help me to not tempt you nor complain so my life and destiny will not be destroyed.

"Nor let us tempt Christ, as some of them also tempted, and were destroyed by serpents; nor complain, as some of them also complained, and were destroyed by the destroyer."
- 1 Corinthians 10:9-10

I pray that for every disappointment, I will have a reason to give God thanks.

"So Moses brought Israel from the Red Sea; then they went out into the Wilderness of Shur. And they went three days in the wilderness and found no water. Now when they came to Marah, they could not drink the waters of Marah, for they were bitter. Therefore the name of it was called Marah. And the people complained against Moses, saying, "What shall we drink?" So he cried out to the Lord, and the Lord showed him a tree. When he cast it into the waters, the waters were made sweet. There He made a statute and an ordinance for them, and there He tested them." - *Exodus 15:22-25*

Father Lord, reveal anyone around me and my family with ill intent towards our life and destiny. Their plan will not succeed over our lives in Jesus Name.

"Then Herod, when he had secretly called the wise men, determined from them what time the star appeared. And he sent them to Bethlehem and said, "Go and search carefully for the young Child, and

when you have found Him, bring back word to me, that I may come and worship Him also."
- Matthew 2:7-8

I pray that star destroyers will not destroy my star. The sound of weeping and lamentation will be far away from me and my family.

"A voice was heard in Ramah, lamentation, weeping, and great mourning, Rachel weeping for her children, refusing to be comforted, because they are no more." - *Matthew 2:18*

I pray that my star and destiny will not remain small but shall break forth and increase abundantly.

"Though your beginning was small, yet your latter end would increase abundantly." - *Job 8:7*

Heavenly Father, help me to know that you are with me and fighting every battle before me. Help me to know that my part is to position myself, to stand still and see your salvation.

"You will not need to fight in this battle. Position yourselves, stand still and see the salvation of the Lord, who is with you, O Judah and Jerusalem!' Do not fear or be dismayed; tomorrow go out against them, for the Lord is with you." - *2 Chronicles 20:17*

Printed in Dunstable, United Kingdom

77973417R00111

Burke in the Peninsula

Tom Williams

First published by Big Red 2020

ISBN 978-1-9162635-5-0

JAMES FLORENCE BURKE

Born Ireland 1771

Enlisted Regiment of Dillon (France). Saw active service in Sainte Domingue. Surrendered to British in 1793

Detached for special duties at the War Office

1793/4: confidential duties in Ireland

1798: confidential duties in Egypt

1805: confidential duties in Argentina

1806: attached to British forces in Buenos Aires

1806: promoted to Captain

1807: confidential mission to the Spanish court

1808: promoted to major

1808: diplomatic posting to Brazil

1809: diplomatic posting to Argentina

1809: attached to General Hill in Spain

1815: confidential work with Allied occupation forces in Paris

1815: attached to the Hussars of Croy. Saw action at Waterloo

For those who like to keep track of these things, the action in this book takes place in 1809, immediately on Burke's return from Argentina at the end of *Burke in the Land of Silver.*

CONTENTS

Chapter 1: Spanish practices

James Burke felt his mission to South America had ended well. He'd been ordered to make sure that the French could not get their hands on the silver Spain mined there. Perhaps His Majesty's Government had not expected Major Burke to achieve this by fighting alongside Argentina's revolutionaries, but the goal had very definitely been achieved. It was, he conceded, a shade undiplomatic to run-off with the Spanish governor's mistress, but the governor beat her and she was more than happy to leave. Besides, she had abandoned Burke before they could find a ship to bring them back to England.

He had convinced himself that he had nothing on his conscience, so he could not understand why his interview with Colonel Gordon was making him so uncomfortable.

"I hear you had an interesting time in South America."

Burke admitted that he had.

Colonel Gordon smiled – or, at least, his lips jerked into what Burke supposed must be intended as a smile.

"Still, all's well that ends well. I suppose we must account your mission a success." The colonel's mouth twitched again, shaping might well have been another smile and Burke realised that his commanding officer was never going to reveal how much he did or didn't know about the details of his man's exploits in Buenos Aires.

"Thank you, sir."

Gordon paused. It was quite a long pause. Then: "Things getting a bit messy in Spain. Lots of irregulars. Civilians joining in the fighting. That sort of thing. Wellesley needs all the help he can get."

"I believe my regiment has left Spain, sir." For a moment he hoped he might have caught Gordon off guard. "The Queen's Royal Regiment, sir," he added, helpfully.

Gordon harrumphed. My God, thought Burke, I had always imagined that to be a turn of speech. He had never heard anyone actually say, "Harrumph!" before.

"I am perfectly aware of your regiment, major. In fact, some of your chaps got left behind. Careless really. They're joining Wellesley." A moment's pause. "As are you."

Burke brightened. It was what he had always wanted: to be back in the lines after fifteen years skulking as a spy, dirtying his hands with the jobs the government wanted done but didn't want to be seen to be doing.

"It's convenient. You can travel out there, ostensibly to join your old comrades in the Battalion of Detachments."

Burke did not like that "ostensibly".

"In fact, you'll be reporting to General Hill. They need a man who can pass for a Spaniard. Someone who can make himself useful with the irregulars." He looked up and fixed Burke with a disconcertingly sharp eye. "Someone who is prepared to fight dirty if it gets things done." The smile again, but this time with some genuine, if malicious, humour. "I like to think I can always rely on an Irishman in a brawl."

So that was how things stood. He was being punished for South America.

Gordon was already pushing a movement order across his desk.

"Take yourself to Tilbury and this should get you on the first vessel sailing out to Portugal. Good luck!"

Burke's boots clattered on the stairs as he hurried from the building and out onto Whitehall. Sent off on more dirty work and damned as an Irishman to boot! He could feel the colour rising to his cheeks. Still, if that was an end to it, he supposed he had probably got off lightly.

* * *

Sergeant William Brown was whistling *The Soldier Boy* when Burke found him at his quarters in the Tower.

"I don't know why you're so infernally cheerful."

That was, of course, not entirely true. Burke's *inamorata* might have abandoned him in South America, but his sergeant had fared rather better in the romance stakes. Molly had returned to England with him and now ran the Crown in Whitechapel, conveniently to hand from William's quarters in the Tower.

“Movement orders.” Burke threw the papers down on William’s cot. As his sergeant read through them, the whistling stopped, but he seemed far from unhappy with what he saw.

“Spain.” William grinned. “I had some fun in Spain.” He was, Burke thought, a natural soldier. Spain would mean heat and hardship and a real risk of death, from disease if not from the enemy, but Sergeant Brown would go there willingly if there was battle to be had.

"Colonel Gordon has us down for more dirty work when we get there, but we're officially travelling to join a detached unit of the Queen’s Royal Regiment, so at least we will travel as soldiers.”

“I’ll give your boots an extra shine then.”

"I think they're polished well enough. You'd best take yourself home and make your peace with Molly. We’re sailing on Wednesday.”

The remains of the grin faded from William's face, and Burke felt a momentary sympathy. Still, Molly had known what she was letting herself in for when she took up with a soldier. He just wished the viceroy's woman had as much sense. He made his way back to his own quarters, shaking his head. Women! Nothing but trouble. He should have learned by now. Still, he wouldn't make the same mistake again.

* * *

The journey to Tilbury was familiar enough. Burke supposed that, as the Navy was to take him to Portugal, the Navy could have arranged transport down the Thames, but there was a perfectly good road and he’d as soon travel by land as spend more time on the water than he had to.

Tilbury was, in Burke’s view, a vile place. It seemed prosperous enough, for docks were always a good source of income for traders licit and illicit. There were chandlers and slop shops where sailors could buy clothes that would be good enough for a voyage or two once they had been boiled to get rid of the last owner’s lice and fleas. Several taverns were doing good business, for all it was only mid-afternoon and the whores were parading shamelessly along the dock walls.

It took a while to find the right gate, for all the gates were guarded and the sentries seemed to take a perverse delight in directing Burke to one wrong entrance after another. Perhaps they had some private arrangement with the porters who carried his campaign chest. The two miserable fellows had been following him for almost half an hour by now and would certainly demand a fair recompense for their time.

William suggested that they pass through with one of the carts or in the groups of workers who came and went without exciting any interest from the sentries, but Burke would have none of it.

"For once I can travel honestly under my own name. I won't be sneaking in like –"

“Like you do all the time by way of business.” William completed Burke’s sentence and earned himself a venomous look. Fortunately, Burke’s attention was distracted by a particularly persistent beggar.

“Old soldier, sir. Fought with Wellesley in India, sir.”

“Not that old.” Burke’s irritation now had another outlet. “If you’re a soldier, why aren’t you still serving?”

The man said nothing, but held up his hand. Where his fingers should have been, there was just a stump. The injury was, as these things went, a minor one, but he would never fire a musket again.

Burke took one look at the hand and dug a shilling from his purse. There but for the Grace of God… The beggar looked at the coin and, drawing himself to attention, threw Burke a salute, which Burke was careful to return.

Burke’s little procession moved on to the next gate where, as luck would have it, the sentry admitted that they were at the right place and even directed them to the quay where they would find the *Statira*.

Burke, William and the porters joined the sailors, dockyard workers, suppliers and general hangers-on who were making their way towards the wharves. They had, though, scarcely walked twenty paces from the gate when there was a sudden commotion behind him.

“Stop! Stop that man!”

The guard had his musket to his shoulder, but was obviously reluctant to pull the trigger. Given the number of people around the

gate and the notorious inaccuracy of muskets, Burke was very glad that he didn't.

People were already responding to the shouts. Burke caught the briefest glimpse of a running figure, but then all he could see was the crowd setting off after it.

William looked longingly in the direction of the excitement. “Shall we join in?”

"I don't think so. There seem to be enough hounds on that particular scent already.”

Tilbury was a big port and they took a couple of wrong turns before they finally saw the masts of the little brig-sloop that was to take them on the first leg of their journey.

The porters, who had rested Burke’s chest on the ground while he had once again looked about for directions, gave an audible sigh of relief as they started toward the ship. At that moment, though, the hue and cry that they had seen vanishing westwards when they enter the gate now emerged running along the dockside towards them.

“Bloody hell!” William sounded quite disgusted. “Have they still not caught him?”

“Perhaps we had best join in this time.”

Burke and William headed for the excitement, while behind them the porters dropped the chest onto the cobbles with a crash designed to demonstrate their unhappiness with yet another delay. Burke vaguely registered the sound, but his attention was now concentrated ahead of him. The running figure saw that his path was cut off and hesitated and in that moment the mob was on him.

“Oh, well.” William sounded resigned to missing out on the fun. “Too late to join in after all.” He turned to head back to the *Statira*, but Burke put out a hand to stop him.

“I think I recognised that fellow. Let's find out what's going on.”

He pushed his way through the crowd, men allowing him to pass out of grudging respect for his red coat. By the time he reached the centre, though, the man they had been chasing had already been beaten to the ground and blows were falling on him from all sides. It was lucky that, many of those around him being sailors, and sailors often going bootless, he was at least spared the kicking he might otherwise have expected. Even so, his face was bloodied and

the cries that had guided Burke in his direction were already fading to whimpers.

"What in God's name do you think you're doing?" Burke's anger checked the mob for a moment and then a dozen voices responded.

"He's a spy."

"A Froggie spy."

"He's going to set fires in the docks."

So that was it. If Burke had a guinea for every story he had heard about French spies, he would be a rich man by now. There were spies of course: agents among the emigres who flocked to the fashionable London salons; messengers who carried ciphered instructions on the boats that smuggled French brandy onto the coast of Kent. He had no doubt that there were men who watched the semaphore towers that carried signals from London to the fleet in Portsmouth. But he did not believe that they had infiltrated cripples to penetrate His Majesty's dockyards.

Burke knelt beside the man and gently reached for his right hand. "He'll struggle to strike a spark with this, won't he?"

There was a moment's silence as people looked at the fingerless ruin of the hand. Then: "He can still be a spy."

There was a murmuring around him. The man looked French, didn't he?

"He's English, you fools: an old soldier begging at the dock gate. Who set up the hue and cry?"

The marine who had been on guard now shuffled through the crowd. Yes, he had challenged him. The man had no business in the docks and had run when ordered to stop.

"You knew him, then?"

Yes, the sentry admitted: he was a familiar figure. "He begs at the gate. He's always trying to get in because he thinks he might be able to beg food off the ships. The sailors can be soft on a cripple."

Who had said the man was a French spy? There was a silence. The mob was already drifting away and those who remained were taking a sudden interest in the ground at their feet.

Burke took a guinea from his purse and gave it to the marine. "Get him a room in an inn. See he's looked after."

"Yes, sir."

The marine did not appear to Burke to be a bad man. He had, after all, just been doing his job. It was the mob's fear of spies that had done the damage. Burke had heard that somewhere in the North they had hanged a monkey as an agent of Napoleon. It seemed to him that the government's propaganda warning of spies was doing more damage than the spies themselves ever would.

The marine was already helping the beggar to his feet and they limped off as Burke went back to recover his chest.

The porters were not happy to have been kept waiting. The taller one spat as Burke approached. "They say you saved some Froggie spy from a beating."

Burke felt suddenly weary. "He wasn't a spy."

"You'd know, would you? Know a lot about spying, do you?" The man spoke with a sneer.

Burke said nothing, but turned towards the *Statira.*

William remained to deal with the porters. "You can bugger off now. I'll get some sailors to carry our kit."

"You'd better pay us now then. Your man owes us a sixpence apiece for all the pissing around we've been doing."

William smiled, stepped close to him and hit him very hard in the stomach.

"Which part of bugger off don't you understand?"

The porters looked at each other and then at William. For a moment they hesitated. William smiled the smile of a man who really, really wants to hurt somebody and thinks he might soon have the opportunity to do so.

"Keep your bloody shilling," the tall man said, and they turned and walked back the way they had come with all the dignity they could muster. Burke, who had paused to watch the altercation, thought they didn't muster much dignity at all.

* * *

The incident at Tilbury was the most excitement they were to see until they reached Portugal. *HMS Statira* was a fifth rater, but quite good enough to get him and William Brown to Lisbon. They made good time, even though they had to pause at Guernsey where a dozen or more merchantmen were gathering. Britain might be

winning the war at sea, but French raiders could sometimes slip past the British blockade to prey on any unarmed vessels they might come across. The ships supplying Wellington's armies must sail in convoys and the *Statira* was to escort this little fleet across the Bay of Biscay until it arrived safe off Portugal.

It was a pleasant enough trip. Burke was allocated a bunk with one of the lieutenants. He was very conscious of the intrusion into the young man’s already cramped accommodation and apologised for the inconvenience he must be causing.

“Do not trouble yourself about it, Major. We sailors are used to living cheek-by-jowl. I am only too happy to have a fresh face aboard. We are a small ship and it is easy to tire of each other’s company.”

The lieutenant’s remark seemed no less than the truth: Burke’s company was appreciated by all the officers. Captain Boys generally dined with his lieutenants and Burke joined them every night. The first night they feasted on a boiled leg of mutton, a roast goose, vegetables and a pudding, and if subsequent dinners were less lavish, they still gave the lie to the notion that sailors subsisted on salt beef and dry biscuits. The meals were washed down with port, which was apparently spoils of war, the *Statira* having intercepted a French schooner laden with liquor on an earlier voyage.

Good company, good food and excellent wine meant the voyage passed quickly and pleasantly. They were blessed with favourable winds and no rough weather and only six days after leaving Tilbury, Burke and William were taking their first steps onto the soil of Portugal.

Chapter 2: The Plain in Spain

Burke sniffed the air of Lisbon and was not impressed. Like so many ports, the place stank of fish and sewage, but Lisbon in June was almost unbearably hot, and the temperature meant that the stench was particularly pronounced.

Still, it looked pleasant enough, and the wharves were busy with sailors and stevedores bustling about the docks. The arrival of the convoy would mean a lively couple of days ahead for all the workers on the water and a profitable few nights for the taverns and brothels that served the port. What Burke did not see was any sign of soldiers, British or Portuguese.

Burke turned to where Sergeant Brown was supervising the porters carrying his campaign chest along the quay. He would have quite liked an excuse to stretch his legs after the voyage, but it wouldn't do for a major to run his own errands in Lisbon. "Leave those fellows, Brown. They'll manage the baggage well enough on their own. Go and find someone who can tell us where we're taking it."

"They're billeting new arrivals in a warehouse over there." William pointed along the harbour.

Burke was, as ever, impressed with the man's ability to find accommodation wherever, it seemed, their wanderings took them. He had no intention, though, of spending any longer than he needed to on the Lisbon harbour front.

"After that, Brown. After that. Find somebody who knows where the Army is and somebody else who knows how we can get the horses we need to catch up with them."

"Sir." Brown produced a fair simulacrum of a respectable salute, which Burke was reasonably sure was ironic. Still, while they were both wearing the King's uniform and in public in a foreign land, it behove them to observe the proper distinctions of rank.

Burke noticed a thread of hemp that had blown onto his sleeve and brushed it away. He wanted to enjoy the resplendent scarlet coat for as long as he could. For a few days he could be an honest soldier, rather than one of His Majesty's Confidential Agents. He

hated the scurrying in dark corners; the betrayals and the knives in the dark. Still, it was work that needed doing and he knew himself to be very good at it. There may be no glory in his line of business, but he did his part in bringing down Napoleon, just as much as any other soldier.

He turned his attention to the porters. As soon as William had left, they had set their load down and started to talk amongst themselves.

Wearily Burke walked back toward them. “Get a move on!” No response. Damn it, Burke thought, they dealt with British officers all the time. He was confident that they understood him. He drew himself up in his uniform and, every inch a soldier of the King, repeated his demand, slowly and more loudly, as British tradition dictated. Only when there was again no response was he reduced to demonstrating the fluid Portuguese that he had acquired from his time living in Brazil. The string of expletives that accompanied his instructions this time included one or two that the porters had not heard before, even from local customers. Without further delay, they heaved the chest to their shoulders and staggered their way toward the warehouse Sergeant Brown had pointed out.

Barely ten minutes later, Burke was sat on the chests waiting for William Brown's return. The walls of the warehouse had been hastily white-washed, but the paint was already peeling away and the building smelled of damp. In one noisome corner, stacks of pallets suggested that several hundred men had once slept here, but now the place was almost empty. A few idle fellows stood nervously, looking at the major who had suddenly appeared in their midst. They were a shabby bunch: men who had, in one way or another, managed to avoid moving off with the Army and were now waiting for the military bureaucracy to catch up with them. They did not look the type who were comfortable in the presence of officers under the best of circumstances and this warehouse clearly did not represent the best of circumstances. Burke had stood them down with a casual "Carry on," but they stayed awkwardly shuffling, their silence broken only by the occasional cough.

Burke was as keen to be on his way as they were clearly anxious to be rid of him. Obviously there was some hotel or other lodgings in the town suitable for officers, for he was sure that none had spent

a minute longer than they needed to in these insalubrious surroundings. Until William came back, though, Burke had little choice but to stay where he was.

In the end William was away for several hours and returned in the late afternoon with unhappy news.

"It's not looking too clever," he said, after he had chased the idling soldiers away with the enthusiasm for discipline that all sergeants seemed to share. "Our lads marched out yesterday and catching them up will be tricky. The Army bought up every horse within ten miles of Lisbon before they moved off."

"Every horse?"

"All the ones that were for sale."

"Then I suggest we find some that weren't for sale and conscript them into the war effort."

William shook his head in a definite negative. "Strict orders from General Wellesley himself: the Portuguese are our gallant allies. Nothing to be seized and all goods taken to be paid for."

"Well that leaves us in a fine pickle. Have you any suggestions?"

"Well…" William Brown hesitated. "The convoy we came in with, sir: there'll be a supply train to carry everything up to the Army. There's not much you see. I had a word with the Quartermaster-General's office and they've got carts and waggons rolling out in a couple of days. They'll let us travel in the carts."

Burke rose to his feet, brushing dirt from his white breeches. "I had hoped that, for once, I might travel as befits an officer and a gentleman."

William looked sympathetic. "Best I can do, sir. I have found somewhere to stay while we're waiting for them to unload the ships. That's something, at any rate."

It was, Burke admitted, something. In fact, William had done him proud. He found himself billeted with a Portuguese wine merchant who was happy to share his cellar with a British officer. And if William's own arrangements meant he found a corner in the servants' quarters for himself, it was, Burke conceded, no more than he deserved.

Two days later, the ships were unloaded and the Army's supplies were ready for their journey into Spain. Burke, William, and the porters with his baggage were back on the quayside before the sun

had risen. The day, Burke knew, would be hot, but at this hour there was a chill coming off the water. Men and horses shuffled to keep warm.

The convoy lacked any air of military smartness. The Army had clearly requisitioned anything it could get hold of that had wheels on. Burke thought of the columns marching towards Madrid and imagined how many carts must already have been dispatched to follow them. Feeding an army was a mighty undertaking. The wonder was that there was any transport left there at all.

He heard William's voice raised in altercation with one of the carters and made his way over to see what the fuss was about.

"He says he won't take the chest, sir. Says there's no room."

Burke looked at the cart. Rickety as it was, it was a decent size and his baggage consisted of a single chest, albeit a huge campaign chest designed to carry everything the modern officer might need in the field. He had, it was true, travelled and fought for months with no more than he could carry, but one campaign chest was, for a respectable major, a very modest amount of equipment indeed. It was bad enough that officers who fought a more conventional style of warfare would sneer at him behind his back, without their also condescending to him because his personal kit was visibly inferior to their own.

"There's room."

The carter was a big man and carried himself with the casual swagger of a habitual bar fighter but there seemed to be something about this major that made him hesitate. Burke reached for his purse and produced a gold sovereign. "Just put it in the cart. I don't want to hear any more about it." He turned and strode toward the head of the column without looking back. Behind him William helped the carter load the chest.

The incident had not improved Burke's temper and when he was unceremoniously allocated a seat alongside a Portuguese driver who stank of garlic and appeared not to have washed for a week, he grew even more irritated.

The convoy would be moving through friendly territory, but it had a small escort nonetheless and Burke sought out the lieutenant in charge.

"I should ride with your escort, not sit on one of the carts." The potential discomfort of several days in the saddle was well worth it to avoid the indignity of travelling on a cart full of root vegetables.

The lieutenant cast a supercilious eye on Burke's uniform. "Infantry man, aren't you?"

Burke admitted that this was the case.

"Then," the young officer drawled, with the insufferable arrogance of the cavalry, "best stay out of the way."

So when, after the inevitable delays attendant upon getting a civilian convoy on the road, the carts finally rattled their way out of Lisbon shortly before noon, Burke was on his way to see General Hill perched uneasily in front of a several hundredweight of turnips.

They started out following the Tagus river – an easy road through prosperous farming country.

The plain gave way to a landscape of hillocks – small enough in reality, but seeming like mountains after the open plain. Fields gave way to olive groves, perched here and there on the hillsides.

Their route followed the path taken by the eight thousand troops who had set off from Lisbon four days earlier. The roads, it seems to Burke, had probably never been that good, and the damage caused by an army – even a small army – marching along them had left them in a miserable state. As the cart lurched and bumped over the ruts and potholes, Burke felt that his buttocks would have suffered much less had he spent the entire journey in the saddle.

For three days they passed nothing larger than the odd hamlet, but late on the fourth day they arrived at Nisa – a small enough place, to be sure, but an opportunity to supplement their travelling rations with fresh food. Perhaps it was the British gold that made the locals so friendly. The traders had every reason to smile as they took their money, but Burke was impressed to see the young women of the place going about their business on the streets. Wellesley must indeed be keeping his men on a short leash if the townsfolk had not got their daughters locked safely out of sight of any red-coated soldiers that might pass through.

They took only the briefest of rests before pushing on north, along roads that were barely passable. Burke wondered how the army had coped. Most of the artillery and cavalry would have travelled with Wellesley's main force, taking the road north of the

Tagus. Those travelling this way would have been infantry. He imagined the lines of men, arms swinging, their red coats faded under dust kicked up from the parched ground. Yes, it would have been hard, but they would have pressed on regardless. He felt a surge of pride in the British fighting man. It was good to be wearing a red coat himself once more.

Burke was happy to be a simple passenger. The cart was uncomfortable, but he could relax and leave the worries of the journey to the lieutenant. His initial meeting with that young man had not gone well, and he had made no effort to improve relations since. The fellow was as arrogant as any cavalry officer and Burke was more than content not to share the responsibilities of command. It was, therefore, not until the route looped back to the Tagus that he considered the problem of how the convoy was to cross it.

The river lay in a narrow valley with steep hills on either side. On the farther side he could see the whitewashed buildings of a township that had grown up at the water's edge but there were no buildings on the southern bank, confirming his opinion that the river was not easily crossed. He squinted towards the town and the driver, noticing this, gestured northward. "Villa Velha," he grunted, and relapsed into silence.

Now, against the glare of sun sparkling on the water, Burke could make out a dark line across the river. It didn't look like a bridge, but there was definitely something there and that was the direction that the convoy was taking.

As they drew closer the dark line resolved itself into a pontoon bridge. Boats were lashed together across the water, planks stretched across them to form a rough roadway.

The carts rattled down the last of the slope toward the river's edge. The carters pulled at the levers that made a crude brake on their vehicles, but Burke was tense for the whole of the descent, readying himself to jump clear should the cart run away on the gradient. It seemed, though, that, rickety as the carts appeared, they were well up to the job and their drivers were experienced men. Although he heard the odd ominous scrape as wheels skidded on the rocky path and there were occasional neighs and whinnies of fear from the horses, they arrived at the bottom without mishap.

Burke could not relax yet. The carts did not pause, but rattled their way onto the planks of the makeshift bridge. The boats bobbed unnervingly and Burke, looking at the thick ropes that moored them to the riverbed, hoped that they were anchored firmly. He could have sworn he saw them moving with the current but, though the planks creaked and the rocking of the boats seemed to increase as they left the bank farther behind them, the bridge held up.

Burke had no idea how long the crossing took. It seemed like hours, but, although the carts had inched carefully along, it was still probably only a few minutes. All he knew was that his heart only stopped racing as the cart bumped up the last of the planks and made its way across solid ground again.

That night they stayed in Villa Velha. Over dinner – another passable stew, sold by the good people of the town, who must have decided that military men were there to make them rich – Burke asked William if he had any idea where they were going.

"You don't know?"

Burke gave William what he intended to be a withering look – though William remained obstinately unwithered. "Our friend from the cavalry seems a very superior sort of gentleman. I'm damned if I'm asking him our line of march. Besides …" He took a mouthful of wine. "… I'm supposed to concern myself with the grand strategy. I expect you to attend to the details like knowing where we are."

William knuckled his forehead and made an effort to look humble. Not much of an effort, though.

"It's a good thing I've picked up an idea of the route, then, isn't it?" As ever, Sergeant Brown was a mine of information. His ability to fall into easy conversation with anyone from a cart driver to a cavalry trooper never ceased to amaze Burke. "We're heading for Castelo Branco. We should make it there in a couple of days. With any luck we'll catch the Army up soon after that."

Brown's information was, as usual, impeccably accurate. They left Villa Velha in the morning and, after one more overnight stop, they found themselves on the main road to Castelo Branco.

This road was wider now. More importantly, as far as Burke was concerned, it showed clear signs of the passage of the main Anglo-Portuguese force. The ruts were too deep to be accounted for by

regular carts, even driving in convoy. No, these were the unmistakable spoor of an artillery troop, dragging its cannon to war. Hasty repairs to bridges showed where engineers had strengthened them to carry the weight of the extra traffic. The detritus of an army on the move lay scattered along the highway – kit that had broken or been lost, yet to be scavenged by some peasant who could use a scrap of leather from a torn cross-belt or a ragged sole, detached from its boot. Burke grimaced at the all-too-frequent signs of inadequate footwear. The Army never had enough cobblers and no new boots were being sent out from England.

It was not long after they joined this road that they passed a row of crosses where freshly dug earth marked the last resting place of some of the men who had marched into Spain. Burke counted them: sixteen. He doubted that there had been any fighting here, but an army always lost men to accident and disease – often more men than it lost to the enemy. They would, he knew, pass many more such memorials as they followed in Wellesley's path.

Castelo Branco, when they reached it, was a disappointment. Burke's driver had been so excited by the idea of the place that he had become, by his standards, quite voluble. It was a Bishop's See with a great cathedral, he said. But both cathedral and town seemed shabby, many of the buildings visibly in need of repair. Burke was not sorry when their escort ordered the convoy to head straight through the town, not camping until they had left the city walls hours behind them.

From here, their path ran pretty well due east towards Spain. They were pushing the horses hard as they tried to catch up with the army and the next day they reached the line of mountains that marked, however tenuously, the border. As the road became narrow and began to zigzag its ascent, the cavalry escort, which had been riding ahead with the air of young men enjoying a day out, closed up around them.

That night, camping on Spanish soil, the cavalry mounted guard through the hours of darkness.

"What was that about?" Burke asked the lieutenant in the morning. "We're well behind the Army. There are surely no French here."

“No French.” The lieutenant spoke gruffly, clearly uncomfortable. “I’m more worried about Spanish bandits.”

Burke was intrigued. So far, all he had heard about the Spanish was how the gallant peasants were risking French retaliation by fighting a war of the common people against the enemy. They even had a word for this ‘little war’ – *la guerrilla*. There was no mention of problems with banditry.

“They’re hardly going to steal from a convoy with a military escort, are they?”

“You have no idea.” The lieutenant shook his head, as if he had trouble believing his own story. “They don’t sneak in and steal. They organise armed raids. Before we started escorting the convoys from Lisbon, we would lose whole columns of wagons. And these are the bastards we’re supposed to be fighting for.”

The lieutenant’s news certainly gave Burke food for thought. In London the talk was all of a nation united. Wellesley’s army, made up of British and Portuguese regiments, would take to the field alongside the Spanish army that remained true to its king and they could rely on the support of the people. The Spanish, according to the men in Whitehall, were fighting for *dios, rey y patria*. There was no suggestion that God, king and country might be less important than booty.

Burke mulled over what he had been told while the convoy rattled its way further into Spain. He had plenty of time for thinking, after all. His companion, driving the wagon, was not a great conversationalist and William Brown was travelling in another cart further down the convoy. It was bad enough two people bumping along on the narrow wooden plank that made up their seat – three would have constantly thrown them into each other. When they stopped for lunch, though, Burke sought William out. His sergeant confirmed what the lieutenant had said: it was common knowledge amongst the drivers that the convoys were preyed on by Spanish bandits.

"Of course, you have to make allowance for the fact that they’re Portuguese and they will never miss a chance to accuse the Spaniards of all sorts of unnatural practices. But there’s no doubt the convoys have been attacked. A few of the drivers have been

killed, so the men are pretty uncomfortable. If it weren't for the escort I think most of them would have turned down the job."

Burke tore a piece of bread from the loaf that, with a bit of cheese and dried sausage, made up their midday meal. "We best keep our eyes open."

"Don't you trust the cavalry?"

"The lieutenant is keen enough, but he's new to this game. You can see he's nervous. He'll do his best, but a couple of pairs of more experienced eyes will do no harm."

They did not start moving again until well into the afternoon. The day was hot and the Portuguese insisted on their siesta. The lieutenant – Burke realised he did not even know his name – looked calm enough, but his impatience was transmitted to his horse, which fidgeted continually. Burke could understand the man's irritation. While the Portuguese lazed in the shadows of their carts the cavalry had to remain on guard, exposed to the sun. Burke, though, was on the side of the Portuguese. It made sense to rest at midday and keep moving into the cool of the evening.

Once they were on their way, Burke forced himself to stay alert, despite the sun and the rocking of the cart. They had left the hills behind them and now they were crossing a vast plain. Occasionally they would pass a village; the few fields surrounding it the only sign of life for miles. The horizon was broken by hills that protruded from the plain as if a giant hand had scattered them here and there for want of anything else to break the monotony. Burke noticed that they avoided these hills. If the road passed near them, the convoy would bump its way along any little track it could find, rather than venture too close. The driver sitting next to him seeming content to follow, despite their already uncomfortable ride being made so much worse by the unevenness of the tracks.

"Why don't we stay on the road?"

The driver shrugged. "With the plain all around us, *senhor*, the *cavalarianos* can protect us. But where there are hills, there is always the possibility of ambush."

Burke looked across the open ground. He understood the argument and he could see that, to a cavalryman, this looked exactly the open ground that favoured a mounted man. Indeed, if a company of infantry were to try to attack, the cavalry would have

no difficulty in keeping them at a distance. Almost any of his fellow officers would agree with that conclusion. Burke's experience, though, was different. He had fought with the Bedouin as they harried the French on their march through Egypt. He had joined rebel raids on Spanish outposts in South America. He did not see a plain, on which units of infantry and cavalry moved according to the drills they would have practised so often. He saw countryside with ditches and little outcrops of rock. There were scrubs that could conceal a man and, here and there, great boulders where three or four men might lie in wait. The lieutenant's caution was admirable, but his lack of experience meant that he was not being nearly cautious enough.

It was late afternoon and the sun was low in the sky. Burke turned back the way they had come and squinted against the light. It was difficult to make out detail with the sun in his eyes. If he were going to launch an ambush, early morning or late afternoon seemed to him to be ideal times.

They passed through another village. Women hurried from their adobe houses and pulled their children indoors. The fields around them were empty. From one of the houses, he heard a child crying, but otherwise there was silence. If he had not seen the women as they called their children, he could have believed the place deserted.

He thought back to the other villages they had passed through. Nobody had been exactly welcoming, but life had carried on around them – men working in the fields, a blacksmith shoeing a horse, groups of women gossiping around the well.

He looked urgently for the lieutenant. Damn! The escort had ridden ahead to take up position on the edge of the houses. There was no danger of them being attacked here, where the men responsible could be easily identified and retribution visited on them. But the menfolk had to be somewhere and Burke suspected they were waiting just far enough from the village for things to be blamed on some random gang of bandits roaming the countryside. The lieutenant, constantly ranging ahead of the carts, looking for the kind of attack he had been trained to fight, would be utterly unprepared for what Burke feared was to come.

For now, he could do nothing. Where the road passed between the houses the convoy was forced into single file. The cart Burke sat

on had to stay in its place, the horse plodding dejectedly along in line with all the other tired beasts.

He looked carefully at the houses as they passed. Might he be mistaken? Now and then, he caught a glimpse of faces at a window. Usually they were children's faces that showed for a moment before their mothers pulled them back inside. It was natural, he supposed – this fear of soldiers. The drivers were not soldiers, but it was a military convoy with an armed escort. People who lived on land that was fought over by Spanish, French, Portuguese and English developed a natural suspicion of all military activity. Wellesley might order his troops not to loot or pillage, but Burke doubted that every private soldier in the Army could be trusted to obey these orders. Even if they did, there was no reason to expect these villagers to believe it.

The few minutes it took to move through the village seemed to stretch. Perhaps he was wrong – perhaps the villagers planned an attack here. Every face that appeared at a window, every half-glimpsed figure vanishing through a doorway – all exuded a sullen hostility underlying their obvious fear. His eyes scanned the buildings, looking for signs of men hiding, his nerves tense in case of ambush.

As they left the last miserable houses behind them, Burke felt a definite sense of relief, though he knew that the risk of attack was greater out in the countryside beyond.

Around the village there were fields – sad patches scratched on the dry earth where a few struggling shoots were all to show for the farmers' efforts. The land here had been cleared of any rocks. There was no danger here and the escort was already well ahead of them, ranging across the plain, passing another of the clusters of boulders, skirting round an area of scrub, keeping their eyes on the hills in the distance.

"Pass the rest of the wagons and go after the cavalry."

The driver looked at him in blank incomprehension.

"Just do it, man. Your horse must be able to go faster than this."

"*Si, senhor*. But why should I tire my horse. It is an old horse and likes to move slowly."

Burke grunted. The horse's preference for moving slowly had been very apparent ever since they left Lisbon.

“I have to speak with the lieutenant.”

“Well, *senhor*, you can speak with the lieutenant when he returns to us.”

Burke had taken off his sword belt when he settled himself onto the seat. The scabbard lay at his feet and now he reached down to it. The driver watched, his face showing, at first, confusion and then, as Burke unsheathed his sword, alarm. He opened his mouth to speak, but before he could form any words the edge of Burke's blade was against his throat. He swallowed nervously and wisely remained silent.

"I want to speak to the lieutenant now." The emphasis was on ‘now’ and the driver swallowed again, already shaking out the reins and reaching for his whip.

It took the horse longer than his master to realise that the time for dawdling was over, but a couple of cracks of the whip and the beast began to trot. There was no enthusiasm in that trotting and Burke was scarcely conscious of moving faster, but gradually they passed the other carts and were rattling uncomfortably ahead of the column.

The escort was a good half a mile ahead by now, but, as he watched, Burke saw one of the men turn and move his horse across to what he supposed must be the lieutenant's mount, though at this distance he could not be sure.

The riders were all turning now, moving back to see what had led to one cart breaking away from the convoy. The lieutenant must have recognised him as soon as he saw the red coat and he galloped over, his anger obvious on his face.

"What the hell do you think you're doing?"

"Saving your convoy, I hope."

The quiet confidence with which Burke spoke checked the lieutenant's anger and he waited as Burke explained.

"Did you not notice that there were no men in the village?”

The young officer frowned, thinking of what he had seen and what the implications were. Then: “Where do you think they are, sir?”

The ‘sir’ was a good sign. The officer may be young, but he was quick to realise he could have made a mistake and, in his own way, to acknowledge that.

"They'll want to attack before we settle for the night. Darkness gives them some advantage, but you post sentries and there's too much risk. So ..." He looked at the sun. "Not that long."

"But it's open ground."

"You're not facing a militia that will appear in ranks, lieutenant." Burke looked at the road ahead. A couple of miles away was one of those boulder fields that appeared here and there on the landscape. The road skirted round it. "I'd say there's a very good chance they're in those rocks."

The lieutenant turned and looked towards them.

"I think," Burke continued, "that their plan is to let you ride past and attack the convoy as it draws level with the rocks. When you turn back the sun will be directly in your faces and you'll have trouble seeing anything. They'll pick off one of the carts toward the back of the convoy and then place themselves behind the rocks to open fire on you as you arrive."

"How do you know this?"

"Because it's what I would do in their place. And trust me, lieutenant, it will work. They will be firing from cover and so long as they stay in the stones you get no advantage from being on horseback. You could make a battle of it, surround them and wear them down, but it will take time and lose you men. In the end, it makes more sense for you to sacrifice one cart, and that's what you'll do."

The lieutenant sat, chewing his lip and watching the rest of the carts creaking their way towards where they waited.

"If you're sure where they are, we can just loop away from the stones."

"We could. Or we could take them." Burke lips drew back into a grim smile. "That would be a feather in your cap, wouldn't it, lieutenant?"

* * *

The sun would be in the eyes of anyone watching now, so Burke was not too concerned that the bandits might see what was happening around the convoy. They might wonder why the carts had all stopped for several minutes, but they would probably

assume that a wheel had come off or some other repair had made them wait. What in fact was happening was that the cavalry were changing clothes with the drivers. Several of the escort took exception to the idea. "They'll be giving us all fleas," one man complained.

"Lice too, maybe," Burke admitted. “Think of it as a sacrifice for your country."

Not everybody stripped themselves of their uniform coats. The last two carts had their loads redistributed among the others and half a dozen men crouched low in each of them.

The drivers were more than happy to don the red of the cavalry. Some argued that they should take the breeches and boots as well, but Burke suspected that he would face a mutiny if he insisted on that. Besides, it didn't matter that most of the coats were on the big side, but baggy breeches and boots that did not fit would be no more convincing than the non-uniform trousers and the shabby shoes that the drivers wore.

"When you get near any rocks, pick up some speed and go straight pass them. Anyone looking will see the red coats and not worry about what else you are wearing."

The cavalry were carrying carbines and they held onto these, even as they surrendered their uniforms. The men who disguised themselves as drivers had their weapons tucked away beneath sacking, their swords riding with the vegetables behind them. The men hidden in the carts had their carbines ready at their sides.

It was all done in a few minutes and the convoy creaked back into movement and carried on eastwards.

Burke had taken the reins of the cart where he had been a passenger as his erstwhile companion galloped into the distance. He had moved towards the rear of the column. It was there, he was sure, that any attackers would strike. He had no carbine, but he had a pistol and his sword and he was damned if he was going to miss out on the fight.

He had worried that he might struggle with the business of driving, but it proved simple enough. A flick of the whip to encourage the miserable nag into motion and it trudged along behind the carts in front. He didn't even really need to touch the reins. It gave him plenty of time to look around at the countryside.

Now that they were committed to his plan, he began to worry that he might have got something wrong. Perhaps the men of the village had all marched off to war. Perhaps they were bandits, but were off raiding somewhere else. Or maybe they had some other plan for stealing from the convoy.

Everywhere he looked he saw places that men might be concealed. Why, they could just lie on the open ground covered under a blanket with dirt sprinkled across it: he had done that himself and it had been effective enough.

Still the carts moved on, untroubled, and the boulders drew nearer.

The horses of their supposed escort were far ahead now, the Portuguese revelling in the freedom to gallop high-spirited animals across the plain. What if he were wrong? Suppose that the Portuguese fell victim to bandits? They were unarmed and had been told that they were in no danger. He strained his eyes toward the horizon, but he could see nothing threatening them.

The first carts drew level with the boulder field. Burke's eyes moved restlessly from stone to stone, but he could see nothing.

Now he was driving past the boulders himself. Some were only a foot or two high, others stood well over the height of a man. You could conceal a hundred men in there, he thought, but he still saw nothing.

For all he kept his guard up, the attack, when it came, was a surprise. A rattle of shots sounded from the rocks and splinters flew from the carts as the balls struck home. As soon as the firing started, Burke realised that he had underestimated the scale of the bandits' attack. He cursed himself for a fool: there had been no men left in the village, so it should hardly have surprised him that they were now coming under attack from a substantial force. There could be fifty or more men in the rocks – it was impossible to say. All he knew was that the ragged firing continued.

With so many men in their force, the bandits had decided that they could take more than one cart. Burke, with no carbine, had anticipated that the attack would be concentrated on the carts to his rear, but as the bandits emerged into view, several were headed for him.

There was a last fusillade and he felt the wind of the musket balls passing his face. There was a sting as one tugged at his arm. It barely scratched him, but it made him realise how vulnerable he was.

The bandits should have taken advantage of their position and continued to fire from cover, but the first of the villagers were closing on the carts now and the firing had to stop as the danger of hitting their own men grew too great.

Before they reached the cart, Burke had leapt down to meet them. He fired his pistol, bringing one man down, but there would be no time to reload. He would have to rely on his sword.

The first seconds, he knew, would be decisive. There were a lot of them – maybe seven or eight – but they had no plan or discipline. They ran forward as a mob, expecting no resistance. The sight of an angry soldier facing them, sword drawn, threw them into confusion.

A tall man, his face shaded by a wide brimmed hat, seemed to be leading the group and was a pace or two ahead of the others. He had no time to react to Burke's sudden appearance. He ran one step forward, the beginnings of surprise showing on his face, and Burke swung his sword viciously across the man's throat. Blood sprayed as he fell forward. The next man tried to turn aside and Burke swung again. The bandit screamed and clutched his arm, his dirty white shirt already reddening.

Burke counted quickly. There were five left. Two had rusty cutlasses; the others just knives. Burke showed his teeth in a grin. Knives weren't going to help them in a sword fight. First, though, he had to deal with the cutlasses. He stepped forward and lunged with the point of his sword. The first cutlass dropped to the ground, a second ahead of the bandit who had been holding it. Burke ignored him as he writhed on the ground, stepping forward to deal with the only other man with a half-way decent weapon. He had no chance, though, to lunge. The bandit was backing away and one of the three men behind him was already running back toward the rocks.

Burke heard another musket ball strike the cart. With only three men now between him and the rocks, at least one of the bandits was prepared to take a chance of a shot past his comrades.

Burke stepped forward again, closing the distance with the robber who was energetically, but ineffectively, swinging his cutlass from side to side in front of him. Burke hesitated. His opponent was a big man and clearly relied on strength rather than skill. It would be easy to pass by his hopeless attempts to guard himself, but, once he fell, Burke would be exposed to the fire from the rocks.

Burke struck out, slicing into the big man's sword arm. As he dropped the cutlass, Burke grabbed hold of him, spinning him to face his fellows. Burke's left arm gripped him around his throat while his right held his sword toward the two knifemen who hesitated, uncertain whether to come to their comrade's aid to run for cover.

His captive began to struggle and Burke squeezed his arm tighter around his throat, but the remaining two men were taking advantage of the distraction to move in closer. He kept the one on his right at a safe distance with a swing of his sword, but on his left he was defenceless. He felt a knife slice into the arm that gripped his prisoner and, as the pain struck, he momentarily released his grip and the man broke free.

There was a moment's pause as his attackers took in their changed situation. Three of them faced Burke, who stood alone, blood staining his sleeve.

The man he had wounded had no weapon to replace his cutlass and his right arm hung uselessly at his side, but he swung his left arm viciously at Burke's head and Burke, stunned, staggered back.

Now all three were on him. The sun glinted on two knives, striking forward. He stabbed towards one, but his erstwhile prisoner struck him again and his thrust missed. Another burst of pain on his left, as he was stabbed again and the big man swung his left fist. Burke staggered back and saw all three of his opponents step forward to finish him off.

So this is how it ends, he thought. Not on some vital secret mission, or fighting heroically against the French. He would die the victim of a petty robbery. To have come so far, and met a fate he could have suffered outside any tavern in London.

There was the crack of a cavalry carbine and the big man fell.

Two cavalrymen, incongruous in their borrowed clothes, were running towards him, swords drawn. The knifemen took one glance at them and were headed back to the rocks. As they ran, musket fire from behind them covered their retreat.

More cavalrymen were running to join the fight and their carbines fired again, forcing the bandits to stay in cover. Burke staggered to his feet and looked to the rear of the column.

There were two carts behind where he stood and, he guessed, fifteen or twenty bandits had attacked them. There had, though, been as many redcoats hiding in the carts and half a dozen bodies showed how effective their fire had been. The area between the carts and the rocks was now a mass of brawling figures, but the redcoats, outnumbering their opponents, were having the best of it and the fight was moving steadily towards the boulders.

One of his rescuers reached to hold him back. "We've got them on the run, sir. You should get that arm attended to."

Burke shook him off. The fury of the fight gripped him, the simple blood-lust that drove on the fighting soldier in the heat of battle.

He threw himself towards the bandits, the pain something that seemed somehow distant, a concern for later, when the fighting was done. His sword was swinging, men falling away as he slashed and thrust. It was a desperately one-sided affair, the bandits mostly armed with knives and clubs, the soldiers swinging cavalry sabres. More men were emerging from the rocks now. They carried muskets but they could not get a clear shot. If they had bayonets, Burke thought, they could have saved the day, but without fifteen inches of sharpened steel the muskets were a liability in this sort of fighting. Some of the bandits held them by the barrel and wielded them like clubs, while others threw them aside and fell on the soldiers with their knives.

With no one left to give covering fire, the fight played out with a grim inevitability. The cavalrymen were disciplined, well-armed and healthy. Their opponents, now Burke had time to look at them, were a rabble of half-starved Spanish peasants. One by one, they fell until just half a dozen were left grovelling in the dirt and begging for mercy.

The lieutenant turned to Burke for advice. "I'm damned if I know what to do with them." He looked at his prisoners and his face showed a mix of pity and disgust. "You're the senior officer, sir. I think they're probably your responsibility."

Burke surveyed the scene of the fight. A dozen or more bodies lay motionless where they had fallen. Almost as many again were showing signs of life: several were screaming, while others moaned piteously. Most, it seemed to him, were unlikely to survive without a surgeon – and where would they find a surgeon here? He thanked God that there seemed to be no serious injuries amongst the British. His wounds were probably about as bad as anyone's and they would heal once they had been washed and bandaged.

"We can't take them along with us. We don't have the men to guard them or the space to carry them. And we need somebody here to bury the bodies – we can't just leave them. Those idiots" – he gestured to the prisoners – "can bury their dead and do the best they can with the living. I think that is punishment enough." He walked over to where the survivors were kneeling on the ground, surrounded by soldiers with unsheathed swords and harangued them in furious bursts of rapid Spanish.

The lieutenant looked on, impressed. "I thought I spoke the lingo, sir, but I have no idea what you said to them."

"I told them that if we ever hear of banditry in this area again, we will return and burn their village to the ground."

"But I'm not sure that we could actually do that, sir."

"I could." Burke turned abruptly away, looking for William Brown. William was the sort of man who would have bandages about his person, or know where he could get them.

The fighting over, Burke was suddenly aware of the extent of his wounds. He'd lost a fair amount of blood and he felt very tired. He swayed and turned to rest against the nearest cart. For a moment, he thought he might fall, but then he felt an arm reach round his body to support him.

"I've got you, sir." It was William Brown. "We won't be going anywhere for a little while. You settle down and I'll fix you up."

Brown was bleeding himself, but when he saw Burke look at the blood on his face, he was quick to reassure him. "Just a cut over the eye, sir. Bleeds like a pig, but no real harm done."

His sergeant produced a blanket. God knows where he found that, Burke wondered. He felt himself propped against a rock and the blanket was wrapped around him.

“We’ll sort out that arm in a jiffy," he said. "But first of all, let's get a brew on."

The sergeant moved away but almost immediately he was back, his fist wrapped round the handle of a tin mug where steam promised hot tea. Burke roused himself. "Good man!" You could rely on Sergeant Brown: a man who could always magic up fresh tea was a man you could trust.

* * *

Sergeant Brown, it turned out, was wrong when he said they would rest where they were for a while. The presence of so many dead and the potential threat if the prisoners were not kept under strong guard made it an unattractive spot to linger. Without all their drivers, getting the convoy moving again was not the smoothest of operations, but eventually the cavalry, with much swearing and cracking of whips, managed to manoeuvre themselves into line and set off eastward.

They did not travel far, however. As soon as a couple of miles of open country lay between them and the sight of their battle they clustered the carts together and made camp.

Most of the soldiers mounted guard, nervous of a repeated attack. A few, who had seen enough action to be familiar with the needs of wounded men, moved among the injured. Men with spare shirts in their packs gave them up to be torn into strips and used for bandages; wounds were cleaned and bound up.

Despite William’s demands that he rest, Burke insisted on talking to each of the wounded men. “I am the senior officer, William. I have a responsibility to the men, even if they are not under my command.” He had no idea if the troopers appreciated his attention or not, but he felt that he lifted some of the load from their lieutenant’s shoulders. It could be hard, being a junior officer: all the responsibility of caring for your men, but little real power.

“You know, lieutenant,” he said, after he had satisfied himself that all was well, “in all the excitement of our journey, I don’t think

I ever properly introduced myself." He remembered their first meeting in Lisbon: himself tired and irritable, the lieutenant disguising his lack of confidence with an insufferable arrogance. It had not been an auspicious start. He put out his hand. "Major Burke. James Burke."

"Lieutenant Johns. Peter." The younger man took his hand and smiled. "I should have let you ride with us."

Burke shrugged. "You didn't have a spare horse. Don't worry about it."

Johns had led the men hidden in the rearmost cart so he still had his uniform coat. Now he drew a brandy flask from his pocket and passed it across.

"Thanks."

They shared the liquor with the easy comradeship of men who had fought together.

"Do you think I'll ever see my horses back?"

"They'll be back. Not until dark, I'm guessing. The Portuguese are having too much fun."

Burke was right. The sun had already set when the decoy patrol finally returned. Their horses were lathered in sweat and the riders were still laughing excitedly amongst themselves. Burke could see the troopers were angry at the condition of their mounts, but their lieutenant took care to thank the riders effusively. They were civilians and had every right to have refused to join in the plan, but they had played their part to perfection.

As darkness fell, they gathered scrub to make fires. Someone had killed a couple of rabbits and the fresh meat, little as there was, was added to the dried beef they carried. (Nobody suggested eating the turnips – they weren't that desperate and, besides, the food was needed for the Army's horses.) The resulting stew, thickened with biscuit, made a meal they could all share. The Portuguese produced wine and toasts were drunk to Anglo-Portuguese unity. It was a good start to his adventures in Spain – except for the inconvenient fact that they had just butchered a party of the men the British Army was ostensibly fighting to save.

The next day dawned bright and clear and the convoy moved on without further drama. Whether it was his concern to get the supplies to the army as quickly as possible or simply a desire, after

the fight of the previous day, to get the journey over with, Lieutenant Johns kept them moving, even refusing more than the briefest of siestas. They pushed on after only half an hour and the carts rattled through the afternoon, despite the complaints of the drivers who said that their horses could not stand such usage. Even as the sun set, the lieutenant showed no signs of allowing them to rest and they bumped along in the growing darkness until, in the gloom ahead they saw the flickering of camp fires.

Burke, who, a few minutes earlier, had been on the edge of sleep, jerked awake, watching the fires grow nearer. Even the horses, which had been plodding wearily for the past few miles, seemed to realise that they were nearing the end of their journey and picked up their feet, managing something that came close to a trot.

More and more fires could be seen burning in the darkness and now the noise of the camp began to make itself heard. It was a dull rumble: part the voices of the troops raised against the crackle of the camp fire flames, but a hundred other sounds added to it. There were the horses of the cavalry, shifting and neighing as they settled for the night. Farriers beat new horse shoes to replace those cast during the day. Somewhere somebody was playing a fiddle and a score of voices were joined in a raucous song. Spoons rattled in mess tins as men ate and every now and then there was the raised voice of a sergeant shouting at someone who had offended his sense of order, for it is the business of sergeants to shout and the men would know there was something truly amiss if they did not. For all his time spent away from regular military duties, this was a sound that Burke associated with home – or, at least, as close a thing as he had had to a home for more years than he cared to remember.

There was some embarrassing confusion as to the password. Lieutenant Johns had ridden ahead of the convoy and the sentries, seeing what they reasonably assumed to be one of their own patrols returning to camp, demanded the password of the day. Johns, of course, had no idea what that was. The arrival of forty wagons, each driven by an unshaven foreigner, confirmed the sentries' suspicions that their camp might be about to be attacked by French agents in some sort of cunning disguise. It was only when Burke produced written orders that he report to General Hill that they sent for somebody who could read and confirm that these really were

British troops with much needed supplies. Indeed, the Officer of the Day was so delighted to see the convoy that he barely wasted any breath berating the sentry. “The Spanish promised us supplies but have signally failed to provide anything,” he explained to Burke. “Rations are tight and every little helps.” He looked again at the convoy and seemed to notice for the first time how few carts there were in relation to the size of the camp. Burke could see him performing some mental calculation and, as he did so, his face fell. More sombre now he turned his attention from the carts and towards Major Burke.

"You have my most profound apologies, sir.” The Officer of the Day was a young captain and he was clearly embarrassed by the confusion. Burke suspected that the sentries escape from his censure might be strictly temporary. “I’ll escort you to General Hill myself.”

They threaded through the organised chaos of an overnight camp. The men were bedded down on the ground, each platoon gathered around neatly stacked muskets that pointed skyward like miniature tepees. There was a mess tent for the officers and a cluster of larger tents for the Staff, but otherwise there was no shelter from the elements. It was fortunate, Burke thought, that the night was mild and promised to be dry.

More sentries – smarter and more alert than the first Burke had dealt with – challenged them. The young captain explained who Burke was and an aide-de-camp was summoned to escort him to the general. William, who had been dutifully following, was abruptly ordered to wait.

Hill had clearly been busy at his map table, presumably discussing the next day’s route, but he drew himself away as soon as Burke entered. Burke saluted and the general returned the salute in an offhand way that seemed almost ironic.

Hill was a solidly built man, but he carried himself well and Burke imagined he looked good on a horse. Burke judged that they were about the same age, but he liked to think that he wore his years better than the general, whose dark hair was beginning to recede. He looked like someone who had kept himself fit leading troops into battle but who years of Staff appointments were beginning to

grind down. Even so, he moved easily to greet Burke and the hand that he offered was firm and strong.

“It's good to have you with us, Major Burke. We've been wondering when you would get here. I must confess I was becoming a little concerned.” The general sounded as if, with all the things he had to worry about, he had really noted Burke's absence and wondered what had happened to him. Burke realised why his troops called him "Daddy Hill". Although, like most senior officers, he could be a harsh disciplinarian, he gave the impression of knowing and caring about the men under his command. Despite his usual cynicism, Burke was instantly charmed.

"You'll be making yourself useful straightaway. I said I needed somebody who spoke good Spanish and I was told you were one of the best."

“I’ve spent some time in Spain and in Spanish America, sir.”

“Good. Because I need someone who can find out what exactly is going on with the locals. They’re all supposed to be desperately anxious to help us see off the French, but they seem a disorganised rabble. When we send any of our officers out, people either vanish away or promise an undying devotion that seems to evaporate with the morning mists. We need someone who can get close to them and find out what they’re really thinking. Can you pass yourself off as a Spaniard?”

“Yes, sir, I can.”

“So how do you fancy travelling around ahead of the army and getting the lie of the land?” This was purely a rhetorical question and before Burke could answer, the general was continuing. “How will you do it? Travelling pedlar? Pilgrim?”

“Priest, I think.” He’d answered quickly, but it really didn’t seem a difficult choice. There would be few travelling pedlars in a country torn by war. Besides, what could he sell?

There was an audible intake of breath from a couple of Hill's officers who were within earshot. Burke’s suggestion that he might feign Holy Orders was clearly shocking, but Hill took it in his stride. “Good idea,” he said. “Expected no less from a man of your reputation."

He offered Burke his hand again, this time clearly in dismissal. Burke, slightly dazed at the speed of events since he had reached the camp, took it.

“There's some stuff you need to know: maps the Guides have produced for us, latest intelligence on the enemy, that sort of stuff. Jenkins will fill you in.”

Hill’s ADC was already beside Burke, ready to escort him from the tent and, moments later, he was out in the night air.

The ADC gave him a sympathetic grin. "You look a bit stunned. Don't worry; that's the effect he has on most people the first time he meets them." The officer held out his own hand "I'm Jenkins, if you haven't worked that out. Show me where you’re bedding down and I'll bring the map over to you. I'll talk you through what we already know, too, little as it is. Will you need anything?"

"A cassock will be useful."

"I can't really help you there, old man. We don't even have our own padre. There are a few women amongst the followers who will be able to run you up something very quickly if you can find the cloth." The idea seemed to amuse him. "Good luck with that, though."

Burke had yet to find himself a place to settle for the night. He would have stayed with the men he had ridden in with, but most of them had dispersed. The supplies had been urgently needed and would already be being distributed around the camp and the cavalry had gone to join their unit. Apart from William – and it was anybody's guess where he was – Burke knew nobody in the place. Used as he was to operating on his own, he suddenly felt very alone.

Jenkins was apparently both perceptive and sympathetic, for he recognised the momentary pause as Burke looked about him and guided him quickly to where a group of young officers were gathered under a rather sorry-looking tree. "There are some good chaps here. You can mess in with them for one night. I won't delay you with introductions; you're a busy man.” Burke appreciated Jenkins’ discretion. He would be away in the morning, and in his line of work the less anyone knew about him, the happier he was.

As soon as Jenkins left, Burke was off to look for William. If anybody would be able to produce a cassock by morning, it would be the estimable Sgt Brown.

Fortunately, William was easy enough to find. A few of the carts were still being unloaded close to where they had first arrived in the camp and William was nearby. He had attached himself to the closest group of redcoats and in an enthusiastic, if tuneless, baritone was belting out one of his favourite songs.

Had she but told me when she did disorder me
Had she but told me about it in time
I might have got salts and pills of white mercury
But now I'm cut down in the height of my prime.

As soon as the men saw him, there was the nervous shuffling of private soldiers in the presence of an officer. Burke decided he might as well play up to the role.

"Really, sergeant. I imagine the men were singing something far more suitable before you joined them."

One man, quicker than the others, was already starting on 'The British Bayoneteers' before Burke had finished speaking and as the others joined in William slipped away from the group. Burke stood listening for a couple of minutes before joining his sergeant. There was no real need for such a precaution, but the mechanics of spying had become automatic to both of them. None of the soldiers needed to know that Sergeant Brown and Major Burke were anything other than their uniforms would suggest, so they waited until they were anonymous in the gloom before they joined each other to discuss plans for the next day.

When it came to subterfuge and deceit, Burke valued William's opinion above all others. Fortunately, he approved of the idea of the priestly disguise. That left the question of how they were to travel.

"If I'm supposed to be some itinerant priest I ought really to travel on foot, but we won't be able to cover enough ground that way. And if we do find something we'll need to be able to carry news back quickly."

"Horses it is then."

"Yes, but once we get near a village, I'll leave my horse with you and take to my feet."

"Best way to do it, sir. And I'll try to get close enough to you that I can help out if things go wrong."

"Not too close, William. I fear that it will be difficult to explain yourself if you are found lurking with two horses."

William grinned. "I'll say I stole them. From what we've seen so far, I'll not be the only one. I've stolen them and I'm trying to get to the British because I've heard they want horses and will pay well for them."

Burke was, as so often, impressed by William's ability to produce a convincing lie. The British were, indeed, in want of horses and it seemed all too likely that there were Spaniards prepared to steal the mounts they needed.

"Better get rid of the uniform and find yourself something suitably disreputable."

"Good as done, sir. I've bought the spare clothes off the bloke who was driving my cart. I thought they might come in handy. I've left them with one of the women to boil up. I don't fancy his fleas. You'll need a change of clothes yourself. Something more priestly."

"Yes, a cassock. No one here is going to have one. Hill's ADC has suggested that I might get one made. He says there should be seamstresses amongst the camp followers."

William choked back a laugh.

Burke looked at him sharply. "It really doesn't seem that amusing to me."

"You know what a seamstress is, don't you sir?"

"I had rather imagined a woman who sews clothes."

"Well, yes, that's what they say when the Army asks them what they do, but generally they earn their money on their backs, if you take my meaning."

Burke looked embarrassed and annoyed, though more annoyed than embarrassed and William took pity on him. "I imagine at least some of them can sew as well. Just best be careful that if you offer them a needle, they know what sort of prick to expect," and he laughed at his own joke.

"Very droll, sergeant. Perhaps I had best leave negotiations to you."

"That may well be true, sir. But you'll have to be there if we're to be sure of getting something that fits."

Burke reluctantly agreed and the two of them set off together to find the women gathered on the edge of the camp.

The area that the camp followers occupied was, as usually seemed to be the case, remarkably well ordered given the bad reputation of the women inhabiting it. In fairness, Burke knew the reputation to be often undeserved. Many of them were the wives or, at least, common-law wives of men in the Army and all the women contributed to the welfare of the troops by helping with cooking and cleaning and, indeed, occasional sewing. It was true, though, that many – if not most – of them helped keep body and soul together by providing, for consideration, the companionship that men on the march would be unable to get elsewhere.

Burke was hardly a prude but, as he stood by listening to William negotiating with the women, he found himself blushing at their conversation. He was pleased that he had left this part of the business to his sergeant who was all too clearly comfortable with this badinage.

Soon things were settled. William introduced Burke to Sofia, a comely wench who had attached herself to the Army somewhere in Portugal. "She's from these parts, you see," explained William, "so she knows what a Roman cassock should look like."

"So she can start now. We need the wretched thing by morning."

"Ah!"

Burke did not like the sound of that 'ah'.

"We need the cloth."

"She doesn't have it?"

"Be fair, sir." There was the slightest tone of exasperation in William's voice. "You can hardly expect her to be carrying a bolt of cloth with her just on the off chance."

"Well that leaves us in something of a quandary, doesn't it, sergeant?"

"Don't you worry, sir. You can rely on me."

Burke nodded. He suspected that he could. William's abilities as a scavenger were second to none. Burke settled down to wait, ignoring the half heard jokes of the alleged seamstresses around him, while his sergeant vanished away into the camp.

He was starting to worry when, half an hour later, William returned with the cloth.

"Well done, William. Where did you find that?"

"Best you don't ask, sir."

Burke looked at the cloth, looked at William, and decided not to ask again.

It was very good cloth and Sofia turned out to be a very good seamstress. She used a knotted string to make some measurements and then told Burke that he could leave her to it. "It will be ready for you in the morning." Burke rose to return to the officers he was to mess with but William showed no sign of leaving.

"Don't worry, sir. I'll bring it to you first thing."

"You don't have to wait here, William. We can collect it in the morning."

"I'm happy to wait, sir. It will be my pleasure."

Burke caught Sofia's eye and she nearly burst out laughing. He pretended not to notice and made his way back to where Jenkins had left him.

Chapter 3: Confession is Good for the Soldier

The next morning saw an oddly assorted pair ride out from the Anglo-Portuguese camp – a ragged good-for-nothing and a priest. Anyone with an eye for horse-flesh would have noticed that their mounts were fine animals, for Burke had insisted that they needed the best Hill's cavalry could supply. Their saddlebags were of a distinctly military design and cavalry carbines rested in their bucket holsters.

Anyone who noticed all this on the road east to Madrid would, in these dangerous times, take care to notice nothing else and to hope that the travellers would pass on and not bother them. As it was, though, there was no one there to notice anything.

The country seemed deserted. There were low hills on the horizon and one or two outcrops of rock nearer to hand, but in most directions they could see for miles. Wellesley was no fool and, like any general leading an army across country, he favoured plains where manoeuvring was easier and the dangers of ambush more limited. Burke screwed his eyes against the morning sun and scanned the landscape. He was not impressed by what he saw. Parched grassland, long turned to brown, was dotted here and there with patches of scrub. Ahead, a few straggling trees clung to life on a rocky slope to the side of the road. In the distance was a patch of deeper green that gave promise of some sort of wood.

He looked at the hand-drawn map that Hill's *aide de camp* had produced that morning. "There are no reliable surveys here," he was told, "so we have to make our own maps. The Corps of Guides have come up with this. They're pretty good."

Burke had heard of Wellesley's Corps of Guides, whose duties overlapped his own. Where he reconnoitred dressed as a priest, though, they could proudly wear their uniforms as they rode ahead of the army. He glanced up at the distant greenery and back at the map. Yes, there was supposed to be water there, which would explain how the land could support the wood. He grunted a reluctant approval. The Guides seemed to know their job. What the

map could not tell him, though, was the mood of the locals and whether they were to be regarded as friend or foe.

Land like this was not going to support much in the way of life. Burke could see no cattle or crops, though perhaps some of the trees in the distance might bear olives. He understood now why convoys of supplies were following the army from Lisbon. They would struggle to live off this land, even if the local people were prepared to let Wellesley have all that they could produce.

William had been making his own survey of the surroundings and had come to much the same conclusion. "Where are we heading, sir? If there's any villages, I can't see them."

"According to the map, there should be a few houses about four miles that way." He gestured ahead and to the right.

Both men stared in that direction. With the sun still low in the sky the glare made it difficult to see but there were rises and falls in the land that could conceal a village. "We'll head along the road a mile or so and look for somewhere to leave you with the horses. I don't want to be caught out riding before I've turned into Father Martin."

Father Martin had ridden in his youth but he'd not sat on a horse since he took holy orders. His family had farmed. They'd lived near Madrid, Burke had decided. He'd spent long enough in Madrid to be confident that he would not give himself away by knowing nothing of the area he claimed to have been brought up in. Madrid was close enough that a priest might have travelled from there, but far enough away for there to be no danger of running into anybody who might ask embarrassing questions about why they had never heard of him when they lived there. He knew the seminary where Father Martin had studied and the parish where he had preached before he had fled the French. Once he had left William to lay up with the horses, he would walk the last couple of miles and by the time he arrived there he would have absorbed the character of Father Martin to the point where part of him would really believe himself to be the priest.

So it was that around mid-morning, a farmer carrying a bucket of swill to feed the family's pig met a priest walking towards the hamlet of Portaje. The holy man's black coat was dusty from the road and he leaned heavily on the staff he was carrying.

The farmer greeted the priest with the respect due to his cloth, but he could not entirely keep the wariness out of his voice, for this was a remote enough part of the world for strangers – even clerical strangers – to be objects of suspicion. Father Martin, though, was reassuring.

"I am pleased to see a friendly face, for I have been two weeks upon the road, keeping to the byways for fear of the French."

"So it is true what they say about the Frenchies persecuting our priests?"

"Indeed it is, for they are a godless race. In Madrid they have looted the churches and flogged the priests at the altar." This was, Burke knew, pure invention, but it was always best to ascribe wanton brutality to the invaders. Such stories were always believed and, in Catholic Spain, tales of the oppression of the priesthood would surely rouse the population to anger. People were also more likely to be sympathetic to Father Martin if they believed him to be fleeing persecution.

The farmer looked appropriately shocked and assured Father Martin that there were no French in the area.

"I am delighted to hear it. Does this mean that there is a priest?"

No, the farmer admitted, there was not. Portaje was too small a place to support a priest. There had been a priest, he assured Burke. "We would travel to Vallepunto. It's six miles or so," (Burke noticed that he did not use the kilometres that the French were inflicting on their conquests) "but we walked there for mass every Sunday."

"And now?"

"Now there is no priest. He was ordered to Madrid and he never returned."

Burke had chosen his disguise to enable him to move from village to village, an itinerant priest constantly fleeing the French. He had not actually intended to do anything more clerical than exchange philosophical platitudes or give the odd blessing to those who felt they needed it. Now, though, the dawning of hope on the farmer's face made him realise that he might end up with a greater priestly role than he had bargained for.

"Is there any chance, Father, that you might stay? For we have had no one to celebrate mass for three months. Father Francisco

promised he would return in a week, but he is clearly lost to us. To send a message to the bishop was always difficult – a matter of waiting until someone was journeying towards Madrid – but now no one travels if they don't have to, saving your reverence." He looked at Burke with new respect as the implications of a priest wandering the countryside struck home. "Not many men would brave the roads with things being so uncertain. And for a priest, with the army of the ungodly controlling the highways …" He was almost stammering as emotion overcame him.

"I fear I cannot stay here, my son. I have to travel to Seville, where I am ordered to join my house there. I will tell them of your plight, but I regret that I am pledged to obedience and I cannot remain with you, however much I might wish it." The story that Burke had prepared was simple enough and would explain his moving on. What it did not do, of course, was give any reason why he could not perform his priestly duties as he passed through and this, he realised, was exactly what the farmer was going to ask of him.

The village certainly needed a visit from a priest. They had not attended mass since their priest had left and their immortal souls were at risk. Esmeralda (the farmer seemed to imagine that Father Martin must know who Esmeralda was) had had a daughter who could not be received into the church. Alberto ("that's Alberto the farmer, not Alberto the baker") had died unshriven and another old man needed extreme unction. Could Father Martin rest in Portaje for a day or two and give them a chance to save their souls?

Burke hesitated. He could get away with it, he was sure: all those hours in church as a child; the books of doctrine he had read in the absence of any novels that might have made it from London to Kilkenny. He had always had a good memory and a lively imagination. He could play the part of a priest well enough. The question was whether he dared. It was many years since he had abandoned Catholicism, but it was one thing to walk away from the church, quite another to officiate at ceremonies he had no business with. What better way, though, to gather intelligence? If he were to celebrate Mass for the villagers, he would first have to hear their confessions. No need to linger in a tavern or make tedious

conversation with the local gossip: in the confessional he had only to listen and all the secrets of village life would be revealed.

But even a lapsed Catholic cannot entirely throw off their respect for the secrets of the confessional. Could he really abuse his position like that?

In the end, it was the pleading of the farmer that persuaded him. The villagers were clearly despairing, convinced that they were doomed to eternal hellfire if they could not secure the services of a priest. As far as Burke was concerned, their fears were mere superstition, but they were no less real for all that. If he celebrated Mass, their fears would be eased, at least temporarily. The old man who was dying might die in peace. Esmeralda, whoever she was, would believe her child to have been received into the church. His deceit would make the whole village happier. And if, in the course of this charade, he were to learn exactly the sort of information he had been sent to discover, then what was the harm in that?

* * *

Portaje was too small a village to have its own mayor. Usually, Burke reckoned, the person who would make decisions would have been the priest – even if he had to travel over from Vallepunto. In his absence, it seemed to be Old Pedro. Everybody referred to him as ‘Old Pedro’, although he can’t have been much more than forty. Presumably there was a young Pedro around somewhere, but Burke never found out who he was. Old Pedro had the biggest house in the village, though this was not saying much. There were two rooms and a lean-to that sheltered animals in the winter and retained the stench into summer. Burke was offered the use of the larger of the rooms, the family moving into the kitchen to allow their priest some privacy. And Father Martin certainly had need of his privacy. The news that there was a priest who would celebrate Mass with them the next day meant that the entire village was anxious to make their confessions.

Burke had wondered if anyone would suggest he press on to Vallepunto, but the people of Portaje were not about to relinquish him to a rival village if they could help it.

"You can hear confessions in here, Father." Old Pedro's son and two of his daughters carried in a makeshift curtain, apparently stitched together from some old dresses and a piece of fabric that may once have been part of a coat. "This will have to make do for a confessional screen."

The son – a strapping lad Burke judged to be in his early twenties – was already balancing on a chair and hammering nails to the roof beam so that the curtain dangled down, concealing a corner of the room. "You can sit behind the curtain and I'll put a stool in front for the penitents to sit on."

It was a rough and ready arrangement, but it preserved the decencies and Burke was happy to agree to it.

"Perhaps you could hear my family now, Father?"

Father Martin had not the heart to refuse him. Old Pedro obviously considered it an honour that his family should be shriven ahead of the rest of the village so Burke settled himself into the chair that the farmer had placed behind the curtain and waited for the first of the family to make their confessions.

When he had been young and forced to undergo this ritual every Saturday, Burke had quite envied their priest. The aged Father Jerome, he was sure, must have drawn a vicarious pleasure from the details of his parishioners' misbehaviours. The reality, he soon realised, was that there was little entertainment to be found in the sad litany of petty misdemeanours that parishioners recite to their confessors. Pedro's wife admitted to looking lustfully at the baker, but looking was all she had done and Burke felt that even the two Hail Marys he prescribed was a little excessive. Pedro himself indulged in no sins of the flesh, but intended to appropriate part of the property belonging to one of the older farmers once that septuagenarian could no longer manage it. Burke, impressed that anyone made it to such an age in this place, informed Pedro that even contemplating such an idea was worth half a dozen Hail Marys and that he should forget any schemes he might have to enrich himself at the expense of his neighbour's family. The son of the household predictably admitted enough lustful thoughts to suggest he passed his days in a state of almost permanent arousal, but his only actual sin was onanism and Burke felt that even the Catholic Church could not take this too seriously.

He had higher hopes of the daughters, for they were young and pretty and the older had a wicked sparkle in her eyes, but this was rural Spain and the girls were well chaperoned. They, too, were sent off to recite their Hail Marys for their admissions of envy and, for the younger girl, gluttony. Perhaps, Burke admitted to himself, he was a little harsh about the gluttony, but he had noticed the girl did seem rather on the plump side and he considered it probably was a sin to waste the figure that God had given her.

After he had absolved Old Pedro's family, he was allowed a couple of hours' rest, during which the females of the family vied to feed him with little bowls of olives, figs, cheese and slices of cold sausage. As the afternoon drew on, though, the village women began to arrive at the cottage and, one after another, they took their places on the stool before the make-shift curtain and Father Martin listened as they confessed to much the same things as he had heard from Pedro's family. It was all domestic stuff. There was little opportunity for real vice in a village where everybody knew everybody else's business anyway.

As the sun sank towards the horizon and the men left the fields and came, in their turn, for confession, Burke hoped for something more interesting, but he heard nothing but the same monotonous stories of unrequited lust and petty larceny, occasionally enlivened by envy, gluttony or sloth.

"My son," he would prompt gently, "you must remember that sins committed at times of war are still sins. Have you done anything beyond the village that you might want to confess?" He could make out the bemused shaking of heads, even through the curtain. Nobody was venturing far from the village, whether to fight the French or to steal from their neighbours. When he asked them directly if they intended to fight ("It is no sin to make war against the godless,"), they all insisted that they would resist the foreigners to their last drop of blood. The issue, though, would only arise if Napoleon's men were to arrive in the village – an eventuality so unlikely that Burke felt they need not fear losing any blood at all.

It was well after dark before the line of penitents had all been duly given their penances. There was no rest yet, though. The old man still needed the last rites and Pedro led him into the darkness to a hut on the edge of the village where Giraldo lay on a pallet

attended by his one surviving daughter. She was sitting by the light of a guttering oil lamp and looked up as Burke entered. “The priest is here, father,” she said, and moved aside so that Burke could sit and take Giraldo’s hand.

He was surprised by the strength of that bony grip. “Father!” The hand pulled him closer. “Father, forgive me, for I have sinned.”

He felt, rather than saw, the girl and Pedro slip out, leaving him alone with the old man.

James Burke was tired and frustrated after a day in which he had learned nothing of use but, as he sat there, he let James Burke slip away in the darkness and all that was left was Father Martin. If Burke could do nothing here for the war effort, Father Martin could at least bring some peace to old Giraldo.

Ten minutes later, he called softly for the girl to re-enter the room. The old man was lying back peacefully, a smile on his face. The girl sat herself down again, reaching to touch her father’s face. There was the merest flicker of an eyelid, but otherwise he lay still.

Burke slipped from the room, leaving the girl watching over her father’s last hours.

“It will not be long, I think," said Pedro. "You did a good thing there, Father.”

“Yes,” said Burke. “Yes, I think I did.”

* * *

The Mass itself was going to be a problem. Every Catholic knows that Mass can only be celebrated at a consecrated altar and the nearest consecrated space was at Vallepunto. That was where the people of Portaje had traditionally celebrated the Mass, but how would people at Vallepunto feel about a stranger taking over their church? And would Father Martin not need to hear their confessions too?

Burke thought about the risks in Vallepunto. They had, until recently, had their own priest. They could reasonably be expected to be more familiar with the liturgy. Could his uncertain recollections from his youth pass muster in Vallepunto? No, there was too much risk and no real prospect of benefit. He would have to explain that

the celebration would not be properly sanctified. There was a war on. Surely people would understand?

There were cooking smells drifting from the kitchen. It had been a long day and Burke was ready to eat. Over the meal he would explain to Pedro that they would have to celebrate the Mass as best they could in Portaje. He could christen Esmeralda's daughter at the same time. Everybody would be happy – more or less.

He had his hand on the latch when he heard Pedro taking to his wife.

"You could see the peace on Giraldo's face. He has been in torment these last days, but I really think that receiving the rites from the priest made all the difference. He was able to make a good death."

"He's dead, then." His wife spoke matter-of-factly.

"He must be by now. And with God."

"Father Martin is a good man."

"He is a gift from our Lord. To have a priest and to celebrate Mass after so long. Our prayers have been answered."

Burke paused, his hand still on the latch. Then he shrugged to himself and opened the door.

"Tomorrow," he said, "we must go to Vallepunto."

* * *

In fact, the villagers did not make their way to Vallepunto until the day after.

In the morning, Pedro sent a messenger over to the neighbouring village to explain the situation. The messenger was back before noon to say that Vallepunto would be honoured if Father Martin would stay in their priest's house and hear confession that evening, before holding Mass the following day. The celebration should be at noon, to allow time for the people of Portaje to travel to join them.

Burke set off straightaway. If he were to do this, it were best to get it over with, he reasoned. But in the end the whole business of hearing the confessions seemed to go very well. There was a small church with a proper confessional box, which somehow made it easier – or perhaps he was just getting more practised at it.

The priest’s house was solidly made of stone and, though far from luxurious, it offered better accommodation than Pedro had been able to provide. More importantly, though, the priest had left his books, which included a missal with all the details of the Mass. For a moment Burke wondered if this was a miracle. It was exactly what he needed if he was to give a convincing performance the next day and, surely if he was going to benefit from divine intervention, then a priest's house must provide an ideal spot. On the other hand, he reasoned, a priest's house was also the most natural place to find a missal. Perhaps it wasn't a miracle after all.

His early start at Vallepunto meant that he was free to begin studying the missal by the end of the afternoon. He settled down to work with an application that would have impressed Father Jerome had he shown anything like the same dedication when that unfortunate cleric had been responsible for the direction of young James's soul.

After an hour or two, Burke's concentration was interrupted by the rumbling of his stomach, which reminded him that studying was hungry work. He wondered if there might, perhaps, be the odd dry biscuit or leftover piece of cheese about the house but he feared this was unlikely. He was reconciling himself to the idea that fasting was traditionally an adjunct to the religious life when there was a knock at the door and the middle-aged man who had welcomed him to the village led in a procession of young women who proceeded to set the table with a feast of bread, cheese, ham, stew, olives, and even some oranges that he imagined must have travelled all the way from Seville. It was, even to a hungry scholar, more food than he could possibly manage to eat. He invited the youngest and prettiest of the girls to join him and shared as pleasant an evening as he had enjoyed since leaving England. As soon as the meal was eaten, though, he sent the girls on their way. Partly he wanted to ensure that he was seen as behaving with the propriety suitable to his priestly disguise but, at least as importantly, he still had a lot of reading to do. Darkness having fallen by now, he settled to his books by candlelight and had worked his way through a goodly number of the priest’s supply of candles before he took to his bed. By then, though, he was confident that he would be able to perform acceptably the next day.

Pedro led the people of Portaje into the village well before noon and by the time the church's bell was ringing out to call the congregation to prayer, the place was almost full.

He was nervous at first, faltering with some of the Latin phrases, but as the service moved on he found himself growing in confidence. The words came with the familiarity of old friends, long neglected but far from forgotten.

As the congregation came forward to take the wafers, Burke was touched with their smiles. What he was doing was, he knew, the highest form of sacrilege, but he had given up believing in God years ago. Besides, if there were a God, surely he would see the joy on the faces of his people and agree that Burke had acted for the best.

The baptism, held in the tiny baptistry at the church door, was conducted after the Mass, when most people were celebrating with an impromptu fiesta in the square of beaten earth that marked the centre of the village. Esmeralda insisted that the child be named Alicia, for her mother, and Martina, for the man who had arrived so providentially to allow the infant to be christened at all. The little girl was so tiny and quiet that Burke could see why the mother was anxious to have her christened, lest she die without being taken into the body of the Church.

Alicia Martina's uncertain future was the only blot on an otherwise cheerful day, as Father Martin joined his congregation at the trestle tables that the people of Vallepunto had put up in the square. Bread appeared as if by magic and beautiful girls put down bowls of olives. Father Martin saw several of his erstwhile penitents glancing towards those girls and wondered if he should have demanded more Hail Marys. The assurances he had been given about avoiding lustful thoughts in the future seemed to have melted away in the Spanish sun.

Burke decided that Father Martin should regard himself as definitely off duty and he helped himself to a handful of olives while yet another of the local beauties thrust a beaker of wine into his hand. He wondered what it was about Vallepunto that produced such lovely women, while he allowed the odd lustful thought of his own to add itself to all the sins he had accumulated since he last made his own confession.

The party had been going for over an hour, the people of the two villages happy enough to enjoy each other's company for all the rivalry between them, when Pedro got to his feet and made a speech of thanks, which seemed to be the signal that it was time for them to set off back to Portaje. Nothing happened quickly in Spain, though, and there was much shaking of hands, kissing of cheeks and hugging before the folk from Portaje finally gathered themselves together to start on their way. As they did so, a horse cantered into the village from the Portaje road, the rider a young man with a musket slung across his back.

Burke tensed, wondering what sort of trouble this meant might be on its way, but the welcoming cries of the locals reassured him and, as the stranger pulled his horse to a halt, he was quickly surrounded by people who threw questions at him. “Where have you been?” “Are you safe?” “Why are you back?”

One wag, louder than the others, shouted, “Hey, Alfredo, you missed the party!”

The rider ignored the other questions and turned to the humourist. “But I hope I haven't missed the priest.”

There were cries of reassurance and several people pointed to where Burke was standing on the edge of the group from Portaje.

The young man dropped easily from his horse and turned towards the visitors. A few minutes of excited questioning revealed that, returning home along the road that took him through Portaje, Alfredo had been surprised to find the village almost deserted. Only a couple of young men had been left to keep an eye on the place together with Giraldo's daughter who had stayed to watch over him as, to everyone's surprise, he had survived the night. "She doesn't need to watch anymore," said Alfredo. "He died soon after you left." He paused respectfully and his audience crossed themselves. "She told me about the priest." He turned to Father Martin. "It has been three weeks since my last confession."

"My son ..." Burke spoke reassuringly. "For your neighbours it was much longer than that. Their sins lay heavy on their consciences, but they were soon shriven. Come into the church and I can put your mind to rest before I set off back to Portaje."

"No, Father." Alfredo was shaking his head, and Burke thought him pale under his tan. "I have not been at home with these honest

souls and my confession will not be the business of a few hurried minutes."

Burke looked sharply at the young man. He was dusty from a long ride, but he moved easily, obviously comfortable after hours in the saddle. Burke had seen only a few tired old nags in Vallepunto and no horses at all in Portaje. Where, after all, would people ride when their world was just the few miles between their two villages and the fields around them? And, though the men left to guard Portaje had proudly carried a musket to demonstrate that they meant business, it was a sad old thing, while Alberto's weapon was polished and looked ready for business. It did, indeed, seem that he might have more interesting things to confess than had everyone else whose sins Father Martin had suffered through.

Burke took care to keep his excitement from showing. Instead Father Martin looked quite severe as he told Pedro that he would catch them up later. Turning gravely to Alfredo, he asked if the young man was ready to start confession immediately. “Or, if your sins are truly so grave, do you want to rest and prepare yourself in prayer before commencing the sacred rite?”

The young man hesitated for a moment, but then shook his head. "You will want to catch up with your friends in Portaje. I will not detain you while I rest.”

Father Martin nodded gravely and led the way into the church. He settled into the confessional and waited while Alfredo knelt on the other side of the screen. Burke had to admit he had never seen the point of this pretence of anonymity. Still, Father Martin would believe in it and who was he to argue with the traditions of the Catholic Church?

"Forgive me, Father, for I have sinned …” Burke hardly listened to Alfredo's routine recital of lustful thoughts and theft and greed. He had heard these so often that he scarcely paid them any heed. He suspected that Alfredo, too, considered them of no great import. He gave the impression that he was reciting these while he gathered himself for the real business of his confession.

It came after about five minutes, when Burke, who the villagers had made sure had eaten and drunk well, was close to dozing off in the heat.

"And then, Father, I killed a man."

Burke was suddenly wide-awake. Father Martin, he was sure, would be shocked.

"You killed a man? That is rather more serious than lusting after Charlotta and envying Carlos because she prefers him."

"Father, this was not in Vallepunto. This was with the guerrillas."

"God is always with us, my son, even when we fight against the French." Father Martin paused and Burke added, "Perhaps especially when we fight against the French."

There was a long pause. Father Martin could hear Alfredo swallow on the other side of the screen. Then, quietly, "We were not fighting against the French, Father."

Burke had no problem in sounding as shocked as he was sure Father Martin would have been. Alfredo seemed a pleasant young man. The sins he had confessed to in Vallepunto were trivial even by the standards of that sleepy little village. It seemed hardly credible that he was riding with the bandits who seemed to be terrorising so much of Spain.

"Who did you fight, my son?"

The reply was so mumbled that Burke had difficulty in understanding it. Even when he asked Alfredo to repeat it, he had to lean close to the screen to catch every word.

"There was a village. It's called Montehermoso. It's about two day's ride north of here. We were camped out there for a week and the villagers said we should move on. There was an argument."

"An argument?"

He could see the shrug of the shoulders even through the screen.

"A fight."

Burke waited, but Alfredo did not seem ready to give any more details.

"What sort of a fight? A fight with fists? With knives?"

"With guns, Father." Alfredo's voice was shaking and Father Martin worried that he might be about to break down in tears. "We killed three of them."

It took a long time to get the whole story but, as far as Burke was concerned, it was time well-spent. And it was only natural that Father Martin would want to understand exactly what had

happened, so he was free to probe for as much detail as Alfredo could give him.

Alfredo, it turned out, was a patriot and an idealist. He was also frustrated by life in Vallepunto and wanted to get out and see more of the world. With no money and no education, though, every year saw his ambition fading. Then came the French invasion and the opportunity to leave his village and travel to join the fight against Napoleon's troops.

"People helped. They gave me a little money and as much food as I could carry to start my journey."

His story confirmed Burke's understanding that there were no guerrilla bands in the area.

"I had no clear plan. Just to head towards Madrid until I found people who were ready to fight for their country."

As it was, he had wandered for over a week, living on the charity of the villages he travelled through. Nowhere was there any active resistance to the French, but everybody was sympathetic to the idea of fighting them. A young man who had left home to take up with the cause need never lack for shelter for the night or a meal before he set off again.

Eventually he heard rumours of a guerrilla leader based nearby and he took up with a man known by his followers simply as *El Jefe* – the Chief.

"They said there were sixty or seventy of them altogether, but when I was with them there cannot have been half that number. El Jefe said that there were other men he commanded but they were away on missions that he could not tell us the details of. He said that we were going to find French couriers and kill them, but we never saw any couriers. We did see a patrol once, but there must have been twenty or thirty of them and El Jefe said we should not waste our lives in a hopeless fight, but wait for a better opportunity."

"So where is El Jefe based?"

"He moves around, staying a few days here; a week or two there. Generally he's north and east of here, towards Madrid. He stays clear of the main road, though. He says it is too well patrolled by the French."

"So he takes care to avoid any actual fighting."

Burke saw that shrug again, outlined through the grille. El Jefe's men had, it seemed, found themselves involved in quite a bit of fighting – just not with the French.

"El Jefe said that people should be proud to give us money and supplies so that we could be better prepared to defeat the invaders. Some were happy to give, but others ..." His voice tailed off.

"And at Montehermoso?"

"We stayed too long. At first people had been happy to feed us, but then they said that we did not fight the French, just rested in their village and stole their food. And there was some trouble with women."

The trouble had not involved him. He seemed particularly anxious to assure the priest that he had not misbehaved in this way. "Some of the men, though... You have to understand that they have been away from their homes for a long time and perhaps..."

"There can be no excuse for such behaviour." Father Martin was firm. "I am relieved that you had no part in it."

Alfredo had, though, been drawn into the fighting once the resentment of the villagers had turned to violence. He wasn't sure how it had started. He did insist that the villagers had been the first to open fire. Burke had his doubts: the self-styled guerrillas would have been well-armed and used to violence, while the villagers would have been totally unprepared to go into battle with them. Still, it hardly mattered. The fact was that the bandits had fired on their hosts, killing three and injuring four more, including a woman.

"And you killed one of the men."

"I think so, Father."

"Was this the first time you had fired your musket?"

"No, Father. I had practised with it many times."

"But this was the first time that you had fired it in battle?"

Alfredo's face was obscured by the confessional screen, but Burke could see him nod.

It was extremely unlikely that the boy had killed anybody. In Burke's experience, muskets were hopelessly inaccurate. The first time Alfredo had used it in earnest he would have been unlikely to have held it steady enough to hit anything smaller than an elephant and more than ten paces away. With the noise and smoke, he would have had no idea of whether his shot had missed or not. Still, Father

Martin would not have known this and Alfredo should pay penance for the intention, if not for the deed.

"It is a terrible thing to take a life, my son. No penance I give you can return the gift of life to the man you killed."

A strangled sound came through the grille and Burke realised that Alfredo was crying.

"You are not suited to a warrior's life, my son. I think your penance is to stay here, in Vallepunto and live peacefully. Try to do in your life all the good that might have been done in the life of the man you killed."

"Is that all, Father?"

"I think you will find it is enough. Though you can say a rosary as well. It can do you no harm and may do good."

"Thank you, Father."

"One other thing."

"Yes, Father."

"Give that musket to one of the older men. I don't want to see anyone else getting hurt."

Chapter 4: Guerrillas in their midst

The next day, Father Martin bade farewell to the good people of Portaje. He should really, he knew, have left as soon as he had finished playing his priestly role at Vallepunto, but 'Old Pedro' had been insistent that he stay one more night to rest before resuming the journey he had told them he was making to Seville. He convinced himself that he was delaying because to insist on rushing away sooner would create suspicion but in his heart he knew it was because he had come to like the people of Portaje and the chance of one more evening in their company was appealing. He suspected, too, that once he left the village he would be plunged into the reality of the war that had so far not touched the lives of the Pedro and his friends. A few more hours of innocence and peace, he decided, was not too much to ask.

To make up for the delay, he set off soon after dawn, walking back along the road that had brought him to the village. A couple of farmers insisted on accompanying him on the start of his journey and he was not left alone until he was almost back to the Madrid road, well past the point where he had left William. When, at last, they turned off the path to tend their olive trees he walked on for another ten minutes and then settled down to rest on a convenient boulder that served as a reasonably comfortable seat. He would wait until the farmers were sure to be well clear of the track before doubling back to William.

Two minutes later he heard the sound of a bridle jangling and he turned to see William riding one horse and leading the other as he walked them quietly along the track.

"Trying to slip away without me?"

"Hardly. I was wondering if you might have given up and left me."

William grinned. "I had begun to worry about you, but sound travels out in the countryside and I heard the church bells. Have you been busy doing priest-stuff?" He sniffed the sniff of an unbeliever.

"I have, indeed, been doing 'priest stuff' as you so charmingly put it. But I've been doing some 'spy stuff' too. Speaking of which, were you seen?"

William sniffed again. "I'd have thought you knew me better than that. I saw you and your two friends pass and make sure you had plenty of space before I followed. I moved the horses up quietly and kept well back until those fellows were clear of the track. No one will have seen me."

Burke nodded. William had an almost supernatural ability for moving unseen.

"Well there is no need to move quietly now. We need to get ourselves to Montehermoso and see what we shall see."

Burke explained what he had learned as the two men set off.

William said nothing while he digested the news. Finally he spoke. "This El Jefe sounds a nasty bit of work." He was sombre for a moment and then grinned. "Can we kill him?"

Burke had been wondering how to deal with the situation, though he had not phrased the question to himself quite so bluntly. If El Jefe and his men had any real intention of fighting the French, it was up to him and William to recruit them to aid Wellesley. There should be some proper liaison. The British should help in locating targets for El Jefe to attack, as Alfredo's story made it seem unlikely that they would find any useful targets on their own. The guerrillas could act as scouts, but only if they had arranged some way of sending information back to the Anglo-Portuguese army. One way and another, even a relatively undisciplined band of fighters could be made a useful part of Wellesley's plans. On the other hand, if they were nothing but bandits, were they any affair of the British?

On the whole, Burke rather thought they were. Wellesley's strict orders against looting were not given purely out of a sense of righteousness or moral qualms about the behaviour of his army. The war in Spain was not a straightforward conflict between the Spaniards and their allies and the French. The French had been able to move into Spain with the tacit support of at least some of the country's rulers and war there had started as a civil uprising. Burke should know: he had been on a mission in Madrid in May 1808 when William had seen the first stone thrown in the riot that

triggered the war. In fact, Burke had his suspicions that William may have been more closely involved with that riot than he ever admitted. If the Spanish were to support the British Army, which was essentially an army of invasion, they had to believe that the British offered them more security and safety than the French. Having bands of roaming ruffians claiming to be fighting the French but really just robbing their compatriots was the sort of thing calculated to drive the Spanish back into the arms of Napoleon. Besides, as Burke had discovered on his journey from Lisbon, the bandits posed a real risk to the British as well as the locals.

William's question was all too pertinent. Perhaps the answer would involve killing. Burke hoped it wouldn't, but the possibility had to be faced.

He said nothing to William, but dug his heels into his horse's flanks and pushed on towards Montehermoso.

* * *

Their arrival at Montehermoso was an anti-climax. They had ridden easily so as not to over-tire the horses and they rested under some straggly pines when the day was at its hottest. Even so, it had taken them little more than a day – Alfredo's horse was presumably less lively than theirs, or he was not a particularly good rider. The place was tiny – even smaller than Portaje. Burke could see that it would have had trouble supporting a band of fighters for more than a few days. He doubted that they grew any more food than they needed for themselves. Perhaps that, combined with their experience with El Jefe, accounted for the surliness of their reception.

Burke had decided that he would not be a priest at Montehermoso. He did not need to probe subtly for information. There had been bloody violence done in the place. There was no reason why the locals should not tell him about it, so he and William rode directly toward the little cluster of houses that nestled together on the top of a rise that qualified as a hill only because of the miles of plain stretching around it.

Alfredo was right about the villagers being armed, at any rate. A musket that Burke suspected had been there since the War of the

Spanish Succession was brandished by one of the men who met the two of them just outside the village. It was only when Burke asked if they could buy food – and backed up his request with the sight of a well-filled purse – that the weapon stopped being pointed in his direction and the men stopped scowling and offered the friendlier greeting that Burke had hoped to find. It had been, as far as he was concerned, a nervous couple of minutes – not because he had thought that the men of Montehermoso intended them any harm but because he didn't trust the mechanism of the ancient musket not to discharge itself accidentally. There was definitely more than a hint of relief in his thanks when he was beckoned forward and the barrel was no longer pointed at his body.

Once reassured that the two strangers did not intend to rob the village, the people were hospitable and friendly. Burke and William soon found themselves sharing a room in one of the larger houses. Burke would have felt guilty, as the son of the family was obviously being forced out to sleep in the kitchen, but the delight on his mother's face as he handed her a few *reales* eased his conscience. It was obviously not a prosperous place and his money would make a real difference there.

It was quite late in the day when they arrived, so as soon as they had had a chance to rest and wash off some of the dirt from the road they were invited to join the family at their evening meal.

There were five of them sitting down to supper. Senora Espindola was a widow and she was joined by her grown-up son and her daughter Sofia. There were olives and bread on the table and as Burke and William sat down the senora served up a dish that seemed to consist mostly of onion, tomatoes and peppers, though Burke was sure he found a bit of dried meat hiding in the stew. It was simple food but, after three days in the saddle, it seemed delicious.

He had wondered how to introduce the question of El Jefe, but, before he could do so, the widow raised the subject herself.

"I'm sorry that you were greeted so inhospitably. It is unfortunate that we have to guard ourselves against honest travellers."

"It was only one man." Burke smiled. "And he was hardly threatening us."

“Even so …” She spread her hands in a gesture of both helplessness and embarrassment. "Two weeks ago we had a group of men ride into our village. They said they were fighters against the French. But we did not see them fight the French."

Her story poured out. It was essentially the same tale that Burke had heard from Alfredo, though with rather more detail about the dishonouring of their women and the theft of their goods.

“When we told them they should leave, they laughed at us. Then came the fighting. I think, when they realised how many they had killed, they knew they had to go. But they were still laughing as they rode away."

“Where did they ride to?”

Again, she gestured with open hands. "I don't know. They took the road north. We don’t know where they went after that.”

That was all Burke could learn. The conversation after that stayed on safer subjects: the weather, the progress of the crops, and the beauty of the countryside.

It was only when they had finished eating and Burke had stepped outside to give the family some privacy that Senora Espindola’s son followed him into the cool of the dusk and plucked at his sleeve. “I think you are more interested in El Jefe than you pretend.”

“I have made no pretence one way or the other. What is it to you?”

The young man paused, looking at Burke's face, as if trying to make his mind up about him. After a long moment, he spoke. "Some of us tried to track them the next day. They did head north, but then they took the track east, over the stream. We followed a few more miles, but there was no sign of them and we were getting too far from home by then.” He shrugged and echoed his mother’s gesture, opening his palms. For a moment, he seemed uncertain what to say or do next. Then, quickly, he said, "I hope you find them. I hope you find them and kill them." He turned and went back into the house, leaving Burke and William breathing in the evening air.

"A fine lad, that," said William. "I think he might have the right idea."

* * *

They set off early the next morning. Somehow word had got round that they were hunting for El Jefe and most of the village seemed to have turned out to see them on their way. Several people thrust provisions at them and, when Burke attempted to pay, they waved his money away.

They followed the track north, crossed the stream (in truth, little more than a trickle at this time of year) and rode on for another half hour. The ground had become steadily drier and more barren as they left the stream behind and now the track petered out. Bare earth stretched in all directions.

Burke consulted the map that Hill's ADC had given him, but there was nothing shown here. "Well, William, do you have any thoughts?"

William was chewing meditatively on a dried sausage that he had been given as they left, but he paused in his chewing to look about them. "There's what looks like it might be trees to the south and some of those hills to the north." He used the remains of the sausage to gesture right and left. "I don't think they'll have turned south. They'll have wanted to put distance between themselves and the village. But I doubt they'd just ride out across the plain, so my money's on north."

Burke nodded. "North it is."

They headed north across the plain. Already the day was growing hotter. There was no shade, nor any prospect of any until they reached the hill. Experience had shown that these outcrops were always ridged with gullies where they could rest from the worst of the sun.

"With any luck," William said, "there will be a few houses there and we can make a siesta with the locals."

Burke grunted. While William had enthusiastically adopted the local custom of siesta, Burke found the idea of a mid-day rest a profound irritation when the chase was afoot. Still, he was realistic enough to accept that resting in the hottest part of the day made sense. The *bandidos*, after all, would be resting too. The two of them could afford to take a short break.

They pressed on, the hill seeming to remain as far away as ever. Burke felt himself drooping in the saddle while William, never a

strong rider, seemed practically asleep, slumped forward along his mount's neck. The horses picked up on the weariness of their riders and moved from trot to walk to weary plodding.

At last, though, they reached the hill. By now the sun was almost overhead.

"I can't see any shade on this side."

Burke acknowledged Brown's comment with a nod. "We'll ride around until we see something."

Like so many of these rocky outcrops, it projected directly from the plain and riding round it was straightforward. This one was larger than many of them, but Burke reckoned you could circumnavigate it in less than half an hour. With any luck, he hoped to find somewhere to shelter from the sun in the next ten minutes or so.

In fact, they had ridden for only five minutes when they crossed a dry stream bed and, turning and following it toward the hill, they soon came to the mouth of a gully. It offered shelter from the worst of the sun and, presumably, some trace of water if you dug deeply enough. In any case, it was obviously a good place to camp, for somebody had built a small adobe house there.

"*¡Hola!*" Burke reined in his horse and waited for a reply. It was best to let people know of your approach in these isolated spots, lest a nervous homeowner shoot first and enquire as to your business later.

There was no answer. The silence was absolute. There were no birds in this heat and no tinkling of water, for the brook had dried up months ago. He called again.

"*¡Hola!*"

Nothing but echoes from the rocky walls of the gully.

Burke drew the carbine from his saddle-holster and walked his horse towards the house. William, true to his infantry training, dismounted and approached on foot.

No call; no challenge; nothing.

Burke stopped when they were still ten yards from the building. He leaned forward and sniffed. What he mainly smelt was horse, but there was something else – something he knew all too well.

He dismounted and walked to the door. He still held the carbine, but casually, his hand gripping the barrel, well clear of the trigger. He would not need it.

The smell was obvious now, much stronger than the smell of his horse. He opened the door.

The sudden light from the doorway disturbed the flies, which rose with a great buzzing. Some flew towards him and he stepped back, instinctively, batting them away from his face with his free hand.

There was only one body that he could see: a man, in early middle age as far as he could judge. He wore the rough clothes of a peasant and he had a knife in his hand. Burke took one step inside and looked down at the corpse. It was no weapon that the man held but a kitchen knife that he must have snatched up in desperation. It could hardly have been expected to help – the hole in his chest showed that his assailants had been carrying firearms.

There was a doorway to a second room and the sound of more flies from there. Burke took one step forward but then turned away, back to the light. What was the point in exploring further? The ground was rock hard, the day was hot, and they had an enemy to pursue. They weren't going to stop to bury these people.

Outside, William was waiting, his carbine ready, scanning the rocks for any potential enemies.

"I think you can relax, Brown. He's been dead almost a week. There won't be anybody still here."

Burke remounted his horse. Neither of the two men spoke as they set off across the plain. They no longer wanted rest and Burke was too sickened by what he had seen to even think about food. All they wanted now was to find El Jefe and mete out some sort of justice. In his report Burke would say something about morale, or strengthening resistance against the French but, in truth, he didn't care whether or not it would benefit Wellesley's army. He thought of the people of Montehermoso and the body in the hut and the other body – or bodies – that he knew were lying in the next room. He even thought of Alfredo and the boy's loss of innocence and he swore that when they caught up with El Jefe, the *bandido* would die.

They headed north again, instinctively sure that their prey would have carried on across the plain. It was astonishing, Burke thought, that here in Europe there could be such a vast area of nothing at all. He remembered his time in South America and the days he had ridden across the pampas. That had been even emptier than this, but the miles of rippling grass had hinted at a land of promise. Here the ground was dry and a few patches of scrub was all the vegetation they could see. On the horizon, a little to the east, was a shadow that might turn out to be another of the scattered olive groves that were the main vegetation. Without conscious thought, he pulled his horse a little to the right and headed in that direction. Alongside him, he saw William doing the same. In his mind's eye he could almost see El Jefe's men, almost a week back, making the same automatic correction to their route.

William spoke for the first time since they had left the hut. "It wasn't a week."

Burke glanced across at him. "What do you mean?"

"While you were in the hut, I looked around outside. There were scorches on the ground where there had been cooking fires. There was a hell of a lot of horse shit, too."

Burke stared at him. Surely he must be misunderstanding what he was being told. "Are you saying that they left the bodies in the hut and just made camp outside?"

William nodded. "Probably cooked up any provisions in the kitchen. Did you see any food there?"

Burke realised that he had not. There had been flies on the body, but no other rotting food for them to desecrate.

"Not a very nice man, El Jefe," said William.

Burke did not reply, but dug his heels into his horse's flanks, urging it forward. Somewhere ahead of them was the bandit gang, and the sooner they were caught, the better.

* * *

They rode for the rest of the day with no sign of the bandits. Burke was beginning to fear that they had lost them somewhere on the plain when they arrived at another tiny village. Santibanez was not unlike Montehermoso. Their reception this time, though, was

friendly enough. A smiling villager had introduced himself as Matías and offered to lead them to a woman who would be able to offer accommodation for the night. “Valentina is a widow, but most respectable. She would be pleased to give you food and shelter.

Burke was happy enough to find somewhere to sleep, but William grumbled as he rode alongside him. “Looks like El Jefe didn’t visit here, then.” His tone betrayed his irritation with the idea of the killers’ escape.

He had spoken in English, but Matías turned at the sound of El Jefe’s name. “El Jefe is your friend, no?” Nothing in the way he spoke suggested any reason why they should not be friends of El Jefe’s and Burke responded cautiously.

“We are following and hope to catch up with him soon. Has he been here?”

“Yes.” Matías smiled, pleased to be able to give them news of El Jefe’s travels. “He was here just three days ago.”

“And he gave you no trouble.”

Matías’ smile faded. “Why should he give us trouble? He is a guerrilla. He fights bravely for his country. Why should he trouble honest Spaniards?”

Burke dismounted and stood face-to-face with their guide.

“We have news about El Jefe. Can you gather the men together so that we can talk?”

* * *

As it was almost dusk, the men of the village were easily summoned. Burke explained who he was and what he had learned at Montehermoso.

It was not an easy meeting. Apparently, when El Jefe’s men had arrived at the village they were sated by the killing at the hut and had been content to claim that they were fighting the French. The villagers had duly welcomed them as heroes. It was difficult for them now to accept that they had been made fools of. Yet here was a man, a gentleman by his bearing, who spoke English and carried papers he said showed him to be a British officer.

The discussion carried on for almost an hour. It had started with angry voices being raised at Burke's suggestion, but in the end his

account of what had happened at Montehermoso had been convincing. Besides, someone said, the band that had visited three days earlier had seemed to show very little interest in finding any Frenchman. Somebody else remarked that one of their visitors had behaved more like a ruffian than an honourable soldier and a third man complained that El Jefe had eyed his daughter rather more lasciviously than had been proper. It was at around this point that the mood of the meeting had shifted, and by the end everyone was convinced that El Jefe was a villain and that, were he to be seen again, he would be sent on his way and the countryside warned against him.

It was Burke's turn, now, to be feted as a hero and the next morning the menfolk turned out to escort him on the path that El Jefe's men had taken as they left the village.

After a couple of hours, the villagers turned back and left Burke and William to carry on the pursuit on their own. At first it had been easy enough. A farmer said that some men had ridden by and insulted his daughter, though she had had the good sense to run indoors and, once they had seen her father at the door with a gun, they had ridden on by. At noon they passed a church where the vestry had been forced open and a silver chalice taken and in the evening they stayed at a village where El Jefe had arrived two days ahead of them. There, though, the people had not listened to any nonsense about guerrillas. The gang had been denounced as thieves and robbers before the villagers opened fire with half a dozen muskets. The bandits had left there in a hurry and not been seen since.

After that, it was as if El Jefe and his gang had simply vanished. The scenery changed, the arid plain giving way to more fertile land. There were gentle hills, the south-facing slopes planted with vines. Villages were surrounded by fields with wheat ripening in the sun. Burke and William stopped at each place they passed and asked for news of horsemen riding through a day or two before them, but there was nothing at all to be learned of El Jefe.

The countryside was peaceful and it was easy to forget that Spain was at war. Not only was there no El Jefe, but there was no sign of any French troops either. When they asked, they were told that the French dared not travel in the countryside because of the

guerrillas. It seemed that these mysterious fighters were having an effect simply by the fear that they engendered amongst the enemy, but there was precious little evidence of their existence. True enough, in a couple of the villages they passed through they heard of another band led by 'El Gato' – the Cat – but the Cat seemed as elusive as the Chief.

"At least this Gato has a bit of imagination." Brown was chewing another sausage – he had acquired a taste for them. "Never trust a bloke what calls himself 'Chief'."

"I'm not sure I really trust someone who calls themselves the Cat. Odd sort of a name for a chap to choose."

"Ah, but what if it isn't a fella? Bloke who sold me this sausage …" He waved what was left of it in the air "… he told me that he'd heard El Gato was a woman."

"People have told me that Napoleon has hoofs for feet and a tail he hides in his breeches. I think we can discount that notion, William. Besides, 'El Gato' is a tomcat. If it were a woman, she'd be 'La Gata'."

Brown shrugged and concentrated on his sausage. It was three days since they had left Montehermoso and the anger that had driven them when they thought they were close to El Jefe had begun to fade. The sun was low in the sky and they were riding side by side along a track that ran towards what, from this distance, looked like a river. There was, in any case, a dip in the land. They could see the tops of trees in the hollow, which was more evidence of a watercourse. If there was a river there, Burke supposed they should follow it and add the details to the rough map they were making of the area. Even if they never contacted any guerrillas, the information about the lie of the land would be of value to Wellesley. Burke thought their course was still carrying them in the general direction of Madrid, which was his excuse for carrying on his pursuit of El Jefe, though it seemed unlikely, by now, that they were going to catch him.

"Leaving aside your friend's extraordinary notions about El Gato, did anybody have any news of the Chief?"

"Not a dickie bird. I think he's knows he's made things hot for himself and he's gone to ground."

“Do you think he could? He's shown a marked predilection for banditry so far. How do you think he's getting by now?"

William looked around. There was just enough of the sausage left for him to use it as a pointer stabbing left and right. "There’s fields there. Proper fields. And livestock nearer the villages. There's more villages than there were before, but it's too easy to get a hue and cry up with more people about like this. On the other hand, it's easier to steal. A goat here, some fruit there, maybe slit the odd throat and steal the odd purse, but quiet like. Send somebody to buy food with your stolen money and then tuck yourself down out of the way until things are quiet and you can ride south and start your banditry again.”

Burke considered what William said. It would certainly account for the way that all traces of the bandits had dried up.

William swallowed the last of his sausage. "We could turn back and let Wellesley know what we found. You're always saying that knowing that there is definitely nothing there is just as useful as finding whatever you're looking for."

Burke could not miss the despondency in William’s tone. His sergeant was no happier with the idea of giving up the chase than he was, but the possibility had to be considered. They had been able to fill in some blank spaces on the map and William was right: they had successfully demonstrated that there were few, if any, active guerrilla bands in the area and, depressing as that may be, it was one more piece in the jigsaw of intelligence that Wellesley would need as he pushed his army forward. "At least we know there's no French here either."

They were almost at the fringes of the wood. To their left the ground rose gently and the trees grew from the hill, following a little gully that seemed to cross their path half a mile or so ahead. The forest – thicker than anything they had seen further south – made it difficult to be certain, but Burke was sure there was a river down that. He even managed to convince himself that he could make out sun glinting on water through the trees.

"You're right. We'll ride as far as the river and see how deep it is. Given this track, I'm reckoning it must be fordable, but we’ll have a look for ourselves. Then we'll follow the stream south and map it. It’s exactly the sort of thing that Wellesley needs to know about.”

They moved into the shade of the trees. It was good to be out of the fierce heat of the sun. If there was water in the stream, they could rest the horses and allow them to drink for a while.

Afterwards he cursed himself for allowing them to relax like that. They were close on the trail of dangerous men, for all they had more or less given up hope of catching them. Yet here he was, thinking about rest and water, when he should have been concentrating – listening for any unnatural sounds in the wood; looking for signs of disturbance in the foliage. As it was, when the attack came he was taken completely by surprise.

Their horses fell with the first shots. Burke was out of the saddle and on his feet in an instant. The horse was rolling and he could not reach the carbine in its saddle holster: besides, it was not primed. He drew his sword as he stepped from the path to the shelter of the trees. Behind him William's comparative inexperience as a rider had betrayed him and he had fallen with his horse in a tangle of stirrup leathers. As Burke watched, two men ran onto the path and grabbed his sergeant, pulling him away from the tangled tack. Burke had a moment of relief as he saw William stumbling in their grasp, but upright. He had, it seemed, managed to keep his legs out of harm's way and the fall had not broken them. Before he could take in anything else three men were on him. Two carried swords and Burke raised his own weapon to defend himself, but the third drew a pistol, pointing it squarely at Burke's chest.

"*¡Caída de su espada o eres hombre muerto!*"

Burke obediently let his sword fall to the ground where one of the bandits (for there was no doubt in his mind that these were El Jefe's men) picked it up. The man with the pistol kept it raised towards him as the other two prodded at him with their swords, driving him further into the wood.

El Jefe's camp turned out to be less than a hundred yards from the track. A dozen or so men lounged about, sprawled on the ground or propping themselves against the trunks of the trees that surrounded their temporary home. A camp fire was burning in the middle of the small clearing. Burke cursed his carelessness. In the clean air he should have smelled the smoke if he had been paying proper attention. A cauldron of something – stew from the smell of it – bubbled away over the fire. Burke wondered where they had

stolen the pot. From the last village they had passed, he imagined: it was too heavy to carry far.

Rather to Burke's surprise, he was sat on the ground and his hands and feet tied. Beside him, William received the same treatment. Given the ruthlessness that the bandits had shown elsewhere, he had rather expected to be murdered out of hand. As it was, he only had to put up with the odd kick from the villains as they milled about the camp, and the blows seemed as much an expression of high spirits as malevolence.

They stayed tied on the ground for what Burke imagined to be close on three hours. Other men came and joined those already in the camp, but he was left with William, more or less ignored by their captors. It was almost dark by now and Burke was beginning to feel the evening chill. That, though, he judged to be the least of his problems.

The bandits were clearly waiting for something – or someone – though there was no air of tension. They seemed quite relaxed.

At last there came a cry from what Burke knew to be the direction of the track, followed by the sound of a horse making its way through the trees.

When horse and rider emerged into the clearing, Burke knew immediately that he was facing El Jefe.

The self-styled guerrilla leader was a big man, running a little to fat, but still well-muscled. When he dismounted from his horse, he moved easily. His clothes were distinctive. He wore the wide-brimmed hat that was favoured in these parts, but his shirt was not the rough cotton of most local peasants. Instead it was fine linen, carefully displayed by an open jacket which itself was dark blue. Perhaps it had been stolen from a military man, though the gold braid that adorned both shoulders and much of the breast was surely not part of any uniform he had ever seen. He suspected that El Jefe had stitched on gold curtain cords to make his outfit more impressive. Most of the men lounging in the camp wore sandals, but El Jefe's trousers (again conspicuously well made, if ill fitting) were tucked into a pair of fine riding boots.

The ostentatious finery would have inclined Burke to laughter but one glance at the man's face quelled any possibility of humorous thoughts. Under thick black brows his eyes were two

dark pools of malevolence that looked at Burke like a butcher sizing up an ox for slaughter. Even if he had not already known of the trail of death that El Jefe had left behind him, he would have instinctively recognised him as an evil man.

The bandit troop was all gathering around El Jefe now, full of news of their cleverness in capturing these two prisoners. For a minute or two, Burke could not see their leader for the excitable group around him. Then the crowd parted and El Jefe emerged to walk over to where Burke sat on the ground.

El Jefe looked down on his prisoner.

"¿Quién eres tú?"

Who was he? Burke could hardly pass himself off as a priest now, and anything he tried would lead to more questions. The safest answer, and one that might play to the vanity of a man who draped his jacket with gold braid, might be the truth.

"I am …" Burke spoke in Spanish, but took care to speak badly and with an English accent. "I am an emissary from General Wellesley, come to seek out allies among the guerrillas of Spain."

There were excited mutterings from the assembled members of El Jefe's band and, for a moment, Burke saw a look of calculation in those eyes.

"How do I know you are who you claim to be?"

"Look in the saddle holsters. Those are British carbines. Who else will be carrying them?"

El Jefe laughed. "These days only a fool does not travel armed. How should I know who you killed to get those carbines?"

"How many men do you know who speak English?" Burke continued in his own language: "I think my tongue proves who I am."

"Huh!" El Jefe grunted, looking to Burke decidedly unimpressed. Among the other men scattered about the clearing, though, it seemed that Burke's response was well received.

El Jefe, too, was looking to see how his men were reacting to his prisoner's claim and their apparent acceptance that Burke might be what he said seemed to sway him.

"Cut him free."

It seems that El Jefe was not the sort of man to stoop to loose a prisoner's bonds himself, but one of their captors drew a knife and,

bending, cut the ropes that tied Burke's hands and feet. Alongside him another performed the same service for William.

Burke rose from the ground and offered his hand to El Jefe, who reached out his own reluctantly. There was the briefest of handshakes.

“If you are who you say you are, what would you have us do?”

Burke thought quickly. His orders had simply been to make contact with the guerrillas and establish their plans. He knew that once General Hill had been told where the guerrilla bands were, he would send officers to liaise with them. Burke had no intention of suggesting this to El Jefe, though. If the bandit leader released them and sent them on their way to the British, Burke had no doubt that they would have moved to plundering elsewhere by the time any liaison officer rode back to them. No: El Jefe had to be kept close under his eye.

"I would have you ride with me to Wellesley's army. There you will be treated with all honour and made privy to his plans for the conquest of the French."

The murmured approval of the other bandits now gave way to full-voiced cheering.

“What’s going on?” William had moved closer to him and now muttered into his ear.

“Have no fear, Sergeant Brown.” Burke spoke in Spanish, loudly enough to be sure that those around him heard. “These brave souls volunteered to fight the French, and they are cheering because we can give them the opportunity to do just that." Then, in English, "Remember Alfredo. He will not have been the only honest man caught up in this.”

El Jefe turned his head, his glance sweeping across all those who were cheering. As the men felt his eyes on them, the cheering died away.

"We do not know if we can trust these men. Watch them.”

He said no more, but turned abruptly and strode away to the furthest corner of the clearing beckoning two men, who Burke judged to be his lieutenants, to follow him.

The atmosphere subdued after his last command, prisoners and guards sat together in an uncomfortable silence.

After a while William asked quietly, “What do you think is going to happen?”

“I think we’re going to ride back towards the army. They may be behaving as rogues and villains now, but a fair number of these men will have joined up to fight the French. While there are no French to fight, they turn to banditry. Now, though, we have given them a chance to show their patriotic fervour. El Jefe may not like it, but I think he’ll have no choice but to go along with it.”

Privately, Burke thought there was a fair chance that El Jefe would arrange an "accident” before they reached Wellesley, but he saw no reason to share his concerns with William. Instead, he relaxed as best he could, joining their captors in eating the stew, which was surprisingly good, and settling down for a night’s sleep on the ground.

* * *

The next morning he woke early. Most of the bandits were still asleep, but one was awake, watching in the direction of him and Sergeant Brown, while ostentatiously whittling away with a suspiciously large knife. It seemed that El Jefe’s orders that they were to be watched were being taken seriously, albeit with a degree of discretion.

El Jefe did not wake until most of his men were already up. Somebody had departed with a bucket and returned with it filled with water, confirming Burke's suspicion that there was a river nearby. Others were busy building a fire, but most stood fidgeting. Burke recognised that nervous pacing to and fro, the twitchy unsheathing and sheathing of swords, the repeated checking and rechecking of harnesses on the horses hobbled under the trees. These were men who thought that they were about to be ordered into action.

Although there was little prospect of any immediate fighting, they were right to judge that, after months of aimless wandering, they were to be given orders to take a more active part in the conflict that was embroiling their country. El Jefe, having eventually aroused himself from sleep, announced that his band was to march south west toward the Anglo Portuguese force.

They moved out at midday. They set off south, following the river, as Burke had intended to do the day before. With their horses dead, Burke and William were ordered to march. "Don't worry though," said one of the chattier of their captors, "we'll get horses for you soon enough."

William nodded his thanks at this news, happy enough to be marching. Burke, though, was less sanguine. Infantryman or not, it had been a while since he had been expected to march anywhere, and he felt the loss of his mount more than, it appeared, did his sergeant.

In the end, they marched until evening. Although the other men were all mounted, they rode easily and paused when Burke and William were struggling to keep up. Even so, Burke was tired that night and relieved, when he woke, to discover that there were now horses for him and William. It seemed wiser not to ask where they had come from.

The bandits had taken the tack from the horses they had killed, so Burke found himself mounted comfortably in his own saddle. The holster, though, was empty. Most of the men seemed to treat him as an honoured guest, but incidents like that made it clear that, as far as El Jefe was concerned, they were still his prisoners. They were not guarded, though, presumably because, in that empty countryside there was nowhere to run to. So Burke and William rode side by side and were able to talk without worrying about being spied on.

"Are we just going to carry on as if nothing is wrong?" William was clearly uncomfortable riding with the men they had been hunting and his concern showed in the questions he kept asking. Burke, on the other hand, was more relaxed. Although his carbine was missing, the rest of his possessions were, rather to his surprise, still in his saddlebags. He had recovered the map he had been working on and added to it at every opportunity, tracking their route. As he and William had pursued the bandits, their journey had taken them first north and then more eastward. Now they seemed to be headed south and would, presumably, later start to head more toward the west. It seemed that their course was designed to avoid those villages that they had pillaged on their outward journey.

"We don't have a lot of choice. If we run for it, we'll have the whole gang after us, assuming that we get out of musket range before we're shot down. And while El Jefe sticks to behaving like an honest enemy of France, there's no reason why we can't all ride together to Wellesley's camp."

"And what do we do then?"

"We make our report, hand El Jefe over to General Hill and, given Wellesley's attitudes to looting, I imagine he'll be strung up the following morning." He paused to call over towards the bandit leader, who had turned at the sound of his name. "I was telling my sergeant that he could learn much from the way that you maintain discipline amongst your men." El Jefe rewarded him with one of his rare smiles and Burke turned back to William. "I'll be up early to watch."

They rode on. El Jefe didn't seem in any particular hurry to reach Wellesley's army and they ambled easily southwards all day. The next day they made better speed and in the afternoon they turned west and the landscape began to look familiar. Burke was not totally confident about his map, but he thought they were north of the outcrop where they had found the murdered man in his adobe hut at the beginning of their pursuit.

As they carried on across the plain, Burke started to recognise landmarks on the horizon. His horse had pulled ahead of William, but now he slowed, waiting for his sergeant to catch up.

"I think we may have a problem."

William sat up straighter in his saddle and looked about him. Burke could see the moment when he realised where they were. "What was the name of that place?"

Burke dropped his voice to reply. "Santibanez."

"What do you think will happen when we get there?"

"You and I will keep a very low profile. If El Jefe is just driven out, we'll express astonishment at the ingratitude of his compatriots and promise that Wellesley shall hear of it."

"And if there's a fight?"

"Let's hope there isn't."

Half an hour later, the little huddle of houses that made up Santibanez was clearly visible in the distance. The riders around them pointed and laughed, clearly looking forward to the

opportunity to rest in the shade and eat a meal that wasn't based around dried beef. They obviously did not expect any trouble, but Burke did not share their confidence. But then he knew that El Jefe had been denounced there as a bandit and their captors did not.

As they neared the village, Burke and William allowed themselves to drift towards the back of the group, but they were still uncomfortably close when a shot ahead of them sent a musket ball close over their heads.

Burke watched as El Jefe rode forward ahead of his men, his right hand raised in peaceful greeting. He was brave: Burke would give him that. Burke would think twice before riding up to a group of determined looking villagers, several of whom had muskets levelled at the bandit leader.

"*¡Hola, amigos!*"

For a moment Burke wondered if this was some sort of bluff but, as El Jefe carried on speaking, he realised that the bandit honestly thought this was a misunderstanding. "It's me. El Jefe. Put the guns away."

The muskets, though, remained conspicuously pointed at him as one of the villagers stepped forward. Burke recognised Matías.

"We've heard what you really are, El Jefe." He pronounced the title with contempt. "Take yourself and your men away and be thankful we don't just shoot you out of hand."

"Amigos! Amigos! There's some misunderstanding. We are riding now to join General Wellesley's army. Look, we have a British officer with us. He will vouch for us." He turned and gestured to where Burke stood at the back of his followers.

"That's torn it." Now that the worst had happened, William seemed remarkably phlegmatic.

Burke moved his horse slowly forward, wondering if some miracle might save him.

It didn't.

"Senor Burke!" The villager sounded genuinely distressed. "What are you doing with these men? You told us that –"

Burke spoke loudly, cutting him off. "This is war, Matías. We take our friends where we can find them."

Both Matías and El Jefe were looking at him suspiciously.

"You know this man?" El Jefe's hand was no longer held up in greeting, but strayed close to the butt of the pistol in his belt.

"We've met."

El Jefe half turned to address his men, but his eyes stayed fixed on Burke. "I warned you that we could not trust these two. They are not as they have presented themselves to us."

For a moment, there was hesitation. Burke allowed himself to think that, in the confusion of the situation, things might somehow end without bloodshed, but then one of El Jefe's men, probably more from nerves than anything else, unslung the musket that he carried across his back. One of the villagers fired and within seconds there was the chaos of smoke and screaming that always attended battle. For a battle it was, or at least a skirmish. Burke flung himself from his horse. Untrained troops, in his experience, tended to fire high, so the closer he was to the ground, the better. Either side of him he saw bandits fall. He was impressed: the villagers were doing well for amateurs. But they must have had less than half a dozen muskets between them. One or two brave men ran forward to stab at their enemy with improvised pikes – scythe blades and kitchen knives mounted on long poles. They covered scarcely half the distance to the bandits before they were shot down.

El Jefe's men fired in ragged, undisciplined bursts and were slow to reload. With a dozen British infantry behind him, Burke could have killed them all as easily as you might shoot a mad dog, but the villagers were not trained infantrymen and they did not have a dozen muskets. In this kind of brawl, numbers and fire power were the decisive factors and it was all-too-clear how the fight would end.

Burke did not have his carbine, but the pretence that he was a guest, rather than a prisoner, meant he had been left his sword. Drawing his weapon he started towards El Jefe. If he could kill the bandit chief, perhaps the gang would flee, leaving the villagers safe.

El Jefe was less than a dozen steps away. Burke was almost there and had raised his sword to strike when he was thrown forward. Something struck the back of his head and he knew no more.

* * *

When he came to, he thought at first that he was blind. Gradually, though, he made out lights – flames flickering somewhere ahead of him.

He tried to sit up but he was tied hand and foot and the struggle to raise his body from the ground achieved nothing more than to awaken a headache that seemed to spread from where he had been hit to produce tendrils of agony right through his skull.

"Take it easy, sir. You've been unconscious for hours." William's voice was reassuring.

"What did I miss?"

He tried to turn to look at William as he replied, but the spurt of pain that induced made him think it was wiser to lie still.

"It wasn't pretty, sir."

"How many did they kill?"

"I wouldn't rightly know. As soon as they brought you down, they turned on me. I think they'd have liked to have knocked me about a bit, but there was a lot going on, so they trussed me up and left me for later. They must have killed most of the menfolk, though, because there are a lot of women screaming and if their men were about, they'd be trying to stop that."

Burke said nothing. There was nothing to say.

He lay there, waiting for the pain in his head to subside. He knew he ought to be trying to keep cheerful, but it was difficult to keep cheerful while a village where you'd eaten peacefully less than a week ago burned around you and the screams of the women made it horribly clear what El Jefe's gang were doing now that they had, presumably, slaughtered the men. And once El Jefe had sated his blood lust and any other kind of lust, Burke was in no doubt that he would return to deal with him. The Chief was not the sort of person to overlook it if you went after him with a sword.

At length the screaming died away and there was the sound of a feast, accompanied by the smell of meat roasting somewhere away to their left. Perhaps El Jefe might forget about them and ride off, leaving his prisoners to free themselves and make their way home as best they could. It was, Burke knew, a vain hope. El Jefe could take his time exacting his revenge and, it seemed, was happy to delay retribution, but that he would be avenged was never seriously in doubt.

The feasting went on so long that, despite his physical discomfort and the trepidation that naturally accompanied his position, Burke fell eventually into an uneasy sleep. He was awakened, he knew not at what hour, by a vicious kick in the ribs.

"Swine! Traitor! It's time you faced justice." He was red faced and slurring his words, clearly very drunk indeed. "Get on your feet."

It is no easy matter to get to your feet when all your limbs are tightly bound and Burke had no intention of even attempting it. When oaths and kicks did not work, he was dragged up by two of his one-time companions and held erect while El Jefe, in a parody of a court-martial, made out the indictment against him. This was an elaborate list of charges which included everything from slandering him as a bandit, through abusing his hospitality, to betrayal and treason.

The indictment, indeed, took rather longer than the rest of the trial, for the verdict was by acclamation and the cries of "Guilty" must have been audible for miles.

El Jefe, who had slumped against a tree while Burke's fate was decided, now drew himself uncertainly to his feet to pronounce sentence.

"You are sentenced to die by firing squad. Sentence to be carried out at dawn. And may God have mercy on your soul. Not that he will." He nodded to the two men holding Burke up who released him and, when he did not fall immediately, pushed him so that he collapsed back onto the ground.

El Jefe, apparently satisfied with his night's work, had already turned away when one of the gang called, "What about this one?" and kicked William sharply in the head.

"Him?" El Jefe clearly could not be bothered with the farce of another trial. "Shoot him too."

Chapter 5: The Girl He Left Behind

"I'm sorry things have turned out like this, William."

"That's all right, sir. We can't expect to be lucky every time."

A voice came from the darkness. "Shut up, English swine."

"Better get some sleep, sergeant."'

Burke heard footsteps approach and then, without warning, felt the blow of a musket stock against his chest. Their guard was apparently serious about them keeping quiet. Burke wondered if he should try to savour the last few hours of life and decided that he had no particular desire for his final memories to be of a night spent lying on the ground with the air full of the smell of burning and the faint sound of a woman weeping somewhere in the distance. Better, surely, to sleep. So, with the practised ease of a military man, he slept.

He woke to a steady thump of mallet on wood. The sun had not yet risen, but the grey, pre-dawn light was strong enough to see the men hammering two stakes into the ground against the wall of the nearest building.

The sound, it seemed, was waking the bandits, who were drifting in ones and twos towards what was clearly to be the execution site. They moved unsteadily, like men who had drunk heavily the night before and were now regretting it. Burke hoped their heads hurt like hell.

When most of the gang had arrived, El Jefe made his entrance, gold braid gleaming even in this light. He seemed in better shape than the others. Either he had drunk less or the anticipation of watching Burke die had cleared up any hangover.

With much shouting of orders, El Jefe and his lieutenants got half a dozen of the men organised into some sort of firing squad. More orders had Burke's guards dragging him and William to their feet. The ropes tying their ankles were cut but, after hours lying tied up, neither was in any condition to walk unaided and each was supported – half dragged, half carried – to the stakes.

The posts were only about four feet high and their escorts simply lifted them into the air while another man guided their bound arms over the top of the stakes. It was crude but effective.

Opposite them the firing squad were taking their positions, while El Jefe strutted up and down, occasionally casting contemptuous glances towards his prisoners.

This was not the first occasion on which Burke had faced execution. That time in Buenos Aires, though, it had all been a cruel joke and the muskets had not been loaded. Now he watched the ragged line of executioners ramming the balls into their weapons and knew this was emphatically real.

The men who were to kill him looked uncomfortable. Most, he knew, would have murdered before, but it is one thing to kill in the heat of battle or rage when the blood runs hot in your veins and another to coldly kill a helpless enemy. They would do it, but they would fumble with their weapons and tremble as they pulled the triggers. He could only hope that they did a half-way decent job and that he died quickly. He turned and looked to his left. William Brown was standing rigidly to attention. Burke knew his sergeant must be feeling fear, but it was hidden. He would die like a man.

For himself, Burke felt a strange peace. He had come to terms with what was to happen. Now he had just to get it over with.

Time seemed suddenly to shift. A moment before the men had been loading their weapons but now they were already firing. The brain, Burke thought, must rush through those last seconds, sparing the condemned man the tedious ritual of orders to aim and fire. The weapons crashed, but there was no shock of pain as the balls hit. Surely they could not all have missed?

Through the mist of smoke that was already drifting across the execution ground, Burke saw the firing squad falling. This made no sense. They should be standing and it was him and William who should be slumping to the earth, blood staining their coats.

Burke shook his head, trying to clear his mind. He wasn't hallucinating. The bandits who had gathered to watch his death were now scrambling to grab up their own muskets, which had been left stacked against a tree. As they ran, though, they too were falling, hands clutching to wounds, blood soaking into the ground beneath them.

Through the smoke, Burke now saw figures moving in the grey dawn light. There was a continued ragged volley of shooting and the smoke around these figures grew thicker.

El Jefe ran towards his men, but a shot brought him down before he reached them. The rest of the gang seemed all to have been hit. Some writhed and screamed, a few seemed to be doggedly trying to pull themselves to cover, dragging shattered legs behind them: most were already lying motionless.

A figure emerged from the smoke. Burke half expected to see the uniform of the British army, for the attack had been smoothly managed and the shooting suggested men who were well practised in the use of their arms, but this man was wearing the same rough trousers, dark jacket and wide brimmed hat that was favoured by most of the peasants hereabouts. In his left hand he held a musket, the stench of powder still on it. In his right, a murderous knife was pointed directly at Burke.

The figure moved closer and the knife flashed towards Burke's bonds. As the rope fell away, Burke thought for a moment that he would fall, but his legs had regained enough feeling to support him. He opened his mouth to thank his saviour, but the man had already turned away and was releasing William. As Burke took an unsteady step to support his sergeant, their rescuer was already stepping back towards El Jefe, who lay alone on the spot where he had stood to oversee the execution. The bodies of Burke's would-be assassins had fallen in the line that they had formed for his execution. They looked far more well-ordered in death than they ever had in life. The rest of the bandits were scattered here and there, cut down as they ran for the cover of the houses.

Burke was wondering if El Jefe had survived when a scream from the bandit captain confirmed that he had. The man who had cut them free gestured to a couple of his comrades to drag El Jefe to his feet and then, for the first time, he spoke. "Follow me. El Gato wants to see you."

He did not wait for any reply, but started back the way he had come, his two companions dragging El Jefe along behind him.

"Chatty fellow, isn't he?" said William.

Burke, taking his cue from their rescuer, did not reply. He hoped, though, that El Gato would be more loquacious than his lieutenant

(for the man's natural air of command suggested that he was El Gato's lieutenant). This El Gato, it seemed, may well be a true guerrilla. He had almost given up hope of meeting such a person. Now, finally, he might be able to carry out his mission and build contacts with the resistance to the French.

They were led out of the village in the direction that their rescuers had attacked from. There was a slight rise overlooking the scattering of houses on this side and two of the guerrillas were standing there, gesturing at the buildings below. Burke assumed the taller of the two was El Gato. A third stood back a little. She wore the same jacket and trousers as the other fighters but her figure was definitely that of a woman, though the wide brimmed hat and poor light meant he could not say whether she was old or young, pretty or plain. He did not look too hard: she was presumably the guerrilla leader's woman and it would be impolite to show too much interest in her.

Burke moved towards the taller man, his hand outstretched.

"El Gato?" he said. "We owe you our lives."

There came a chuckle from the woman. "Lieutenant Burke, it would appear I have the advantage of you."

Burke stood in some confusion. The man he had approached seemed almost as uncertain as him, but took the proffered hand.

"I am Major Burke, sir. I'm very pleased to meet you."

The woman spluttered, as if trying desperately not to laugh. Burke could hardly avoid turning to look at her, but she had her hand over her mouth. She was young and, apparently, vastly amused, but that was all he could make out.

"I am pleased to meet you, Major Burke, but I fear you are under a misapprehension. I am not El Gato."

Embarrassed, Burke turned to the other man.

Now the woman took her hand from her mouth and laughed out loud.

"*¡Hombre tonto!* It's me that's El Gato."

There was something familiar about that laugh.

"No!"

El Gato took off her hat. "Yes, James. It is, it appears, my turn to rescue you."

"Bernadita!"

She stepped towards him. It was, indeed, Bernadita: older than she had been when they rode together in Egypt, but still young and still, it seemed to him, beautiful.

"Carlos!" She spoke to the tall man. "Get the prisoners digging graves for the dead and then we'll decide what to do with the living." She pointed towards El Jefe, whose escort had dragged him up to join them. "Guard that one well. Make sure his wound is tended. I don't want him to die and rob us of the privilege of killing him. But first," her voice softened, "I need some time with this handsome British officer."

"Very well, ma'am." Carlos's words were respectful, but Burke could not mistake the ironic tone. "Best treat him with respect, though. He's a major now, apparently."

Bernadita stifled a laugh. She hardly seemed the same woman as had, only seconds earlier, pronounced sentence of death on El Jefe. "Come along, Major Burke," (she placed, James thought, an altogether unnecessary emphasis on the 'Major'), "we have some catching up to do."

They had indeed. Just over ten years had passed since the young Lieutenant Burke had saved Bernadita López Covas from a life of slavery in Cairo. He had grown very fond of her in that brief mad-cap adventure, but when they had bid farewell off the coast of Spain, he had never expected to see her again.

"A major." She was walking beside him and once out of sight of her men her hand slipped naturally into his. "And a very handsome major. Have you been fighting the French all this time?"

"Mostly." It was, perhaps, not the moment to tell her that at least some of his time had been spent encouraging the South American rebels to rise up against the Spanish. "But that's by way of being my job. How on earth have you ended up leading a band of guerrillas? And I thought you were from Granada. That's almost 300 miles away."

"You're thousands of miles from your own country. You've come here to save Spain from the French. Is 300 miles so far to save my own nation?"

"A fair point, senorita, but few of your compatriots seem to be as enthusiastic to engage the French. And amongst the fairer sex, I

suspect you are the only one. And, 'The Tomcat'! How did that happen?"

"Well, as to my fighting here, I blame the man who had me riding through the desert when he was fighting the French in Egypt. I learned there that a woman could be as tough as any man. But not many men know that. Better to be 'El Gato' than a fluffy little 'La Gata'. I think I've earned the right to be taken more seriously than that, don't you?"

Burke said nothing. He was remembering those days of apparently endless riding and the nights when they had held each other. It had been a special time and she had a special place in his memory. It seemed she, too, was reliving those adventures in her mind, for she was silent as well as they walked together away from the stench of burning.

Burke was the first to speak. "When I left you, you were going to make your way back to your family."

The smile that had been playing around her lips faded. "They were pleased I had survived, of course. But we value the purity and innocence of our women-folk in Spain. I could not disguise that I had been a slave in Egypt. No one said anything to my face, but I knew they could never forgive me for that."

"Surely there was nothing to forgive. It was hardly your fault that your ship was taken by pirates."

"But it is my fault that I did not throw myself into the sea to drown."

Burke let go her hand and took her arms, turning her to face him. "You cannot mean that."

She shrugged, dismissing the horror of what she had said. "A woman without honour is, as far as many men are concerned, no better than a whore. And my honour was lost in the slave markets of Cairo."

Burke looked at her, studying her face. There was no obvious sign of the distress he knew must be there, except, perhaps, for a brightness in her eyes that might have been the faintest trace of tears.

He reached out and held her and she clasped him in return, and for a moment he felt again the girl he had known in Egypt. Then she freed herself from him and wiped her hand across her eyes and was

again the warrior. "Enough of such things. What are you doing here?"

Burke explained his mission.

"It's no wonder you have struggled to find any true fighters against the French." Bernadita spoke matter-of-factly, not judging her compatriots but making a cold military assessment of their situation. "The land here is open and it does not favour the sort of warfare that we Spanish patriots must fight. Most of the guerrillas are in the hills, where they can ambush the French in narrow passes and disappear before the enemy can hunt them down."

"But you are here."

Burke was not at all matter-of-fact, and, for a moment, her voice trembled as she started to reply. "I have nothing to lose, James. Honour, remember? Most of those who fight against France stay close to their homes. In part, this is because they know the terrain there. You could say they do it for tactical military advantage. But they also do it because they have to be able to tend to their farms. They will fight the French and then they will vanish into the mountains and, when the French come in force to kill them, all they will find is farmers working in their fields. They have families to care for and they can't simply leave everything to fight the invaders. I have no one."

"And your men?"

"They are men who hate the French more than they love life. Some have had their families killed. Carlos's wife was raped. She hanged herself. There are a couple who were priests but their churches were robbed by godless soldiers who stole the plate and pissed on the altars. They decided that if God could not strike these men down Himself, He must expect them to fight on His behalf. They all wanted to find someone who would take the fight to the enemy and they heard of El Gato and now here they are."

"And they are happy to follow a woman?"

"I am here. I am fighting the French. And I am, as I think you have seen, very good at what I do. Besides, I am not 'a woman'. I am El Gato."

Burke looked at her with a new respect. She had always been beautiful, but as she had grown older that beauty had changed. This was a strong, proud woman, whose striking good looks almost hid

the girlish charm that he remembered from Egypt. If it had not been for her laughter when he did not recognise her, he might have thought that girl was lost. He was quite unreasonably happy that she was not.

"Anyway," she turned to walk back to the village, "we cannot talk about the past for ever. What do you think we should do with El Jefe and his men? I think you said that Wellesley would have hanged him."

"There's very little doubt of it."

"It seems a quick, clean death. I remember that in Egypt they said the desert women could make a man's death last for hours."

"I don't think that will be necessary."

She looked at him thoughtfully. He realised that she was considering possible alternatives. Finally, she tossed her head. "Oh well, if you're sure. We don't really have the time anyway. What about the others?"

Burke remembered Alfredo. "I think many of them are good lads, but led astray."

They were back where he had first seen her, looking down over the village. Below, her men were searching through the buildings. Two or three women accompanied them, gesturing here and there. Every so often they would look into a hut and emerge weeping. Bernadita gestured towards the women. "Let's ask them if they think they were good lads."

* * *

Bernadita's approach was more matter-of-fact than El Jefe's. There was nothing like a trial. The men were lined up and the women who had survived the rapes walked along the line and pointed at those they would denounce. Almost all were pointed at by one or another of the women. No, they agreed, not all the men had violated them, but all had been there and held them down, or just watched.

What penalty did they demand? Why, death, of course. Or castration, right there, on the spot. Two women offered to wield the knives themselves.

Burke watched, horrified at Bernadita’s casual acceptance of what the women were saying. “You can’t be serious. That’s barbaric.”

"You wondered why the men will follow me." She looked him in the eye, waiting for him to nod. "They do not see any weakness in me. I cannot afford them to think of me as gentler than a man would be."

"But castration ..."

“Yes.” She nodded. “I think that’s unrealistic. They’d end up dying anyway. We’ll shoot them.”

Carlos grunted. "Waste of ammunition."

Bernadita appeared to give his comment some thought. "Cutting their throats is messy and garrotting that number will take a while. Best just shoot them and have done with.”

Burke listened with growing disquiet. “What about the ones they didn’t point out?”

Bernadita hesitated for a moment. Then: “Carlos – tell those four to head north. Tell them that if we see them again, we’ll kill them.” She waited to see her order carried out, but when the men started towards their horses she called down to Carlos, “No horses. Make them walk.”

“There are no villages for miles.” Burke was shocked at her harshness. “They could well die.”

“They have been part of a gang that has raped and looted and murdered for over a year. We’ve been looking out for them for months. If you’re worried to see them sent off on foot, I’m happy to bring them back and shoot them with the others.”

Burke said nothing more, but watched while the guerrillas loaded their muskets and lined up opposite their prisoners. El Jefe’s men seemed numbed by what was happening. Most stared blankly as the firing squad formed up. One fell to his knees in prayer. Another wet himself, his urine puddling at his feet.

Bernadita herself gave the order to fire. At that range every shot slammed home, although one man was merely wounded and Carlos, checking the bodies, bent down and cut his throat.

For a moment it all seemed to be over. The men who had done the killing stood in a group talking quietly amongst themselves, as

if trying to take in what they had done. Carlos cleaned his knife and looked toward Bernadita.

Bernadita turned. Everyone followed the direction of her gaze and saw El Jefe under the olive tree where they had left him. He had fallen to the ground and lay there, moaning.

"Get a rope."

Somebody went to the horses to get a rope. The rest of the men gathered together, drawn by the sight of the bandit chief, whose whimpers were broken by occasional babbling in which Burke could just make out desperate appeals for mercy.

The rope was passed to Carlos, who tied a rough noose in one end and threw the other over a branch of the olive tree.

Burke watched, struggling to understand what he was seeing. Like most of the trees on this desiccated plain, the olive was short and squat. The branch could not have been more than eight feet from the ground – far too low to hang a man from.

Too low to allow a quick drop and a merciful death, but not too low for what the guerrillas planned.

El Jefe was pulled to his feet and the noose tied round his neck. Four men took the other end of the rope and hauled until he hung just clear of the ground.

They stood and watched as he swung, his feet desperately scrabbling to reach the earth inches below them. His weight stretched the rope and Burke saw a toe touching the ground, but the wretch could not get enough purchase to relieve the weight on his neck. His face purpled as he fought for air.

They ate in the village. They sat out of sight of El Jefe, but throughout their breakfast Burke was haunted by the image of that body, in its preposterous gold-braided uniform, struggling at the end of the rope. Had he died yet, or was he still slowly strangling? The knot, he'd noticed, had not slipped tight about his neck. He could live for hours.

Beside him, Bernadita ate without, apparently, any concern for what she had done. Burke decided it was easier not to think about it.

Bernadita was careful to ask the women for permission for her men to scavenge a meal from the abandoned houses. It was all too easy, she explained to Burke, to begin to take food and hospitality

for granted. It seemed to him that she was even more careful in this regard than was Wellesley.

"I have to be careful, James," she explained. "El Jefe was no more than a bandit, but many of those who start out honestly intending to fight the French end up by finding it easier to steal from their own people. I need the help of the people if I am to be successful, so they have to know that El Gato can be trusted."

There was, Burke knew, no doubt of her sincerity or her desire to strike a blow against France, but he struggled to see how she could achieve anything where she was. Where, after all, were the French?

"Hiding in their forts, mostly," she admitted. "If a courier is sent with a message for another fort, thirty men will ride with him. You won't find a Frenchie travelling alone and we cannot take them on in force in this open country."

"Then what can you hope to achieve?"

She gave a wicked smile. "I'm hoping to catch them travelling in their thousands."

It took Burke only a moment to realise what she meant. He thought back to the way that he had fought in Egypt. When the enemy moves through the country in small numbers, they stay close together, constantly aware of the threat. But when an army marches through, men get careless. They fall behind the column because they are tired; they slip aside to answer a call of nature; they allow themselves a few minutes' sleep when they should be standing guard. These were the moments when Burke and his Bedouin allies had struck at the French troops marching to Cairo and this was a lesson Bernadita had clearly learned.

"You know that the French 5th Corps is on the march?" She spoke confidently. Wherever her information came from, she clearly believed it reliable. Which was worrying, because the last General Hill had heard of the 5th Corps it was over a hundred miles away.

"Are you sure of that?"

"Trust me," said Bernadita. "I used to spend time with a great spy. He taught me how to find out the positions of an enemy."

Burke recalled some of the techniques he had used in Egypt and hoped Bernadita had not learned too many of them. He didn't want to have more slow deaths on his conscience. On the other hand, his

methods were certainly effective. Perhaps, he decided, it was best to accept what Bernadita told him and not enquire too closely how she had come by the information.

"Where is it now?"

"Heading towards Madrid. The French know that your General Wellesley is coming, James. They think he will march along the Tagus and then head towards the capital. Our so-called King" – her voice dripped contempt for the man the French had put on the throne – "is pulling the armies back. He knows they are no use north of Madrid."

"How many men are we talking about?"

"Eighteen thousand."

She spoke matter-of-factly, but Burke was shocked. The Anglo-Portuguese army was less than two hundred miles from Madrid and moving forward rapidly. They knew that they would have to face the French marshal Victor in battle on the road, but Victor commanded only twenty thousand troops and the British were confident of victory. Eighteen thousand men being pulled back towards Madrid was eighteen thousand more that stood between Wellesley and the capture of the capital. And if the 5th Corps could join up with the Victor's twenty thousand men, Wellesley's army could well be in trouble.

"General Hill needs to know this."

"So tell him."

Burke hesitated. "Is there other intelligence I should know?"

"That's all I know for certain. There's talk that Marshal Soult is on the march and we were planning to ride north to see what we could learn. I had rather hoped you might come with us."

It was so tempting. Even without Bernadita's presence, the idea of riding with the guerrillas was attractive. El Gato clearly meant business and fighting alongside her would be real soldiering, even if he would not be wearing the King's uniform. And then there was Bernadita herself. He remembered those Egyptian nights, her body pressed against his. It seemed so unfair to have been reunited after all these years, just to lose each other again.

Burke pulled himself together. His duty was clear. He had to make sure the British had this information as soon as they could. Riding against the French would be fun, of course, and he might

learn something valuable. But there again, he might not. He could not justify any delay.

Bernadita was watching him, as if she could read his mind. "It's good to see Senor Brown again, too. Is he as reliable as always?"

That, of course, was the answer. William would return to General Hill with Burke's report. The report would conclude with the news that Burke himself was continuing to travel with the guerrillas in the hope of gathering new information.

“Thank you, Bernadita.”

“Why?” Bernadita’s expression was carefully blank. “I haven’t done anything.” But Burke was already hurrying to recover his saddlebag and start to put his notes together as a report for Hill.

Chapter 6: Killing Time

They moved out at around ten. Bernadita took care to explain that they were delaying their start to allow him time to write his report in a careful script suitable for presentation to a general. “We usually set off soon after dawn. It does not pay to allow the French time to work out where we might be. Still…” She allowed herself a tight smile. “I think we can be confident that there are no French near here.”

William spent his time arguing that he should be the one to stay with the guerrillas while Burke made the report. “It’s not right, sir. I'm a sergeant. It's not my job to be talking to generals. I should be out here doing the fighting while you go and do all the clever stuff."

"Well if you stop moaning and let me get on with this report, Hill will have no reason to speak to you.”

“But you can draw him maps and …”

Burke cut him off. “I’m drawing the maps now, and then you’re taking them to Hill. Don’t worry: Wellesley wants a battle, so I imagine you’ll get to see action back with the army.” Privately, he had his doubts. Wellesley was fighting a desperately cautious campaign, playing a long game that entailed a lot of marching in and out of Spain while the French manoeuvred their armies in increasingly desperate attempts to cut him off. The British would not fight unless they were sure that they could win and this news might well send Wellesley running back for cover in Portugal. There was no need, though, to tell William that.

Despite William’s interruptions, Burke had his report ready in an hour. Burke knew that his sergeant was as capable of reading a map as he was himself, but he accepted Bernadita's offer to have one of her men ride with him as a guide. There was always the risk of something going amiss in a strange country and if they ran into any trouble an armed escort might make all the difference.

“I’ll send Cristian. He can be a bit hot-headed, but he’s a useful man in a fight.”

El Gato’s band was already mounting up, ready to ride north as William followed Cristian away to the south. Burke raised a hand in

farewell. The two men did not speak. There was nothing to say. These were dangerous times: best just to accept that and hope for the best.

* * *

The dust from William's horse could still be seen settling in the distance as the guerrillas moved out, riding easily north. The sun was already well above the horizon, but they were spared the worst heat of the day.

Burke was impressed by the way that they moved. Bernadita commanded almost fifty men and she deployed them like a professional commander. Although no one had seen any French soldiers within a hundred miles, three of her best-mounted riders scouted ahead, while the others travelled in a block with a screen of outriders to guard against any sudden attack. Burke thought ruefully that if he had only exercised the same caution, they would never have been ambushed in the wood.

Burke, riding alongside her, congratulated Bernadita on her approach.

"We're at war," she said. "The French do not treat guerrillas as soldiers. If we are captured they kill us. If we're lucky, it doesn't take too long." Her voice was harsh, her expression unaccustomedly hard. "In these circumstances, you learn quickly."

They camped that night in the open. Sentries were set but they did not expect to see any French patrols.

"You're very confident that there are no French near here."

Bernadita nodded. "Our scouts have ridden some miles ahead and spoken to those they have met." She returned Burke's quizzical look with her own raised eyebrows. "Yes, Major Burke, Spain may look empty but people do live here. Perhaps they are more visible to those of us who are ourselves Spanish."

She had a point. The British might well be the allies of Spain, but a peasant minding his own business somewhere in the centre of the country might well fail to distinguish between one mass of uniformed men and another. Both, after all, would trample his crops and steal his olives. Both, if they could get away with it, would abduct his livestock and, in cooking it, were likely to throw any

wooden tools they found onto the blaze, and if the fire spread and damaged his orchard, they would not care overmuch. They might tempt his sons to quit the farm and join for a soldier and what they might tempt his daughters with did not bear thinking about. No, it was hardly surprising if a British army found the land strangely empty.

"People talk to us, too. They tell us things. They know we are of the people and they trust us. That's why it is necessary to deal harshly with men like El Jefe. Once we lose the trust of the people, we will lose our fight."

They were stretched out beside a fire as they talked. The survivors of the previous day's massacre had been happy to provide them with food enough to feast on fresh vegetables together with some rather tough meat that Burke thought he recognised as goat. Bernadita was picking at her teeth with a nail that Burke noticed had been bitten to the quick – the only sign of tension he could see in her body.

She noticed him looking. “You don’t think I’m eating elegantly.” She raised an eyebrow. “We’re not in a fine dining room with toothpicks in a holder on the table.”

He shook his head. “I was thinking that you look beautiful. Even when you’re picking your teeth.”

For the first time, he saw her looking uncertain, as if fearing some sort of trick, but she recovered quickly to talk about the meal and how they had come by it.

"You see, James, we rely on people for everything. Without their gifts of food, we would have been eating dried meat and olives and precious little else tonight."

They'd unsaddled the horses when they stopped and now she spread the saddle blanket on the ground. There was a poncho bundled against the saddlebow and she unrolled it and settled down under it to sleep. Burke was happy enough with no covering, for the nights were warm but he looked at her as she curled up on the ground beside him and decided that it looked very snug under that poncho.

"Bernadita …”

She cut him off before he could say anything else. "No, James. I am a soldier and a commander. I have to maintain some sort of

discipline." She turned towards him and, even in the shadows, he could see the glint of her teeth as she smiled. "I'm glad that you remember, though, James. And there will be other nights."

Burke slept soundly and, if he dreamed, they were pleasant dreams. He thought that perhaps Egypt might have featured.

In the morning, with no villains to hang, they were on their way soon after dawn. Another easy day of riding ended in a village where they were welcomed by the inhabitants who were quick to tell them that French scouts had been seen some miles further north.

The security of walls around them and the knowledge that friendly eyes kept watch on their behalf more than made up for any concerns that they might be nearing the enemy and Burke again slept the sleep of the just.

The next day, though, was marked by a distinct change of mood. The easy chatter that had characterised the ride up until then was gone. They travelled in silence and, though a screen of scouts surrounded them, everyone remained constantly alert, their eyes scanning the horizon and carefully examining every woody grove or rocky outcrop that they passed.

Early in the afternoon they started to look for a place to camp. Burke could see the wisdom in this: they didn't want to get caught in the open so close to the enemy. In the end, they bivouacked in a dry streambed. It offered little in the way of shelter from the elements but, given the continuing dry heat, this was hardly necessary. What it did do, was conceal them from the view of anybody on the plain.

There was no cooking that night. They did not dare risk the smoke of a cooking fire, so their dinner was the dried meat and olives that Bernadita had threatened Burke with two nights earlier.

The next morning, they stayed in the shelter of the riverbed while scouts rode out to establish exactly where the French were.

They had breakfasted on stale bread and a handful of olives apiece and waited, increasingly impatiently for the scouts to return. By mid-morning, people were definitely getting nervous. Burke recognised the symptoms: raised voices here, extended silences there. A card game started and ended with accusations of cheating. Relief came when a shout from one of their lookouts marked the sight of the first of their scouts trotting towards the camp.

The French, it seemed, were still some way off. “We rode about ten miles out before we came on any sign of them. There were a few scouts who were useless – we gave them a cheery wave and sauntered past as if we were locals checking our goats. Then there were foragers – lots of foragers. There's many an honest family will go hungry tonight after the French have finished with them.”

Several men had gathered to hear the news the scout brought and already they were grinning. It was not, Burke realised, that they did not understand the grief that the French were bringing to the people but rather that foraging bands provided just the sort of target the guerrillas were looking for.

Horses were saddled and weapons checked. They broke camp and moved out across the plain, no longer a solid block of horsemen, but a staggered line, less obvious from a distance. Bernadita rode alongside the scout, who was gesturing ahead as he described the countryside beyond their view. Burke pulled back. These were Bernadita’s men and she would not thank a British army officer – even him – for presuming to ride in a command position.

Soon after noon, they stopped in the shelter of an olive grove. Even Bernadita's strict rules on looting did not extend to forbidding her men to take olives from the trees and everyone was soon scattered about the ground with a handful of olives to eat. Bernadita beckoned Burke over to her. "The French are close. We'll rest and wait for it to get a little cooler. Fighting is hot work and we will be better off doing it when the sun is a little lower in the sky." She smiled. "It won't be long now, James. You will enjoy it. You always liked a fight."

Burke nodded, trying to share her enthusiasm. In truth, he had seen a lot of fighting since Egypt and increasingly saw it as a regrettable necessity more than anything else. Bernadita, though, was still relatively new to warfare. Perhaps, too, with her country occupied she had more reason than him to look forward to the prospect of killing Frenchmen.

One of the scouts now slipped back into the olive grove. He gestured north. “There’s a village tucked away in the trees at the foot of that hill.” Burke couldn’t see the hill from where he was sitting, but he had noticed it as they had ridden towards the olive

trees – another of those clumps of rock that often provided shelter for a few houses. "These olives probably belong to a farmer there. Anyway, the French are in the village. I reckon they're doing the same as us – resting up until the heat dies down and then they'll be back to the army."

"How far away is that?"

"Another five miles. The foragers have mules to take off whatever they plunder."

"Is there a good spot north of the village?"

"About a mile out there's a grove like this one. There's a track passes less than a quarter of a mile from the grove. That's the track they'll take. The trees provide a decent screen. You won't be seen."

Burke was impressed: the man was good at his job. He hadn't just found the enemy but he'd reconnoitred their likely route and found an ambush point. In fact, he seemed to have done much more than was needed, as Burke was quick to point out to Bernadita.

"You won't need the ambush, though, will you? Better to take them in the village, the way you took El Jefe."

Bernadita did not reply immediately, but turned back to the scout. "How are things in the village?"

"It seems calm. The French have rounded up any livestock they can find and taken stores of food, but they don't seem to be looting the houses."

"Any killing? Rapes?"

"There doesn't seem to have been. We heard no shots or screams."

Only now did she turn back to Burke. "We'll go with his suggestion and ambush them on the road out. If we take them in the village it's likely that women and children may be caught up in the fight. Even if they are not, the French will blame the villagers and take reprisals. We've seen it happen before. They've been known to kill every man in the place when a French soldier has died there."

She had spoken matter-of-factly, without any suggestion of criticism, but Burke felt more chastised than at any meeting where he had been dressed down by senior officers. Bernadita's immediate understanding of the situation, and his total failure to recognise the realities of this sort of warfare, had shown quite clearly who should be in command here. He did not say anything, but bowed his head

in acceptance of her remarks and stood quietly by as she gave the orders that saw her men mount up and move away on a route that made a wide loop around the village. At one point, Burke caught a glimpse of it, tucked away among the rocks. Then it was gone as the scout led them, using every tiny depression in the ground to keep them out of sight of any French sentries. They moved with care, and it was almost an hour before they came upon the track that ran north and the trees that would provide cover for their ambush.

They had heard nothing untoward and there was no sign of the dust that would be kicked up by even a handful of mules taking forage away from the villagers. "We've plenty of time." Bernadita spoke quietly, for sound carried in the still, dry air. "Take up positions well back in the trees."

The men moved calmly. Bernadita and her lieutenant, Carlos, moved from man to man, with a few words for each. Here and there they urged one forward or moved another back. Looking at the size of their horses and the way that they had ridden, Burke judged that the faster riders were being moved to the fore, ready to strike the first blow quickly. It made sense and he admired the quiet professionalism of the preparations. Once everyone was in place, they dismounted. There was nothing to do now but wait.

It was not until mid-afternoon that they heard the peculiar haunting sound, halfway between a bray and a whinny that could only be made by a mule.

"Lazy buggers, keeping us waiting like this." It was one of the men towards the front. Everyone was mounting up and there was some laughter, quickly hushed.

There was quiet for a few minutes until that strange cry again. Soon after that they could hear voices in French. Bernadita moved her horse alongside Burke. "Can you make out what they're saying?"

"They're too far away. I think they're just joking." A distant laugh confirmed the truth of his guess. “They sound relaxed, anyway."

The sounds drew nearer. On the edge of the olive grove, the scout stood in the shelter of a tree. Peering out, he seemed part of the landscape, moving less than the branches that shifted in a wisp of breeze.

Burke could hear hoofs on the track when the scout raised his hand and where, a moment before, there had been silence in the grove, now there was the thunderous sound of horses charging out towards the track and men crying with savage delight as they saw their prey fumbling for weapons.

Burke rode with them. Bernadita, he realised, was at least partly right. He no longer looked forward to battle, but once the enemy was engaged, he lost himself in the sheer, cruel joy of it. There was a vigour that possessed him in the heat of battle that he knew only there or in the arms of a woman and he feared that the thrill of battle was, perhaps, more exciting than the thrill of sex.

One or two of the Spaniards had muskets in their hands and tried a shot as they rode. There was no real chance of hitting anybody from the saddle of a galloping horse, but the crack of the gunpowder and the sound of shot flying above them must have further confused and terrified the enemy. There were about twenty of them – enough to bully villagers into co-operating – but they were not expecting to fight and it was not as if any general put his best troops into foraging parties. These men were fat and slow and past first youth. Some were desperately trying to load muskets, others were drawing swords that, he suspected, had seen no action for years, but they were still the enemy and they would still try to kill him – except that he would kill them first.

One of the Frenchmen managed to get a shot off, but he was panicking and fired without aiming and now the first line of the Spanish was on him. No muskets now but sword blades catching the harsh Spanish sun as they rose and fell and rose again, no longer shining bright but dark with blood. Ahead of him, Burke saw a blue-coated figure, his uniform stained with sweat, running towards him, swinging wildly with his sword. Burke didn't even bother to block him, but rode inside the blow and hacked directly at the man's wrist. The sword fell to the ground still gripped in the hand that had held it, while the soldier looked disbelievingly at the blood that spurted from the end of his arm.

Burke did not pause to finish him off but rode on. There was some sort of melee around the mules, but it was entirely one-sided. Most of the French had already broken and run and Burke joined the rest of the band in riding them down and finishing them off.

It was over so quickly that, by the time Burke remembered that he should be taking prisoners to interrogate, there were no Frenchmen left alive to capture. Never mind, he thought. It was not as if this lot were going to be able to tell him anything he didn't already know, and if this was an example of El Gato's methods, he was confident that there would be more opportunities soon enough.

They took what they could carry from the food the French had stolen. "We need to eat and we can't take it back to the village. There must be no connection between the killing and the people the food was stolen from." The food they couldn't take was scattered across the ground. Locals might gather it up, but it was unlikely that the French would take the time, even if they found it.

On one of the empty grain sacks, one of the men used a bloody dagger to sketch a rough drawing of a cat before pinning the sack to a dead Frenchman with a sword thrust into his guts.

Bernadita caught Burke's look of disapproval.

"It makes them less likely to blame the locals and take reprisals. And –" she showed her teeth in a smile that was utterly devoid of humour – "it makes them more frightened of me."

He nodded. She was, again, right. He might be an officer in the British Army, reporting to General Hill, but this was the sort of dirty fighting he had done in South America and Egypt. He could forget all that nonsense about an officer and a gentleman.

Carlos rode over to them. "We're ready," he told Bernadita.

"Good." She raised her hand. "Move out."

They headed away from the track, north into the empty plain.

* * *

That first attack set the tone for the next couple of days. The next morning they found a foraging party on its way out from the French army. This time they kept one alive and when they rested from the noon heat, Burke passed the time in questioning the man, but he learned only that this was the force commanded by Marshal Soult, which came as no surprise. The Spanish troops had long known that Soult was lurking somewhere in the area, but his force, wandering and harassed by continual attacks, consisted of less than ten thousand men, apparently in a pitiful state. Hill's ADC had

mentioned that the British had doubled this estimate, on the grounds that Spanish intelligence could not be relied on, but, even then, Soult's army was no threat. Nothing the prisoner told them left him any wiser than he had been before. He knew nothing of any use, Burke decided. He cut his throat before they moved out, for they did not want a prisoner in the way as they attacked the next party on its way home. The attack was virtually a repeat of the previous day, leaving them with so much food that they had to make a detour to a gully one of the scouts had discovered, where a small cave allowed them to store some of the provisions they had recovered from the French. At night, though, they found a new resting place, for the French would by now be taking them seriously.

Just how seriously became evident the next morning, when they found the foraging parties all escorted by twenty fighting men. Bernadita, riding ahead with the scouts to confirm the first reports, returned and shook her head. They could not afford the casualties an attack on such a force must produce. They would have to adapt their approach.

Now Burke had something to contribute. He had, after all, experience of harrying a French army on the march. He remembered those nights in Egypt, leading the Bedouin as they picked off stragglers from Napoleon's army. It would be trickier here, he knew. In Egypt the army had had to march in the cool of the night, so getting close enough had been easy. He needed to see how the French were managing their army if he was to plan any attack.

How close, he asked Bernadita, could they get to Soult's column?

Bernadita summoned one of the scouts. How close had he been able to get?

"We can't ride within a mile of them," he admitted. "They are well screened by cavalry outriders and if we came close to any of them they would kill us. They are not going to allow an armed Spaniard on a horse anywhere near that army."

Burke considered the options. He could set out on foot and pass himself off as a simple peasant, but, even so, he could not get too close. Armies were known to be made up of dangerous men. Honest peasants gave them a wide berth. He could wait somewhere where

they might pass him (people are always less suspicious of those they pass than those who pass them) but as soon as it approached he would need to scurry nervously away if he were to be convincing. And what would he see? An army passing, the odd outrider, perhaps one of Napoleon's Eagles being carried somewhere in the mass of men. It was better than no information at all, but hardly worth the time that would be spent getting into position, waiting for Soult's men to pass and, afterwards, walking back to wherever it had been safe to leave his horse.

The answer, when it came to him, was obvious. A Spaniard would be viewed with suspicion, but a Frenchman might well be accepted. But what sort of Frenchman would be riding alone in the middle of Spain? Had Bernadita ever come across such a person?

It turned out she had. "There are deserters from the army, of course. There used to be tax collectors and some government officials, but nowadays they always travel with an escort."

"What happens to the deserters?"

Bernadita did not answer immediately, but looked up at the sky. Then: "You must remember, James, that many Spaniards have suffered horribly at the hands of the French."

She did not need to say any more. "So," said Burke, "a deserter might well decide to try to rejoin his regiment and take his chances?" Bernadita nodded.

That, Burke decided, was a possibility. He knew that he could pass himself off as a French soldier. After all, back before England had been at war with the French, he had served in King Louis' army.

Bernadita could clearly see the way his mind was working and didn't like it. "Don't they punish deserters in the army?"

Burke agreed that they did. "But I'll be prepared. I don't intend to hang around and wait for a flogging."

It was, Burke knew, hardly a plan – just the merest outline of a plan. But he was sure that, given time, he could shape it into something that could work.

Given the impossibility of raiding the foraging parties, Bernadita had announced that the day was to be spent relaxing. They had therefore ridden off a few miles to a small valley the scouts had found where the river still had enough water to offer refreshment.

There were even a few trees, under one of which Burke settled himself to think out the details of his plan.

It took him an hour or so to decide how he intended to proceed. The first thing was to check his saddlebags again. To his relief he found that there, at the very bottom, were the picklocks that William had taught him how to use. Burke usually left this sort of prestidigitation to William, who was suspiciously good at it. Now, however, he was glad that he had taken the precaution of packing some of the tools into his own kit. Rather to his surprise, he discovered that El Jefe's men had left his boot dagger there as well. He retrieved it from the saddle bag and slipped it down his calf.

It took him a while to find anybody in the guerrilla band who owned a locked chest, but eventually Christophe – one of the youngest of El Gato's men – admitted that he had a small box that he kept locked.

"He keeps his sweetheart's letters in it." The other men mocked and Christophe's blushes suggested that they might well be right.

"Can I borrow it? I only need the box. You can keep the key."

Christophe accepted Burke's assurances at face value and handed the box over. Once he saw Burke produce his lock picks and start to work, he reached to snatch the box to safety, but half a dozen of his laughing comrades held him back. The men watched grinning as Christophe squirmed with embarrassment and Burke concentrated as he pushed the pins free. It took, he reckoned, less than three minutes until, with a satisfying click, the lock opened.

There were cheers from the watchers, which turned to groans as Burke pushed the lock close again, withdrew his tools and handed the box to a relieved Christophe.

William would have been unimpressed with the time it had taken. It was an easy lock and Burke knew that Sergeant Brown would have opened it in seconds, but it didn't matter. The locks he was expecting to work on would be crude affairs and he would have more than enough time.

He moved away from the other men and sat down on a convenient rock. Bending, he twisted the heel of his boot. It swivelled out to reveal a hollowed space, big enough to take the picks.

He twisted the heel back in place. He was as prepared as he would ever be. He walked down the gully to find Bernadita.

* * *

The next morning Soult's scouts brought in a deserter. He'd ridden up on an exhausted horse, clothes dirty and torn and a face that showed signs of a beating. The beating had been administered by El Gato's men the previous afternoon, but the French weren't to know that. They saw the blood and the bruises and accepted the man's story that he had been captured by guerrillas but escaped.

He was, he claimed, a private soldier from General Sebastiani's 4th Corps. He had deserted to take up with a Spanish girl he was in love with. They had fled to a village near Salamanca where they had lived quietly until someone informed on them to the guerrillas. "El Gato's men came to the village and seized me. They dragged me from my home and beat me. They took me to their camp and beat me again and showed me the tree where they said they would hang me in the morning. But that night they celebrated my capture with hard liquor and, while they were drunk, I stole a horse and escaped. I had heard them say that the French were on the road to Salamanca, so I have returned to serve my Emperor."

"Well, you can hardly serve him here." The older of the two troopers who had captured him looked disdainfully at his ragged clothes and battered body. "The 4th Corps is still buggering about in Madrid." What was to be done? The two cavalrymen worried at the question for a while and decided to refer it to their lieutenant. Burke was escorted to that officer, who decided that it was a decision to be made by his captain. For a while he was led from one scout to another until they tracked down that officer. Like his men he wore a green uniform, a red fronting to the jacket the only splash of colour. There was, Burke knew, some red in the plume of his shako helmet, but the dust of the Spanish plain had long since dulled any brightness it might once have had. The captain, like his uniform, was business-like.

"Send him up to Captain Lafon on the Staff. He can sort him out."

So Burke and his escort trotted the two miles between the screen of scouts and the main column of Soult's army. It gave Burke his first view of the enemy and he could not help but be impressed. He could not see the entire army, for the end of the column stretched out of sight, but there were clearly more than twenty thousand men there and Burke saw no evidence of the ravages of sickness or enemy action that the Spanish had assured Hill had reduced Soult's force to an irrelevance. The lines of blue uniformed figures seemed to be moving easily and there were none of the ragged gaps he would expect to see in a column of sick or exhausted men.

He had the opportunity to see the condition of the men at close quarters as he was led towards the front of the column where the Staff officers kept their positions close to Marshal Soult himself. They looked, it seemed to him, quite ridiculously fit. He thought of the convoy that he had travelled from Lisbon with. It was quite obvious that it was not bringing enough food for the Allied army. Here, though, the French foragers were doing an excellent job in keeping their men fed. Some were singing and the sergeants needed only the occasional bellowed oath to keep them marching in time. It was amazing what you could learn just by listening to an army march. The leaden tread of a struggling force was quite different from the sound of men confident on the march and these, he knew, were men who trusted their commander and had no serious complaints about their conditions.

One of his escorts pushed ahead and saluted an officer in the blue jacket and white breeches of the general staff. Burke could not hear what was said, but the officer fell out to the side of the column and Burke was ordered to dismount and stand to attention in front of him.

He stood there smartly, arms at his side, while the men of his escort and the captain all looked down at him from horseback. He was reminded, yet again, of how much he hated the cavalry. The arrogant bastards would never pass up the opportunity to lord it over the unfortunates who were not on horseback and who, as Burke and every infantryman firmly believed, bore the brunt of the real fighting.

"Well, Thierry, what have you to say for yourself?"

Burke snapped out of his reverie about cavalrymen and what he would like to do with them. "I've seen the error of my ways, sir. Want to do my bit to fight the British, sir." He sounded, he thought, appropriately pathetic.

Captain Lafon did not deign to reply, but instead turned to the stream of men marching behind him. "Sergeant!"

A large man with a scarred cheek stepped aside from the line of march. "Yessir!"

"This man is a deserter, sergeant. Have him march with your men today and have him brought directly to me when we stop for the night."

"Yessir."

The captain and the two men who had escorted him this far wheeled away. Burke noticed that they took his horse with them. It was no more than he had expected, but it was annoying nonetheless.

Only now was he addressed directly and that was just a brusque order from the sergeant to make his way into the front rank and march alongside the others, an order that was reinforced with a blow from a musket butt.

It was a long time since Burke had marched in an infantry column, but he fell back into the way of it easily enough. Even if he had wanted to escape, and escaping was not yet any part of his plan, he couldn't have. The sergeant marched alongside the first rank of his men and Burke was under no illusions as to what would happen if he fell out of step with those around him.

His journey along the column had left him with a good picture of the general condition of Soult's army. Now he was actually marching alongside the French he could learn more. The first thing he noticed was that these men did not march like an army on its way to battle. There was none of the tension, none of the dark humour of men who knew that in a few days they could well be facing death. They were relaxed – happy, even. When they stopped at midday, to rest in the heat and eat and drink from their packs, Burke asked if they knew where the English were. Seeing he had no food or drink of his own, the men were happy to share and to admit that they had no idea where the "god-damn rosbiffs" might be. All they knew was that they were marching under the finest Marshal in Napoleon's armies and he must, inevitably, lead them to victory and

glory. One or two did mention Salamanca, saying that they believed that Soult would be stopping there. "We'll have the other corps join us and then we'll be invincible," opined one of the older men, but whether he knew for certain or whether this was just a rumour, Burke had no way to tell. It was, though, exactly the sort of gossip that was the bedrock of all good intelligence work and he stored it away for future reference.

Burke paid particular attention to the way that sentries were set during the midday break. Because the army was simply resting, sentries were posted in a fairly casual way, but the screen of scouts still seemed to be riding a mile or two out from the column and there was little danger of attack across the plain. Men drifted away to relieve themselves but, again, this did not leave them vulnerable given that there was no real chance of guerrillas getting anywhere near the column. It had been the same as they marched: the column had stayed tightly packed, the sergeants alert to any breach of discipline. There were no isolated individuals to pick off, even if there had been anywhere for an attacker to hide. Any attack would have to come at night.

The march in the afternoon was much the same as in the morning: the same easy pace; the same relaxed banter amongst the men.

Soult called a halt early. That made sense, Burke knew. Their overnight camp would be a much more formal affair than their lunchtime break. Tents would be erected for the Staff; cooks would set up field kitchens; a perimeter would be established and guards placed to protect it. Burke was not to see all this activity, though, for he was, as instructed, taken directly to Captain Lafon. The captain was supervising the erection of his own tent and was visibly irritated by the necessity of dealing with a deserter – and not even a deserter from his own Corps. Still, he seemed to be a conscientious officer and he had soon recruited another captain and a passing lieutenant to make up a drum-head court-martial. The lieutenant worried a bit about the legality of such an informal arrangement with such junior officers but the captains agreed that the matter was straightforward and senior officers had more important things to do ("Like fighting the war," Lafon said) so as soon as a table and chairs had been found for the tribunal, the court was in session.

“Charge is desertion. How do you plead?”

“Guilty, sir.”

"Anything to say before sentence?"

"I regret my actions and returned voluntarily, sir."

Captain Lafon turned to his colleagues and there was the briefest of discussions. Then: “Scum as you are, we can't afford to waste soldiers. You are sentenced to twenty lashes to be carried out immediately. Tomorrow you will fall in under the careful eye of Sergeant Salvaing, who brought you before us. If you fail to maintain your position in line tomorrow, Sergeant Salvaing will shoot you on the spot. Do you understand?”

The look of horror on Burke’s face was not an act. His plan had relied on at least a night in irons. An immediate flogging followed by being placed under Salvaing's watchful eye gave little opportunity for escape. He wondered if it was worth praying for a miracle.

It was the thought of prayer that did it. He held out no hope of divine intervention, but perhaps he might find a priest to get him out of this hole. Revolutionary France had turned against the Church, but there were enough Catholics in the army for him to hope that a plea for a priest might be sympathetically received.

"Your sentence is just, sir, but there is every chance that I will not be strong enough to march after my flogging and that I will be shot out of hand tomorrow. If I am to die, I would beg that I may die shriven. I have not seen a priest for more than a week and I beg you might let me make my confession before my flogging.”

Burke could see a sneer forming on the lieutenant's lips. He was a young man and clearly committed to the atheistic philosophy of the Revolution, but the two captains looked sympathetic.

The other captain – no one had thought it worth telling Burke his name – spoke up. "There's a priest somewhere at the end of the column, isn't there?"

"Father Pierre, yes.” Burke was amused to see the change in the lieutenant’s expression. He looked the sort of subaltern who was good at seeing the way his seniors were thinking and adapting his views to fit theirs. Burke imagined he would go far. “I can probably find him."

The two captains nodded their agreement and Lafon turned his attention back to Burke. "You realise how hard it will be to take your flogging in the morning and then march all day."

Burke nodded. "My body will suffer, yes. But it is more important to protect my soul."

The captain nodded. "Very well. We'll send the priest to you once he's been found. But you'll spend the night in chains. I'm not wasting men on guarding you. You can mess with Sergeant Salvaing's men but we'll have you chained hand and foot. That way everyone can sleep sound in the knowledge that you'll still be here in the morning to take your punishment."

Burke accepted his fate with bowed shoulders, the picture of a broken man forced to accept all that fate threw at him. In truth, though, he thought things could hardly have gone better. He had feared that there might be some sort of stockade that he would have to break free of. Instead, though, it seemed that the French army had so few men in his position that they made no real provision for them. How Napoleon's officers maintained discipline without the plentiful use of the lash he could not begin to imagine. Nor, at the moment, did he care. It was enough that he was to spend the night surrounded by sleeping troops with only shackles between him and escape.

Salvaing escorted him back to their place in the column. He seemed to have been quite impressed with Burke's showing before the tribunal and his judgement was reflected in the attitude of his men. All were friendly towards Burke and one went off to find a uniform to replace his tattered civilian clothes. "The guy who wore it won't need it any more. Kicked in the head by one of the pack mules but it's hardly left a mark on the coat." Burke agreed that it was, indeed, a good coat and a bargain for the five sous that were being asked for it. "You don't need to pay me now. I know you've got no money. But I think you're good for it." It was the honest companionship of the fighting man, both open and generous and, at the same time, never about to pass up the chance to make a few sous. Burke felt quite sorry that his plans did not involve ever paying for the coat.

A blacksmith arrived at about the same time as the uniform. "Are the chains just for tonight?" Salvaing confirmed that this was the

case. "I'll use padlocks then. No point in hammering them together for one night." Burke allowed himself an almost imperceptible sigh of relief. He had not anticipated the possibility that the fetters might have been fixed without locks. He had had a narrow escape from spending the next few weeks serving in the French army.

The priest turned up as they were finishing eating. Burke had been disappointed with the food. He had thought, based on the quantities that he had seen the French foragers steal, that the army must eat well. He had forgotten, though, just how much food an army this size could eat. The French passed through the country like a plague of locusts, stripping it of anything edible, but it was only enough to keep them healthy and far from a feast. He had eaten a stew which he suspected was based around goat with a liberal portion of vegetables of one sort and another, the whole mopped up with bread. The bread was fresh and good and he assumed that the French travelled with their own bakers.

The priest was a little, round man who refused offers to share the last of the stew. Looking at his girth, Burke suspected he must have already eaten a rather better meal before joining them, but he did agree to a drink from the flask of wine that Salvaing passed among the men. Those niceties observed, the priest took Burke, his chains rattling noisily, to sit a discreet distance from the others, though still, Burke noticed, under the watchful eye of the sergeant.

Burke was tempted to tell the priest the truth, admitting to being an English spy, just to see how far he could push the sanctity of the confessional. He knew, though, from his own turn as a man of God, that priests were not always what they appeared to be. It was better to play safe. He had heard enough confessions to have no difficulty in concocting the usual litany of bad behaviour, petty dishonesty and minor sexual peccadilloes. The priest looked unsurprisingly bored and prescribed five Hail Marys as a penance.

All Burke had to do then was wait until dark. With his new comrades sleeping, he swivelled the heel of his boot to reveal the pick locks. He had to move carefully, for the noise that his chains made seemed terribly loud, but it was hardly as if he was working in the silence of night. All around men snored and snorted, some twitching in their sleep. Further away some groups showed no interest in settling down and there came laughter and occasional

snatches of song. Further still, the horses of the officers whinnied softly to each other. Somewhere a girl was giggling. Burke wondered where on earth she had come from. It was a mystery to him how every regiment had its followers, but the truth was that soldiers always seemed to find women somewhere. It was just one of the things soldiers did.

He had the pick locks out now and had started work on the padlocks that secured his ankles. Once his feet were free, he had at least a chance to run. No point in freeing his hands if he couldn't make his escape.

There was one padlock on each foot, menacing great things with shackles a quarter of an inch thick. He smiled as he started on the first one. As a general rule, he knew, the bigger the lock, the easier it was to pick.

Less than a minute later there was a sharp 'click' and the first padlock was open. The second was even quicker. Carefully, Burke slipped them clear of the fetters and cautiously freed his feet, laying the chain quietly on the ground.

The locks on his wrists were more of a problem. The chain that connected them was a decent length, but it's still difficult to reach a padlocked wrist with a hand that is, in turn, padlocked to it. The task was made especially difficult because picking a lock should involve two hands - one to lift the wards and one to hold them in place. Fortunately, the lock was so big that there was room to manage with just one hand, the other twisted round to balance the picks on during the most delicate part of the operation.

It took a good five minutes to open the first lock and when it came free it fell to the ground, clashing against the manacles on the way. Sergeant Salvaing, who had taken care to lie down near to his prisoner, turned in his sleep. Burke froze and it was several minutes before he dared to move at all. Then he eased the manacle off his left hand and started on the other.

Working on the manacle around his right wrist proved more difficult than the left. Working left handed was not easy and, though he no longer had his hands fettered to each other, he had to keep the right hand still as every movement rattled the chain that now hung loose from it. Twice Salvaing stirred in his sleep and each time Burke had to stop work and sit motionless until he was sure that the

sergeant was soundly back asleep. A full quarter of an hour must have passed before the second lock came undone and he was able to ease it gently to the ground.

He picked up the bundled uniform. He was still wearing his torn civilian clothes, as he had had no chance to change into the uniform before being chained up. Now though, he slipped silently away in the darkness and, as soon as he was a safe distance off, he discarded his jacket and trousers and became just another soldier in Soult's army.

Though most of the men were sleeping, there was always movement in an army on the march. Men woke and moved to quiet spots to relieve themselves. Messengers moved up and down the column carrying late night orders from tired and harassed Staff officers. Sentries returned as their duties ended and others moved out to take their place. And, of course, the girls responsible for the giggles he had heard attracted paramours who risked leaving their positions for a quarter of an hour or so of illicit pleasure.

The secret, Burke knew, was not to try to avoid being seen. A man who is trying to hide excites suspicion. So as soon as he was clear of Salvaing, he walked openly along the column of sleeping men. If anyone had challenged him, he would have been carrying a message from Captain Lafon. No one did challenge him, though.

He had no watch, but the night sky was clear and he used this to judge the time. It took him, he reckoned, over two hours to reach the baggage wagons at the end of the column. Here he had to be more circumspect, for the wagons always attracted thieves and a passing stranger was less likely to go unchallenged, but he saw enough to tell him that Soult's army was well supplied.

Long before he had reached the baggage train, Burke's reconnaissance had established that the British intelligence on Soult's strength grossly underestimated the reality. There must be close to fifty thousand men in this column. Added to what he had learned about the artillery (neatly camped in ordered lines that made it easier to count), his perambulation along the column more than justified his adventure. Now, he decided, the most important task remaining was to look at the organisation of the sentry posts. This was not just the ostensible reason for the whole exercise, but it was

essential if he was to be able to escape with any of the information he had gathered.

Gathering intelligence about sentries would not be achieved by simply walking up to them with the insouciant air he had adopted in the column. With no immediate threat from an enemy army, the sentries would be as concerned to ensure that deserters did not get out as much as preventing anyone from getting in. If he were seen by them, he would be challenged and no nonsense about taking messages for Captain Lafon would save him.

He walked to the edge of the column, carefully stepping over the sleeping figures on the ground and passed beyond them, doing his best to vanish into the darkness.

A few yards into his reconnaissance he decided that vanishing into the darkness would be easier said than done. When he had raided enemy posts under cover of darkness in the past, he had always been suitably dressed for the occasion. Slipping through the pampas grass in the loose trousers and shirt of a South American cowboy had seemed natural enough, and the robes he wore in the desert had been almost purpose-made for the business of sneaking up on enemies in the dark. The blue uniform that was supposed to impress the enemy on the field of battle was not designed to let you crawl silently along the ground. The fabric was heavy and Burke found it murderously difficult to crawl in. He had to negotiate his way across the open ground, a few painful inches at a time. He had, of course, removed his shako, but he could not abandon it if he was to pass himself off as a Frenchman again, so after every few inches he wriggled forwards he had to drag the ridiculous headgear along with him. His buttons kept snagging on the ground; all the metalwork that the uniform's last owner had religiously polished threatened to reflect any light there was; and his belt and ammunition pouch weren't just hideously uncomfortable but the leather kept creaking with a noise that Burke was certain would wake the whole camp.

Despite all these difficulties, he managed to get close enough to two sentry positions to establish that piquets had been set up at regular intervals and that the men on duty seemed awake and alert: too alert really, for the second man had heard something and moved towards Burke in the dark. Burke's hand was already reaching for

the knife in his boot when the guard, having peered into the darkness, turned and walked away.

The reconnaissance, Burke decided, was turning into a nightmare. All he seemed to have done was establish how difficult it would be to get past the sentries while coming far too close to being spotted himself.

He started to edge back towards the camp when he heard another soldier walking in his direction. Had he been seen? Apparently not, for as Burke froze flat to the ground he heard the steps pass him and a few seconds later the challenge from the sentry.

"Password of the night."

"*Merde,* Jacques. It's me. I'm relieving you."

"I'm still supposed to ask you the password."

"Has anyone ever told you you're an arse-licking little toad?"

"Often. And I'm still supposed to ask you the password." Then, when he got no reply: "Look, if you've got it wrong, you'll shoot the next poor bugger that turns up. Just say it."

"It's *La Gloire*, all right? Now bugger off and get some sleep and maybe you'll not be such a bloody prig in the morning."

Burke stayed absolutely motionless as Jacques set off for the column to sleep for what was left of the night. He hardly dared breathe as the Frenchman walked within a yard of where he lay, but Jacques obviously had his mind on his rest and he passed Burke without looking in his direction.

It was a close run thing, though, and Burke lay still for a while after Jacques had gone on his way. It gave him the opportunity to think over what he had learned. First and foremost, of course, he had learned the password for the night. That would make things a lot easier when the time came to escape back to Bernadita. Almost as importantly, though, the exchange between the two sentries suggested a certain carelessness about learning the password for the day. It was hardly surprising. They were in the middle of nowhere and nobody took the idea of somebody trying to sneak into the camp at all seriously. The sentries were tired, bored young men, conscripted into the army and now trying to make the best of their time in Spain by stealing anything that wasn't nailed down and fornicating with as many of the local women as they could. They

had no interest at all in the silly games their officers played - games like issuing sentries with a new password every day.

Burke thought about the possibilities this opened up while he watched the shadow that was the new sentry move to and fro. New sentries, in his experience, fidgeted and some of their fidgeting included looking about them more carefully in the first ten minutes of their watch than they would at any other time. Burke was in no hurry: he would wait, and while he waited he would plan.

A quarter of an hour later, the sentry was motionless at his post. Burke would not accuse him of sleeping, for if an officer were to make an inspection he would find his man upright and coming swiftly to the salute. Still, he was as close to sleep as a man could be while still standing with his eyes open and Burke was not much concerned about him as he wriggled his way back to the column.

He needed two things now, he decided. The first was a horse. His had been taken from him and he had no intention of walking all the way back to Bernadita.

He remembered the whinnying he had heard as the men around him settled for the night. It had sounded towards the front of the column, which made sense because that was where the Staff officers were and Staff officers needed horses. There must be cavalry somewhere towards the front, too, though Soult's force seemed light on cavalry. The horses belonging to the Staff would be easier to steal, in any case. Cavalrymen generally slept with their beasts and tended to take it amiss if you tried to steal them. Staff officers slept on camp beds in the luxury of tents and their horses were guarded by sentries who had no particular interest in them.

It did not take long to walk back to the area where Thierry had faced his impromptu court martial and, in the still night air, it was not difficult to hear the movement of horses shuffling in their sleep or the peculiar 'harrumph'-ing that, Burke assumed, was a sort of equine snore. Burke had until then walked directly through the column, skirting groups of sleeping men and exchanging casual greetings with anyone who was awake. Now he became cautious again. He did not crawl along the ground, as he had when approaching the sentries, but his movements became smoother and his steps quieter, until he seemed to glide along. His path became

more indirect, slipping from shadow to shadow before, silently, he was swallowed by the darkness.

There were two men guarding the horses. In Burke's experience, there was a lot to be said for having just one man on guard. A man standing watch in the night feels proud and scared. Proud because he has been entrusted to guard whatever he is watching over, and scared because a man alone in the dark watching for enemies is naturally nervous. The combination of fear and pride keeps a man alert but, Burke believed, as soon as there were two guards pride and fear were both reduced. It was just another boring duty, with a comrade to watch your back if you were to sleep at your post. Neither man would stand guard as conscientiously as a sentry on his own. And so it was here.

The first guard stood near the horses. Too near, for the sounds they made as they shifted covered any sound from Burke and the guard's attention was continually distracted by the movement of the animals. Burke was only two paces from him when the Frenchman realised he was there. Even in the starlight Burke saw the whites of the man's eyes as they widened in horror. He drew breath to shout a challenge. Or a warning – Burke would never know which: his boot knife was already slicing the guard's windpipe and whatever he had intended came out as a gurgle of air and a choking sound as he began to inhale his own blood. Then he fell to his knees and, toppling forward, died.

Burke felt he had made a good job of the killing. It had been quiet and neatly done. The horses, excited by the smell of blood, edged away, stamping their hooves and whinnying nervously. The noise drew the second guard, but he seemed curious rather than alarmed.

"Hey, Jean-Claude, what's up with the horses?"

Burke had stepped past the body and was now standing between the horses, his own shape hidden in a mass of dark, moving animals.

The sentry saw Jean-Claude where he had fallen, and stepped forward, apparently almost unable to believe what he was seeing. Burke moved quickly towards the body and as the sentry bent to look at it his knife was already slashing towards the man's throat.

The Frenchman must have sensed the movement at the last moment and jerked to his left, so the knife sliced at his shoulder. The man started to swing his musket towards Burke, but he had no time to get the momentum he needed to use it as a club. Burke smashed it aside and stabbed again, this time into the man's body. He went down screaming. Burke kicked him onto his chest and then, leaning over him, pulled back his head and administered the coup de grace, slitting his throat. It had been a much noisier killing them the first, but it did not matter. There were no other guards and nobody else close enough to be concerned.

The killings, especially the second, had produced, it seemed to Burke, a quite inordinate quantity of blood. One of the advantages of the British scarlet uniforms was the troops could bleed profusely before the effect was obvious at any distance. This was definitely not the case with the French blue coats. Burke's was covered in gore.

He had already decided that he should try to get hold of an officer's coat. Password or no password, a private soldier riding alone out of camp would be likely to be challenged. An officer's coat would make things easier. By now, with his coat so bloodied that the stains were visible even at night, a new coat was a necessity.

It was simple enough to decide that a coat was needed: getting hold of one was going to be less straightforward. He could hardly cut another throat, for there was no point exchanging one blood drenched uniform for another. The officer he killed – he could think of no other way to get hold of a uniform in a hurry – would have to die without shedding blood.

Fortunately, the officers' tents provided plenty of rope. They had been well pegged out, and Burke had no trouble cutting himself a length of guy rope without the tent visibly sagging.

The next thing that he needed was an officer about the same size as him. As to this, he already had somebody in mind. Captain Lafon was about his height and build. He would do. And Burke had seen where his tent had been pitched. He had an excellent memory for details like that: it was his job.

Leaving the bodies where they lay, he slipped away to find Captain Lafon. He moved carefully through the shadows, for he had

no wish to run into anybody before he had a chance to get out of this uniform. Even so, he was able to wind his way quickly through the tents. It took only around five minutes for him to arrive at the point where he had been court-martialled. He turned about. Yes, that was the tent Lafon had been watching his men pitch.

Burke walked towards it as if he had every right to be there. Perhaps he was carrying an urgent message to the captain. Perhaps the officer had demanded to be woken in the middle of the night. (Burke hoped he hadn't – he had no wish to meet an angry Frenchman who was not sound asleep.) Yet, though he strode along as if he hadn't a care in the world, Burke's steps were almost silent and when he opened the tent flap and stepped inside Captain Lafon's temporary home he was confident that that officer's sleep would be undisturbed.

A single candle guttered in a lantern to provide enough light to make his way across the tent. Burke had no problem in working out where, in the gloom, Lafan's bed was. The man snored. He snored so loudly that Burke suspected he could have thumped his way across in best parade ground style and still not woken him. Even so, he moved cautiously until he was standing next to the camp bed where Lafon was about to spend his last few minutes on earth.

Burke took the guy rope he had cut and wrapped each end firmly around his fists. Then he slipped the rope around the sleeping man's neck and pulled sharply. Lafon woke, but it took him a moment or two to realise what was happening, and by that time the garrotte was tight around his windpipe. He struggled, arms and legs jerking haphazardly. Burke stood at the head of his bed. It's very difficult for a man lying on the ground to land an effective punch on somebody behind his head. For a man woken from a deep sleep and already weakening, it's nigh on impossible.

It was all over in a couple of minutes, but Burke kept up the pressure while he counted to a hundred, just to be on the safe side. It wouldn't do to have Captain Lafon make a miraculous recovery.

The captain's servant was clearly a man who knew his job. Lafon's uniform was hung neatly on a stand at the foot of his bed. Burke quickly stripped off his own bloodied clothes and put on the officer's uniform. It was a little loose around the stomach – Lafon obviously enjoyed eating well – but Burke was happy with the fit.

Putting on his sword belt he stepped back out of the tent and walked confidently back to the horses. He faced a few nervous minutes when he realised that the beasts were not tacked up and he had no idea where to find their bridles and saddles. In the end, though, there were not too many places they might have been. A small tent nearby proved to hold saddlery for all of the officers.

Saddling an unfamiliar horse in the dark was challenging, but hardly his most challenging task that night. About a quarter of an hour after Lafon had died, Burke was walking a fine chestnut gelding southward, away from the camp.

A sentry loomed out of the darkness. Seeing his rank, the man saluted.

"The password, sir." He was little more than a boy and seemed nervous of challenging a captain.

Burke was reassuring. "Good man! We need men like you – alert at this ungodly hour. It's 'La Gloire,' man."

The sentry saluted again and Burke set off, at a slow but steady trot. He should, he reckoned, be back with Bernadita soon after dawn.

* * *

It said a lot for the discipline that Bernadita had instilled in her troops that Burke was not shot before he could report his success. He made sure not to approach her camp until daylight and, when he did, he rode slowly and made sure to keep his hands in clear view on the reins. Even so, he thought there must be a real danger that a nervous sentry would open fire on anyone wearing the uniform of a French officer, whether they seemed to pose an immediate threat or not. As it was, nobody shot at him at all, but three men with muskets in their hands rode out to meet him. Only once they were close enough to recognise his face did they relax and escort him into camp, where he was soon surrounded by guerrillas who wanted to know every detail of his adventures.

Burke would have preferred to be able to tell Bernadita ahead of everyone else. Since she had saved him from El Jefe he had felt that he was always following on behind. It was not a situation he was used to and the chance to describe an adventure where he had been

able to take charge of the situation and emerge as something of a hero would have given him, he felt, a much-needed boost to his self-esteem. Still, his self-esteem was definitely boosted by the admiration of the men who clapped him on the back and applauded the bloody details of his adventure. And when he looked past them to Bernadita he saw her listening too, a quiet smile on her full lips.

It was a while before Burke was allowed to stop talking and settle to breakfast. It was dried meat and olives, for they dared not risk the smoke from a fire. For Burke, though, basking in the admiration of the men around him and, he had to admit, somewhat relieved to have survived unscathed, the meal seemed delicious, more so as Bernadita settled beside him and helped herself to some of his olives.

For a few minutes Burke hoped that his daring with the French might induce Bernadita to relent and allow him to rekindle the spark of their old affair, but then Carlos moved to join them and they were all business again.

At least Carlos was suitably impressed with Burke's efforts. He understood the vital importance of the intelligence that the exercise had provided. "I imagine you'll be off to Wellesley with your news. After all," – and for a moment he looked more sombre – "it looks as if there'll be little that we can achieve if the French are as well organised as you say."

Burke allowed himself to finish chewing a strip of unidentified meat and swallowed. "I'm not so sure about that."

Bernadita's eyebrows raised and the beginning of a smile returned to her lips, but she said nothing, allowing Carlos to ask the question that Burke was clearly waiting for.

"You have a plan?"

Yes, Burke had a plan. And, as Bernadita and Carlos leaned in to listen, he explained what they could do.

* * *

That night, Burke rode slowly back towards the French column. It had crawled just over ten miles during the day. Moving an army was always a slow business but it was clear that the French were in no hurry. They were taking it easy, moving through territory which

they considered long subdued. For two days, they had seen no attacks from the guerrillas. There had been some excitement when a deserter had killed an officer (two sentries as well, but they hardly counted) and made off on a stolen horse, but the troops would still be relaxed. Discipline would be a bit slack. Burke was counting on that.

In the darkness he could just make out the shapes of men on foot – El Gato's band, moving silently towards the French, still invisible somewhere ahead.

"Halt! Who goes there?" The sentry had seen him before he had seen the sentry. That was only to be expected, a man on horseback being rather more obvious than a man on foot. Around him Burke sensed the guerrillas sinking to the ground. He rode forward, confident in his stolen uniform.

"A friend," he said.

The sentry saw an officer approaching and stood to attention.

"The password, sir."

"La Gloire."

Burke spoke confidently, still moving forward.

"Beg pardon, sir, but that's yesterday's password."

"Damn. Is it really?" He was level with the man now and slipped from the saddle. The forgotten password was a minor embarrassment, something to be sorted out face to face.

The sentry never saw the knife in Burke's hand; hardly felt it slicing his throat, opening his windpipe before the scream could start. There was a gurgling that would hardly disturb the next guard on the perimeter and then he fell to the ground and thirty shadows flitted through the gap in the French defences.

It was so easy that Burke almost felt guilty about it. Even as these things went, it was a dirty business. They must have killed a dozen or more men in their sleep until somebody woke and the screaming started. Frenchmen, still half asleep, had little chance. Confused in the darkness, by the time they realised the enemy were already in their midst, another dozen were dead.

Bugles sounded. Officers came running. Sergeants shouted orders to wake and take up their arms. And as the camp came alive the Spanish were already vanishing in the darkness.

They moved back the way they had come, as shooting broke out behind them. The French were, in their confusion, firing on each other.

Occasional shots could still be heard as they mounted their horses which had been left a good half mile away where neither sight nor sound of them could have given warning to the French.

They rode hard until the dawn. Soult was hardly going to forgive a raid like that. His cavalry would be riding out looking for them and infantry patrols would be searching every house or barn within ten miles of the French line of march. Their own scouts, though, had been exploring the area since they first encountered the enemy and El Gato was now established in a camp in a narrow gully where a stream provided a ready supply of water. The gully widened twenty yards into the hill where the stream had its source, allowing space for a few shady trees and even some grass for their horses to pasture. It was as secure a spot as could be found for miles and they were happy to relax and celebrate their coup against the French. Their hiding place was far enough back into the hill for them to risk a fire: the smoke would not be visible to anyone near the entrance to the gully. They enjoyed the luxury of a hot meal and the wine that they had liberated from the French foragers was passed around and drunk more liberally than usual. Songs were sung and two of the younger men, whose families came from the South, strutted some of the steps of a flamenco dance while the others clapped a beat.

The day passed with songs and stories – some of them legends of old Spain, some stories of the war against the French, which Burke was sure would pass into legend soon enough.

By evening the songs were quieter and people stretched peacefully beside the flames, talking over the events of the previous night or dozing. Bernadita usually held herself a little aloof from the men – a wise move for any commander, Burke thought, but especially for a woman in her position. This evening, though, she relaxed, joining the others beside the fire, swigging from the wineskin and passing it on. It seemed perfectly natural for her to end up alongside Burke.

Perhaps it was the wine. Perhaps it was a day of relaxation after the excitement of the night before. Perhaps it was the romance of a warm Spanish evening, but Burke was suddenly very conscious of

her closeness. Living as they did, El Gato and her men seldom had the chance to bathe, yet Burke was aware of the sweetness of the body that was now pressed against his own. When he put his arm around her, drawing her yet closer, there was no resistance.

They lay together in silence for what seemed to Burke a very long time until Bernadita rolled away and stood in one fluid movement. Burke allowed himself a silent sigh. It had been a pleasant interlude and now it was over. Then he realised that she was still standing there, her arm stretched towards him. He reached up and took her hand. Laughing she pulled him to his feet.

They walked further up the gully. It grew narrower here, but there were still patches of flat ground where the grass grew close by the stream.

"Do you remember that afternoon at Alexandria?"

Burke remembered it. "How could I forget?"

"There was no grass there. Just bare rock."

"I'm older now," he said. "The grass will be appreciated."

She wrapped her arms round him and pulled him with her as she slipped to the ground.

His lips found hers. As his tongue explored her mouth, the years fell away. He remembered her taste and the feel of her flesh on his.

He had no recollection of their undressing, but, without any deliberate effort, he found himself naked in a tangle of clothing and she was laughing and he pressed his face to her breast and breathed the scent of her again.

He pushed her gently towards the ground, but she twisted free and straddled him. He looked up at her, dark against the fading light of the evening sky and she lowered herself onto him and he was lost as she swayed above him, intoxicating and magnificent.

He thrust upwards and she fell on him, holding him and kissing him as he emptied himself into her and then they were lying, sweating and exhausted.

He pulled a shirt from the mess of clothing and draped it over her and she pressed her heat against him and they slept.

* * *

They woke, unromantically, in the pre-dawn cold and scrambled for their clothes. Spain was, as far as Burke was concerned, fiendishly hot at midday but distinctly chilly at night.

They lay holding each other.

"I suppose that now that you've had your way with me – again – you'll be off."

Burke turned and kissed her. "How can you even think that?"

She kissed him back. The sky was beginning to pale and there was just enough light for him to see the sadness in her eyes. "I know you. In the end, you will always do your duty to your country, and your duty now is to tell Wellesley what you know of Soult's army."

He did not reply immediately and she watched him in silence for a while before she spoke. "We will not be able to attack the French like that again. You can't achieve anything by staying here."

"I don't know. There must be something we can do. I'd wager your men are as useful a group of fighters as the British will find in Spain. I can't believe we can't damage the French somehow."

She nodded and bent to kiss him again. "Maybe. But you still have information you need to take back to your army."

"Will you ride with me?"

She shook her head. "Wellesley has fifty thousand troops. My little band can't achieve anything alongside his army. But out here we may yet do something of use. I'll send one man to guide you and to help if you run into trouble on the way, but the rest of us are going to head north to see if there are any more French making for Madrid."

Burke couldn't argue, for there was no doubt at all that she was right. So they made their way back down the gully and joined the others for a breakfast of sausage and olives and some cheese they had stolen from the French. Someone had made a sort of chapatti by baking dough on a flat rock. Altogether, it made a good breakfast, but Burke's mind was not on the food. He watched Bernadita as she ate and thought of the night before.

Young Christophe was to be his guide and, as the last of the olives vanished, he nudged Burke.

"Best be off," he said.

Bernadita was sat talking to Carlos and she looked up as Burke stood, but she did not rise. She smiled and waved, but she clearly had no intention of making any public display as he walked to where the horses rested under the watchful eyes of two guards. Burke and Christophe mounted and prepared to follow in the path that William had taken over a week before.

Chapter 7: Sergeant Brown Reports for Duty

When William Brown had left the guerrillas to rejoin the army he had been glad of the guide Bernadita had dispatched with him. His intention had been to ride south until he hit the road that ran towards Madrid before making his way westward back towards the point where he had set out from Hill's camp. His guide, though, soon veered towards his left, heading south-east.

"The army has not been idle while you have been away," he explained. "They are well on the way to Madrid by now."

That made sense. The Anglo-Portuguese force had been moving with remarkable speed when he and Major Burke had finally caught up with it. He counted back the days since they had set out to Portaje. It was, he realised, almost a fortnight ago.

"We'd better get a move on, then. General Hill will be needing this news before he learns where the French are the hard way."

William kicked his horse into a trot and the two men started out towards Madrid. He was not looking forward to this journey. During his years with Burke he had become a better rider, but he knew that the next few days were going to leave him stiff and sore.

After only a few miles riding on narrow tracks across the open plain, they arrived on the main east-west road to the capital. They made their way openly along the highway. William wore his sword and had a pistol tucked in his belt, while Cristian carried a musket slung across his shoulders. It was obvious that they were guerrilla fighters, but they had no fear of running into a French patrol. The margins of the road were, once again, strewn with the detritus discarded by an army on the march. Any Frenchman hereabouts would have been fleeing eastward days ago.

The only excitement on their journey came on the second day. They were riding past an olive grove when they heard the sound of musket fire to their right. William had no intention of getting involved in any fighting he could avoid. His message was more important than any adventures *en route*. He put his head down and pushed his horse forward into a gallop. Beside him, though, he saw Cristian turn. For the Spaniard, it seemed, blood and honour had a

more immediate appeal than the mundane practicality of courier work.

For a moment, William hesitated, but then he saw half a dozen men emerge from the trees and head towards his guide. To William's disgust, he saw that their attackers wore British uniforms.

"Deserters!"

There was no question now of riding on. As far as William was concerned, deserters were the scum of the earth. Once separated from their army, a band of deserters like these had no choice but to live as outlaws, every man's hand against them. These fellows would be as cheerfully killed by the English soldiery as by the French, while to the Spanish they would be just another gang of bandits to be hunted down and destroyed.

William was not surprised that he and Cristian had escaped unscathed from the ragged volley that had marked the start of the attack. Muskets were inaccurate weapons at the best of times and infantrymen were trained to shoot at other infantry marching towards them, not at men on horseback moving fast across their line of fire. The deserters had not paused to reload but were running forward with bayonets fixed, intending to stab Cristian's horse and bring him down.

Cristian had no time to unsling his musket. He had drawn his sword, but William could see that he would not have the reach he needed to strike his assailants before they were able to stab his mount. Fortunately for Cristian, William had spent years in the sort of dirty fighting where being prepared to kill at a moment's notice was almost second nature. The pistol in his belt was already loaded and as he charged towards the deserters he drew it and fired.

One of the soldiers span round. Blood was already soaking into his coat from a wound in his chest, staining the scarlet a darker red. That left five, but its main effect had been to break their attack on Cristian. The sound of the shot had them swivel away from the Spaniard to face this new enemy and Cristian was not slow to take advantage of the distraction. The long barrelled muskets with their bayonets were instinctively turned towards the new threat. Cristian pushed his horse forwards and his sword arced through the air towards the nearest of his assailants.

Now there were four men left. Cristian pulled his horse away as a terrified deserter swung his musket back, fifteen inches of steel threatening to cripple the horse. The other men, though, continued to face William as he galloped towards them. They held their muskets braced for the impact, three bayonets ready to tear into the horse's chest.

Barely a yard from the three men, William swerved to the left. As he passed, he stooped low from the saddle and his sword swept towards the nearest man. He hardly had to move his arm – the horse did all the work. He just had to brace himself for the impact as his blade tore through the deserter's neck.

The three men left standing had given up any attempt to attack by now. They huddled together, bayonets pointing outward. It was a pathetically miniature version of the classic infantry square, but like a proper infantry square it provided a surprisingly effective protection against attack on horseback.

William pulled his mount to a halt and sat, looking on as Cristian dismounted and, slowly and methodically, loaded his musket. The deserters could only watch. If any of them tried to load their own weapons the other two would be unable to hold off a rider, for loading a musket takes space as well as time and their tight cluster of bayonets was all that was protecting them.

Cristian finished loading, slipped the ramrod back into its place under the barrel and took aim.

One of the deserters threw down his musket and fell to his knees, weeping.

Cristian shifted his aim slightly and, before any of them could react, one of the other two fell forward, blood gouting from his chest. At that range, Cristian could hardly have missed.

That left one man on his feet, staring in horror at his comrade. William pushed his horse forward and, almost lazily, stabbed him in the back.

The man who had thrown his weapon down was gabbling something. William was sure he heard the word "mercy", but Cristian did not speak English – not that it would have made any difference if he did. The Spaniard walked over and knelt beside the man in the scarlet coat. Like most of the guerrillas, Cristian kept a

knife in his belt. He drew it and, taking the man's regulation pigtail in his left hand, he pulled his head back and cut his throat.

They did not stop to bury the bodies. William's excuse was that they did not have the time, and this was probably true. More importantly, he did not feel that they deserved a decent burial. Such men were mere savages. No: worse than savages, for they had taken on the uniform of their king and betrayed that trust. He knew that men might slip away in ones and twos and try to lose themselves amongst the people and he understood that. But marauding bands of deserters were dangerous creatures. They were like packs of wild dogs, to be hunted down and killed. No, he would not stop to bury them.

Cristian made no comment when told that they were riding straight on. He cleaned his knife and sword on the coat of the last man he had killed, crossed himself and remounted.

They travelled for a while in silence and then Cristian began to sing. It was a love song and William found himself thinking of Molly and all the other women left behind as their men marched away to war. Was Cristian thinking of a girl? Was she still waiting for him or was she another of the untold victims of this war? William felt it was better not to ask, so he rode on, listening to Cristian's fine tenor lamenting a woman who lived far away and (or so the song said) who might yet leave him for another.

"You know what I really miss?" Cristian said, when the song ended.

This girl, thought William. Or peace. Or your mother's cooking.

"What I really miss," he said, "is my guitar."

* * *

The next three days blurred in William's mind. They would wake, set off at a canter and then rest the horses at a walk until they were fresh enough to start trotting. Then it would be walk, trot, canter, with only the shortest of breaks for siesta. Whenever they passed a village they would ask for news of the army to discover it days ahead of them. They were catching up, but so slowly. William's back ached, his arms ached, even his legs ached – and the state of his buttocks was unthinkable. He remembered the wide,

high saddles of the horses in South America and the sheepskins that cushioned the rider. Why did Europeans insist on using saddles as an instrument of torture?

Walk, trot, canter; walk trot, canter. And then, as night was falling on the third day the flickering of camp fires in the distance and the noise and stench of a vast army carrying to them on the breeze.

They pushed the horses until they were almost at the camp before slowing to the gentlest of walks, their mounts steaming in the cool of the evening.

“Halt. Who goes there?”

“Friend.”

“Oh, aye.” The voice was from somewhere in England’s north and dripped with the traditional English suspicion of Johnny Foreigner. “What's the password, friend?”

William’s buttocks were crying out for the opportunity to get out of the saddle. He didn't have the patience for this. “Urgent despatches for General Hill. Get the officer of the day.” Then, when the man hesitated: “And I’m not your bloody friend. Call me ‘sergeant’ and stand up straight when you speak to me.”

The man didn’t hesitate any longer, but hurried off. Cristian, who had not understood a word of the exchange, but had followed the tone of it without difficulty, had drawn his knife and was ostentatiously cleaning his nails. “So that is how you maintain discipline in the British Army. No wonder the French are running away. Marshal Soult would run away if you shouted at him like that.”

William grinned. "That's nothing. You should hear Major Burke when he's crossed. Napoleon would run away if he met the major on a bad day.”

The two men laughed, good humour restored. They were still laughing when the officer of the day arrived. It was not the same man who had led Burke to the general on their first meeting, but he shared the smooth manners and calm efficiency that William was beginning to think Hill inspired in most of his officers.

"You say you have dispatches for General Hill. He has been waiting on some information. Can you confirm who the message is from?”

William had dismounted as soon as he saw the officer on his way and now he snapped off one of his best salutes. "Major Burke, sir."

"Ah, yes." The officer returned his salute. "And I imagine you are Sergeant Brown."

"Yes, sir. And this gentleman has been assisting us. His name is Cristian, sir."

Cristian was still mounted but, hearing his name, he waved his hand in what a generous observer might take to be a salute of his own.

The salute was carefully returned. "*Muchas gracias por su asistencia. Estoy seguro de General Hill querría verte cuidado muy bien.*" And then, to the sentry, "Make sure this man is fed and his horse looked after. Then find him somewhere to sleep."

William watched as the Spaniard was led away. He thought he had kept his expression carefully neutral, but the surprise must have shown. "You don't have to be shocked, you know. Your Major Burke isn't the only chap who can speak the lingo." He turned and strode off. "Follow me. I think Hill will want to see whatever you have as soon as he can."

Sergeant Brown's particular line of work had brought him into contact with a wider range of officers than the average NCO, but he was still a little over-awed by the idea that he was to meet Hill himself – the man who, after Wellesley, was the most important British general in Spain and therefore, as far as Brown was concerned, pretty much the most important general in the world. 'Daddy' Hill, though, was as careful of his sergeant's feelings as he had been of Burke's. "I'm glad to see you here," he said. "I trust that this is not because Major Burke has met with an accident."

"No, sir. The major is fit and well, sir. He thought he should remain with the guerrillas in the hope of gathering more intelligence, sir. He sent me with his report."

He reached inside his jacket – he was still wearing the unsavoury garment he had bought from the carter who had driven them from Lisbon – and produced Burke's notes.

Hill read them, a small frown of concentration on his face. "It's useful stuff, sergeant, though it tells us nothing we had not suspected. It's natural that the French forces to the north should withdraw towards the capital. What really worries us is where

Marshal Soult is skulking. He's Napoleon's best man in Spain and I'd sleep easier if I knew exactly where he was. Did Major Burke have any thoughts on that matter?"

William had to admit that he had not. "But that's why he stayed with the guerrillas, sir. They were planning on hunting for Frenchmen."

"That's all to the good." Hill nodded approvingly. "I hope they find them. But I think that there's little point in you returning to join him. Things here are coming to a climax. It will come to a battle whether we want it or not. You'd best be attached to one of the regiments here." And, almost before he knew what had happened the Officer of the Watch was whisking him out of Hill's presence and had passed him on to a Captain Farquarson. "You're in the 48th Foot now, m'lad," that officer told him, not unkindly, before passing him, in turn, onto Lieutenant Sykes.

"Brown, is it?" said Sykes. "Not a lot of experience in the line, I understand." Then, when William admitted that this was true: "Well, we lost a sergeant to fever last week, so I'm sure we'll be able to use you somewhere. He sniffed disapprovingly at William's clothes. "We can't have you in the lines looking like that. Best get yourself over to the quartermaster and see if he's got anything you can wear."

It was dark by now, but the camp was still a bustle of activity. There was that sense of anticipation that runs through an army on the eve of battle. Brown passed the armourers, where sparks were thrown up from their grinding wheels as officers presented their swords to have the edges honed. Extra ammunition was being distributed and officers and NCOs alike moved from company to company checking their men were present and their equipment was in good order.

William found the quartermaster back with the baggage train, arguing with a captain about the availability of additional musket balls. When, finally, the captain had been sent on his way with barely half the ammunition he had asked for, the quartermaster turned to William with an expression that did not bode well for any hope of a sympathetic hearing.

William, of course, was in the right. Absolutely, unarguably, correct and proper. He had no uniform, through no fault of his own

and he had been ordered to get himself equipped. One look at the quartermaster's face, though, reduced him to the position of a terrified supplicant begging for any dispensation that the keeper of the regiment's supplies might allow him.

The quartermaster's surliness was understandable. Here he was, in the middle of a war, and some pathetic excuse for a soldier was demanding new uniform. Uniforms, as every fool knew, were issued at Christmas. In between times, you looked after your kit. If it tore, you repaired it. If you lost things, you found – which usually meant stole – replacements. A quartermaster's job was not to provide a clothing store for men too careless to look out for themselves. William, though, was a persuasive soul and had, after all, been confirmed in his NCO's position by no less a personage than General Hill himself. With much muttering and complaints about the imbecility of sergeants in general and Sergeant Brown in particular, the quartermaster finally produced a tunic and a pair of trousers.

"I can't help with the boots."

William was hardly surprised. The army was always famously short of boots and cobblers. In his case, it was not a problem. The boots he was wearing may not have been regulation issue but they were sturdy enough. He did beg for a belt, though, for without the cross belt he hardly looked like a soldier at all. The quartermaster took pity on him and found a shabby old belt and, from somewhere at the bottom of the wagon, pipe-clay to whiten it. He even produced – god knows how – some sergeant's chevrons for him to sew on his sleeve. "You can borrow a needle but you'll have to sew them on here. I'll not part with it."

William was happy enough to sew on the chevrons on the spot: like most soldiers, his needlework skills would have disgraced many a housewife.

Job done, he returned the needle and turned to go.

"Aren't you forgetting something?"

William turned back, uncertain what the quartermaster could be talking about, only to see him waving a pike at him.

A sergeant's pike. Of course.

William had not served in the line since he had been promoted, so he had never had the dubious pleasure of wielding a pike before.

Over six feet long, it looked like a ceremonial weapon from the Middle Ages. He knew it could be used to defend against cavalry and that the sergeants tasked with protecting the colours often put it to good effect. For most NCOs, though, it was more a symbol of authority. You could wave it about to direct your men when the noise of battle meant that they would not hear your shouted orders, but, most importantly of all, you could use the wide blade to drive forward any who were reluctant to step directly toward the enemy and a hail of incoming fire. Some officers believed that an army would succeed only if the men were more frightened of their own sergeants than they were of the enemy and, looking at the pike, William considered that it might well be true.

He returned to Lieutenant Sykes in a rather more sombre mood than he set out. Carrying that pike made him walk more slowly and, walking more slowly, he looked about him more. He noticed the glances that the men gave him: apprehensive; resentful; or just plain scared. The pike represented authority in its purest, most physical form. Argue long enough with a man with a pike and you would end up dead: that was the message that it sent.

William thought of some of the sergeants he had known all those years ago before he was plucked from the ranks to serve alongside James Burke. There hadn't been that many, but he remembered one he had feared, one he had loathed with an intensity that still raised bile decades later, and one he had respected. There had never been, though, a sergeant he had seen as a friend.

He reported back to Lieutenant Sykes feeling very alone.

Sykes appeared to him to be a decent man. He was introduced to the other three sergeants – Hargreaves, Kemp and Collins – and the four NCOs listened as Sykes explained their situation. Most of this, it seemed, was not news to the others, the Army's rumour service being, in William's professional opinion, one of the finest intelligence systems in the world. For him, though, cut off from British military news for over a fortnight, this was his first chance to find out the position the Anglo-Portuguese army was in.

It quickly became apparent that Lieutenant Sykes had little time for the Spanish army. In theory, the Spaniards were gallant allies, bravely resisting the French on their own account while giving the British all possible assistance. In practice, Sykes considered (and

William was confident that he was not alone) that the Spanish were lazy, cowardly and untrustworthy. William's own experience suggested that they were far from lazy or cowardly, but this was based on El Gato's guerrilla band. Unfortunately, Bernadita was not in charge of the army. In fact, William was never sure who was in charge of the army. There seems to be several generals who might well have been more concerned with jockeying for position against each other than with fighting the French. The most successful was General Cuesta and his force was supposed to be fighting alongside the Anglo-Portuguese effort. "But the silly sod ran off after the French without any proper reconnaissance first, and found rather more of them than he wanted to. So he's come running back to us for protection with a goodly chunk of the French army following him. They are probably going to arrive here tomorrow. We should have the measure of them, for there's over 50,000 men here, but …" and here Syke's tone became one of utter contempt, "… 35,000 of them are Spanish." The other sergeants groaned, apparently sharing their lieutenant's disgust.

"As we can hardly rely on the Spaniards to advance against a substantial French force, General Wellesley has established a defensive position. We'll be just below the ridgeline on the hill over there." The lieutenant gestured into the darkness. William had very little idea of where he was. Cristian had told him that they were close to a place called Talavera de la Reina, but that had not really left him any wiser. He was happy to accept, though, that there would be a hill and that the British would put their forces on top of it. It was, after all, one of the most common defensive positions and no less effective for being conventional.

"We're anticipating that the French will mount a frontal attack up the slope – it's not so steep that they'll try to do anything clever like go round it. We'll stay at the top and shoot them as they climb up. So long as you keep your men in line and make sure that none of the lazy bastards let their firing rate drop, it should all be straightforward enough. Kill the Frenchies in the morning, and a celebratory supper that night. Any questions?"

His tone indicated that he did not expect or want any further discussion and his sergeants took the hint.

As they made their way back to their men, Kemp took William under his wing. “I’ll introduce you to your section. They’re not bad lads.”

They were sat around a fire. A cooking pot was balanced above the flames with some anonymous meat slowly singeing to provide their evening meal. Obviously none of the men had a woman among the camp followers who, William knew, would be settling down with the baggage train somewhere toward the rear.

“This is your new sergeant.”

The men turned to look at him, their faces carefully blank. William remembered that look: assessing the new sergeant. Is he strong? Is he weak? Will he be cruel? Will he be able to control his squad?

William wasted no time. The men were sat or sprawled around the fire. Sergeant Brown, still holding his pike, spoke quietly, but every word was distinct. "When you first meet your new sergeant, it's normal to stand to attention."

This was an outrageous lie. He had only known one sergeant to expect this, but he remembered that that particular NCO had been one he most respected. Perhaps it had been because he was a good soldier and cared for the men under his command, but that first order had set the tone.

All the men scrambled to their feet, standing in a reasonable semblance of being at attention. All but one who eased his way up from the ground into a relaxed slouch. There's always one, thought William, and one way to deal with him.

The staff of the pike was moving almost before Brown had consciously decided what to do. It slammed into the man's stomach. Doubled up, he staggered back and it took only another, gentle, push for him to be lying on the ground again.

"Let's try to get up faster, shall we?"

He lurched to his feet. To be honest, he was barely any quicker than the first time, but the blow had left him gasping for air and if he slouched now, it was from pain and no sign of insolence.

Kemp stood back and watched. He said nothing directly about what he had just witnessed. "Well, Sergeant Brown, you seem to be settling in. I'll leave you to it."

Kemp's departure seemed to lift some of the tension that had been building. William allowed his body to relax a little and the men, already sensitive to any shift in his mood, relaxed a little too. He learned their names. There were only sixteen of them and he was good at remembering names. He reckoned he would have them all off pat by the next day.

There were generally between twenty and twenty-five men in a squad. Perhaps Wellesley had been under-manned when he left Portugal but, even so, William imagined there had been a few deaths on the way. He thought of the crosses they had passed on the roadside and decided not to ask what had happened to the others.

"I'm interrupting your meal, lads," he said. "Best save that bit of meat while you can still eat it."

He would eat with other sergeants. On the march, the sergeants would usually eat with their men, but tonight would be an exception. Tomorrow, he might be leading these men to their deaths. Tonight, he was going to spend with Hargreaves, Kemp and Collins, learning as much about the section as he could.

* * *

Dawn the next morning was deceptively cool, but the clear sky promised another blisteringly hot day. William had learned from the other sergeants that the men had been kept busy for the past few days, digging ditches, felling trees, and making up breastworks to provide a strong defensive line. Today, though, they were to be rested. Today, they needed to be fresh for battle.

In the daylight, William could see the rising ground to their north. Lieutenant Sykes summoned his sergeants to order them to get their men in position towards the top of the hill. William found himself, like the other NCOs, bellowing orders as men were lined up, inspected, shouted at for whatever failings were found in their turn-out (there was always something) and eventually marched northwards. It seemed to him an elaborate way to move a group of men a mile or two, but he understood the reasoning. The men he commanded now were not like the men he had served with all those years ago in the Regiment of Dillon. Those who had made the journey to that regiment did so because they wanted to be soldiers.

The Regiment of Dillon did not actively recruit: it relied on those who sought it out. These men were different. A few, perhaps, had always wanted to join the Army, but after so many years of war, the Army would take what it could get. Some had joined in a drunken stupor, signed up by ruthless recruiting sergeants who knew the value of a few pints in easing a man into thinking the Army might be a fine life. The next morning, these recruits would wake with a fierce headache and a conviction that they wanted to return to civilian life, but their escort would explain the penalty for desertion and march them under guard to the nearest barracks. Others were the sweepings of the local gaols. The cost of prisons fell on the rates and magistrates were happy to allow a convicted felon the option of serving under the Crown rather than a regular sentence. Most were stupid: a few verged on simpleminded. Yet constant discipline with clear orders shouted at them very loudly turned this rabble into what William was happy to believe were some of the finest fighting soldiers in the world.

Shouting done and men marched smartly to their positions, all they could do now was wait. Lieutenant Sykes' company was in the reserve, about half a mile back from the men who would bear the first brunt of any French attack. There was, in any case, no sign of the French yet, so there was unlikely to be any fighting that day. At mid-day the troops lunched on food from their packs.

William left his men to eat undisturbed and settled down with the other sergeants. He looked at the oatmeal and dried meat that seemed to be all he had been issued with and he remembered the enthusiasm with which their convoy had been greeted when it first arrived.

"The Spanish still not giving us the food they promised?"

Kemp paused from his chewing to spit emphatically on the ground. "I give that for the Spanish," he said. "They say Wellesley is refusing to advance further on Madrid until the whole business of proper supply has been sorted out."

"That's true," said Sergeant Collins. "We've strict orders not to take any produce we don't pay for, but there's nothing here to buy. The French have been pillaging for months and Cuesta takes what's left for his own Spanish troops. All the promises they gave us about

supply have come to nothing. We're left to bring food up from Lisbon and the bastards in the commissary never send us enough."

Silence fell as the four men contemplated the sad slice of dried beef that was the only meat they would see that day.

"I've got some olives," offered William, digging out a handful left from his journey.

Sergeant Collins twitched his lip at them but eventually conceded that they would be better than nothing. William divided his handful between them. It was, when you saw them counted out, a pathetically inadequate gesture, but his comrades seemed to appreciate it.

After they had eaten, everybody settled to sleep. "I don't hold with kipping in the middle of the day," said Collins, "but the Spanish do it and the habit seems to have spread."

William had taken easily to the idea of siesta and slipped quickly into a contented slumber, but he woke abruptly about three in the afternoon, with the sound of shooting drifting from the plain, somewhere to the east.

"Damn!" Kemp was already on his feet. "It sounds as if the French caught up quicker than we'd hoped."

The lines, which had been full of slumbering figures only moments before were now frantic with men grabbing up their weapons and falling into their platoons. William, arriving at his own section just as the last man fell in, was pleased to see them lined up and standing to attention. It suggested that they had a certain amount of respect for their new sergeant. His sore throat, hoarse from a morning's shouting, seemed a small price to have paid for that.

Lieutenant Sykes strode towards them, as fast as he could without seeming to run. Officers, William knew, never ran.

"Tell the men to stand easy."

William obediently told his men to relax, as if they had not heard the lieutenant for themselves.

They were lined up below the summit of the hill, so any enemy on the plain beneath could not see their position. It meant, though, that William could not see what was going on to the east. He watched Sykes hurry past his men and stand further up the ridge, drawing a small telescope from his pocket and looking in the

direction of the firing. The shooting seemed less intense than it had been, but the crack of musketry could still be heard in the distance.

William held his position, fighting the urge to join Lieutenant Sykes and ask exactly what was going on. Major Burke would never keep him in the dark like this! But his work with Major Burke was out of the general line of soldiering. Now he was just another infantryman, there to go where he was told and shoot when he was ordered. There was no need in this work for him to know anything of the strategy of the battle.

Eventually the sound of shooting died away entirely and Sykes closed up his telescope and replaced it in his pocket. Turning, he spoke generally to his men.

"It seems that the French light infantry are already with us. Our forward outposts were surprised, but the enemy has been checked and our troops have withdrawn to their positions on this line. I do not anticipate that there will be any further action today, but you will remain where you are and prepare for battle tomorrow."

He paused and then, as if desperate for some stirring way to end, he added, "God save the King!"

God save us from inexperienced lieutenants, thought William. Still, this grandiloquent finish from a young officer who was almost certainly facing his first major battle did produce an ironic cheer from the men. No harm done there, in William's opinion. Sykes might well turn out all right.

The men were stood down and settled on the ground. Someone produced a pack of cards. Someone else had a penny whistle and started a tune. There were, William decided, worse ways to spend an afternoon.

Lieutenant Sykes, though, seemed to find it difficult to relax. He kept pacing to and fro towards the ridge line, stopping every now and then to survey the scene through his telescope. Eventually, apparently tired of his own company, he called on William to join him and the two men started to walk further forward, looking for a better view.

"I thought you might enjoy watching the French manoeuvre."

Below, in the distance, there was a scattering of trees, such as might pass for a forest in these parts. They were near the Tagus – William could see the sun catching on the river far off to his right –

and he supposed that the water meant the land hereabouts could support more vegetation.

At first, he saw nothing. Then, squinting against the light, he saw figures beginning to emerge from the trees. As he watched, an entire French division, together with artillery and light cavalry, marched out from the forest with the precision of a parade ground tattoo. They moved at speed, drawing up on a rise in the ground opposite the British line, just to William's left. As they watched, the cannon were unlimbered. Tiny figures busied themselves around the batteries and he saw puffs of white smoke rise from the cannons' mouths. Seconds later the crash of artillery fire rolled across the plain. Behind him he could hear nervous shouts from his men.

"You'd better return to your section, sergeant. They sound as if they need reassurance."

William did so. Fascinating as it was to watch the French deploy, he had a job to do.

"Nothing for us to worry about, boys. The Froggies are practising with their cannon over on the left. It will be a while before they get round to us and at this range they're not going to be doing any real damage." He had no idea if that last remark was true. Napoleon had started as an artillery officer, and the French army generally made very good use of its cannon. Still, his section was at the top of the hill and had cover from the lie of the land, so maybe the value of the artillery would be limited. There was no point in worrying his men about it anyway.

When firing started on the right, he was more concerned. Lieutenant Sykes was still watching the activity below, and seemed to have no objection to William again joining him.

The French who had formed up on the left were still there, their cannon firing regularly. Despite himself, William could not help but be impressed with their efficiency. There seemed no sign of any other troops, though. He looked to the right but the view was obscured by trees and the lie of the land. He could see nothing on the ground but, beyond the trees, white smoke was rising into the air, like misplaced clouds. There was fighting going on down there somewhere, but who was fighting whom was not at all clear.

Sykes gestured in that direction. "That's where Wellesley put the Spanish – safely out of the way." He put the telescope to his eye

again. "Well, if it's the French, it's just a scouting party. There is no sign of anyone else except Victor's men over there – he gestured to the artillery." He snapped the telescope closed and did his best to look like a man in command of the situation. "You can go back and reassure your men, Brown."

William did so. Gradually the sound of firing died away again, but the mood was changed.

"You reckon they'll come at us, sergeant?" It was the youngest of his men who asked. Brown struggled for a moment to remember. Yes, Peters, that was it: a new recruit. This was probably his first battle.

"I doubt it. The French like to organise themselves first. They'll come at us tomorrow."

He could see Peters trying to phrase another question, but then looking nervously at his hands without saying anything.

"You'll be fine, Peters. Keep your place in the line, remember your musket drill and think of your mates either side. They'll look after you."

It was feeble reassurance, but it seemed to work. Hardy – one of the older men – slapped Peters on the back and the boy seemed cheered by the reassurance.

William wondered himself what it would be like. He had seen plenty of action and danger in his life, but this would be different. The job of the infantry in a set piece battle like this was, essentially, to stand and take fire. Wellesley had at least put them in a position where the contours gave them some protection, but eventually they would have to step forward to face the French, repelling them with volleys of musketry and all the time standing, scarlet targets against the sky. There would be artillery, musket fire from the infantry, perhaps cavalry riding at them with sabres. The Army's job would be to stand and not to break and his job would be to stand behind his men and force them forward if any threatened to turn and run. He looked again at that wretched pike, lying on the ground beside him. He'd rather be firing at the French than threatening his fellow countrymen with this cruel blade, but he knew that in war all had their part to play, and this was his.

There was no point in worrying about it. Tomorrow would be a long and bloody day. William stretched himself on the ground and dozed through what was left of the afternoon.

He roused himself when it was time to eat. There were to be no fires, for anything that might show where the troops were concentrated could give useful information to the enemy. The French were moving their regiments from here to there on the plain, trying to place them in the best position for the next day's attack. "Looks like you were right, sergeant," said Peters. "The Froggies do like to fuss about while they get up the nerve to do the business."

There was some laughter and someone said, "Well, at least they're not going to run away as soon as the first shot is fired."

There was an uncomfortable silence. During the afternoon the story had spread about the fire over on their right. The excitement seemed to have been triggered by a patrol of French light cavalry that had run into some of Cuesta's troops. What had started as a few shots fired by the French as they withdrew had turned into a mass panic as the Spaniards, most of whom were well out of range, returned fire. The Spaniards can have had hardly any idea what they were even firing at but, hearing shots all around them, they had panicked and broken.

"They said ten thousand of the buggers ran." Hardy spat on the ground.

"Well," said William, "it's just as well General Wellesley was to hand to get our troops into the gap." He didn't like the way the talk was going. Whatever the truth of what had happened, his men (for he already thought of them as his men) needed to believe that the Spanish would stand firm in a fight. "General Cuesta got his lads back, didn't he?" He looked behind them to the west where the sun was beginning to sink. "We can relax now, lads. There'll be no more excitement today."

He could not have been more wrong.

* * *

The hill that they were stationed on was the key to the British position. William's role here might be that of a simple sergeant in the infantry of the line, but he assessed the terrain with the eyes of

an experienced intelligence agent. The hill, he noted approvingly, was steep and rugged on the side towards the French and rendered more inaccessible by a ravine at the bottom. It seemed a good strong point to anchor the left of the line.

Perhaps because the position seemed so strong, there were no troops on the summit. At the time, William saw nothing untoward in that, but that evening he was to realise that Wellesley might have made an uncharacteristic error.

The French had noticed the absence of troops on the high ground and taken this as an indication that the ridge was not properly defended. As the light began to fail, with the British trying to rest ready for the next day's battle, the enemy, departing from their usual careful preparation, made a sudden dash for the hill.

The assault fell mainly on the troops to the left of Lieutenant Sykes' company, though near enough for the odd badly aimed cannon ball to land uncomfortably close.

The whole company was now lined up in two ranks behind Sykes, who had drawn his sword. That, William thought, did not bode well. Either Sykes was far too excitable – a worrying trait in an officer – or the 48th was about to be ordered into battle.

Shots were coming now, not from ahead but from the summit of the hill on their left.

"Company will wheel on the centre, to the left; on the centre, left wheel. March!"

William thanked the Lord that he was near the centre of the line. Sykes' order was designed to turn the company from two lines of men facing east to two lines facing north. It was one of the harder manoeuvres, especially for those on the ends of the line who had to march with very long steps to keep in position with those who were essentially shuffling round in the middle.

William watched as his men moved neatly to face the enemy to the left with only the occasional correction from him. At either end of the line, though, he could hear Hargreaves and Kemp bellowing and he could swear he saw Hargreaves swing his pike dangerously close to one poor fellow who was falling behind his comrades.

Seconds later, the apparent confusion turned neatly into two lines of men facing the French at the top end of the ridge. All their hours of drill were paying off.

"Dress the lines." Sykes was obviously not that impressed. William hurried behind his men, moving one a foot in this direction and another foot in that until they were spaced perfectly evenly, each man almost touching those on either side.

He waited for the order to move forward, but no command came. Ahead all seemed chaos. In the failing light, he could not see which of the figures on the hill above him were British and which French. Then, in the gloaming, the melee seemed to take on some sort of order. British troops were moving in line up the hill – the 29th, he thought. Shots came from above them where it was clear that the French had now captured the summit. Surely the battle could not have been lost, even before it had properly begun?

"Forward the 48th!"

Perhaps William imagined hearing the order, for surely one voice could not have been audible over the din. But now the drums had begun their steady beat, colours were moving forward and Lieutenant Sykes' company became just one tiny part of a mass of two thousand men, tramping steadily up the slope.

William braced himself for when the first men began to fall. His job would be to dress the line, ensuring that there were no spaces between the men, even as bodies fell to the enemy. The line must never break. Their lives depended on that.

A hundred yards. Two hundred, and still nothing.

A horse was coming towards them. By now it was too dark to see if the rider wore a red coat or the blue uniform of the French. Peters moved to level his musket but Hardy struck it down before William could respond. "Try not to shoot any of our own officers, boy," the older man said.

The drums fell silent and William was suddenly aware that the noise of firing had stopped too. The rider spoke, his voice carrying in what seemed by then an unnatural quiet.

"The 29th have recovered the summit. 48th is to form up in the rear of the 29th to provide support if the French come again."

That was it, then, thought William. For a few minutes, it had seemed as if they were going to see action, but now they were back in the reserve. He didn't know whether to be relieved or frustrated. It was, of course, a good thing that his chances of survival until the morning had just substantially improved. On the other hand he had

been a soldier most of his adult life and a soldier is seldom happy to miss out on the prospect of a good fight. It wouldn't be like the French to attempt a second night assault, so all the 48th had to look forward to was a cold night of waiting for a fight that was unlikely to come.

In fact, things did not turn out the way William had expected – nor, had he known it, the way the French had planned. Two more French regiments had been committed to the attack but, in the darkness, they had lost their way in the ravine. With the failure of the initial assault, it might have been wise for them to have retreated, but Napoleon's army was loath to pull back once it had started out toward the enemy. So the 48th had barely taken up its position when a fresh wave of Frenchmen started up the hill towards the British lines.

The 29th started firing down the hill as soon as the French were in range, with William and his comrades held back, but it was soon obvious that the losses they had taken in the initial attack had left their line far too thin. The horse loomed up again out of the darkness and more orders were issued. The 48th was to move forward and plug the gaps in the 29th's ranks.

Companies marched towards the ridge, their officers leading them as best they could, occasionally tripping on the uneven ground as they could barely see their way. William, with the other sergeants was kept busy keeping his men together and in line. Those on one end of the rank could barely see those on the other, but somehow they kept the two ranks in order and they marched smoothly into one of the gaps ahead of them.

It was, William thought, as neat a manoeuvre as he had ever seen on a battlefield. Two regiments merged with neither able to see properly. Orders had been issued which had been almost drowned out by the noise of firing from 29th. Most of the men had no idea where they were and little notion of what was going on, but the genius of the British Army had placed them in exactly the spot they needed to be to repulse the French.

Now William would see how his men performed in battle. Down below he could make out the shapes of men struggling up the slope towards them. It was too dark to be able to aim at any individual, but that made no difference. A musket is not a precision weapon. A

line of troops would point their muskets in the general direction of another line advancing towards them and would fire as a volley. Most of them would hit something. Then they would reload and fire again.

William was confident of the outcome for two reasons. Firstly, the constant drilling that his men were subjected to made them able to load very quickly. William believed – and his officers told him he was right to believe – that the British infantryman could load and fire significantly more quickly than the French. That meant that, other things being equal, they would kill the French faster than the French would kill them. But other things were not equal. The French were advancing up a hill. They could not struggle up the slope and fire at the same time. So the shots coming from the French would come in ragged volleys with long intervals between them. The British, though, stood firm in two lines.

"Front rank, shoulder arms!" Lieutenant Sykes issued the order and the front row of his company brought their muskets to their shoulders. All along the line, lieutenants were shouting orders and muskets were being brought up.

"Make ready." There was a ripple of sound as over a thousand men cocked their weapons.

"Present!" Over a thousand muskets pointed towards the enemy.

"Fire!"

The noise was deafening and the line vanished for a moment under the rolling smoke of the volley. The stench of bad eggs caught in William's throat, but he did not allow himself to cough. He listened as the front row of his section knelt to reload. Two seconds to lower their muskets, three seconds to reach for the cartridge and tear it open with their teeth. He heard eight men spit the torn paper onto the ground. Two seconds to prime the pan, seven seconds to ram down the cartridge.

The second row had fired by now and started their own ritual of reloading as the first rank responded to the order, "Shoulder arms!"

So it went on. Every twenty seconds each man would shoot. Twice in every twenty seconds the French advance would be swept by a thousand lead balls, ripping into flesh, shattering bones.

William could hear the screams of the enemy before there was any damage inflicted on the British ranks, for the redcoats had the advantage in range, firing downhill.

Now, though, the French began to reply. Ragged as their volleys were, they were effective. Not as effective as the British fire, but William heard screams that were far too close to be those of the French. From the corner of his eye he saw men to his right and left fall, though his section were, so far, unhurt.

The enemy were all too visible now, even in the near-dark, for they had reached twenty yards from the top of the hill. William started to wonder if, against all the odds, the French could recapture the summit.

The British muskets fired again and now William could sense that the French attack was breaking. The enemy was battling up the hill carrying packs that weighed about eighty pounds and struggling with their muskets – another ten pounds that had to be held clear of the ground as they stumbled over rocks and hollows and the bodies of their dead. That was demanding enough in daylight without anybody shooting at you. In the dark, listening to your comrades screaming as they fell, it must be hell. William felt almost sorry for them.

* * *

Finally, they could rest. They were even allowed to make fires, for the French assuredly knew by now exactly where they were. They stretched exhausted on the ground, the living alongside the dead. Tomorrow, after the battle, burial parties would clear the corpses, but now it was too dark and the men were too tired.

By around eleven, William had finally settled to sleep, but there was to be one final burst of excitement that night. At around midnight the Spanish troops on the right opened fire. Perhaps it was a French cavalry patrol that had ventured too close, but nobody was ever able to confirm its existence. Given the behaviour of the Spanish so far, most of the British were more than happy to say there had never been an enemy at all. Whatever the truth of it, the Spanish opened fire on a grand scale. Volleys of musketry were joined by artillery, the noise continuing for twenty minutes.

What the French made of it William could only imagine. In the British ranks, where troops were stood to, ready to face a surprise attack that never came, there was nothing but contempt and derision. The whole affair had had an unsettling effect, though. While the Spaniards' fears were easily dismissed, they left everybody on edge. Suppose there had really been some Frenchmen? For the rest of the night the sentries were discharging their muskets at any sign of movement in the darkness and, while there was no evidence of any dead Frenchmen as a result, several British officers and men were indisputably killed by their own side.

By dawn, no one had slept properly. They had been promised bread for their breakfast and beer. This should have been part of their normal rations, but with the Spanish still failing to honour their pledge to supply the Allied army, it was a while since any food, let alone fresh bread or beer had been supplied. The promised feast was by way of a treat to prepare them for battle and William hoped it would restore some good temper to his tired squad, who were grumbling that there was no water at the top of the hill and precious little firewood to heat it with if they could find some.

"You don't have to worry about that. You've no cauldron to boil it in."

William spoke an obvious truth. As the men had moved forward under fire, they had had to abandon such unmartial luxuries as the cauldron that had been painstakingly carried up the hill to the original bivouac site.

"I'll see if I can find it, sarge." Peters was young and anxious to impress, but his fellows jeered.

"It's been there all night. Best you can hope for is that someone else in the 48th nicked it. Otherwise it will be those bastards in the 29th."

"Or some bloody dago."

That last suggestion came from Franklin, the man whose introduction to his new sergeant had been a pikestaff in the gut.

"They're our gallant allies," William reminded him, to general jeering. "All right," he conceded, "not that bloody gallant. But remember we're supposed to be on the same side."

The temper of the men seemed to be improving, William reckoned. Get some food in them and all would be well.

At that moment, with no warning, the French guns opened up on them.

* * *

At first, William's mind refused to accept the evidence of his eyes. The French were far below on the plain, so there was no possibility that the shells bursting above the British lines could be French artillery.

A cannonball hit the ground ahead of the 48th and bounced towards them. It struck Peters, who had been standing waiting for permission to search for the cauldron, and neatly removed the bottom of his leg. He fell to the ground screaming, while the other men in the company stood frozen in shock.

"Form up!" William was shouting as sergeants to his right and left ordered their own men into line. For a moment he allowed himself a glance at Peters. Where the boy's right foot should have been, there was just a bloody stump.

"Hardy! Get his belt off and tourniquet the leg."

Hardy fell out of line and stooped to give the lad what aid he could. "He needs a surgeon, sir."

Of course he needs a bloody surgeon, William thought. But the surgeons were back in Talavera and it would take two men over an hour to get him there and he couldn't spare two men. And there wouldn't be enough surgeons anyway. For the officers, perhaps. Not for the likes of Peters.

"Tourniquet the sodding leg and get back in line. We'll get him to the surgeons once this is over."

It was the best he could do. At least with the tourniquet, Peters stood some chance of surviving through the day.

The shells were still exploding in the British ranks. Most hit the 29th, who were positioned towards the front, but enough overshot them to give the 48th a bloody nose.

How were the French getting their shot so high? William screwed his eyes against the smoke. Ahead he could see the muzzle flashes of the French artillery. But how could they have got their guns so far up the mountain?

He thought back to the day before, when he had looked down at the enemy on the plain. Above them, opposite the British positions, there had been one isolated hill. He realised what they had done. In the night they had pulled their artillery to the top of the hill where it now fired across the heads of their own army directly onto the British positions.

Yet again, the French had proved that when it came to the placing of artillery, they were, as William grudgingly admitted, really very good.

The British had little in the way of cannon at the very top of the mountain, having chosen to rely on the advantage that their height gave them over any advancing infantry. Until the French came within range of their muskets, the 48th could only stand there and take it. Which, William reminded himself, the British infantry did better than anybody else in the world.

Under cover of their guns, the French pushed up the hill, until they were too close for their artillery to fire without danger of hitting their own men. Then, at last, the horror of the bombardment ended and the redcoats were in a position to do what they did best. The 29th started to fire volleys at the French, the 48th moving close behind. Sykes' company was soon moved to the front line as the soldiers of the 48th were pushed forwards to fill the gaps the French cannon had punched in the 29th's ranks.

The morning soon seemed a repeat of the previous evening, the volleys ringing out every ten seconds. This time, with the sun by now well above the horizon, they could at least see their enemy. Every ten seconds the blue ranks below them would stagger with the impact of a thousand musket balls. But every time they would recover and move that little bit closer to the summit.

Now, over on the left, more Frenchmen were moving up the northern slope of the hill. The enemy were beginning to return musket fire and, as the British faced attack from two directions, the line faltered. On the uneven ground, companies were separated from each other and the battle at the top of the hill degenerated into dozens of close combat fights. Sykes' company exchanged a volley with a French company that had come within yards of the summit and then, neither side allowing time to reload, they fell on each other with bayonets. As the fight degenerated into what seemed

little more than a brawl, musket butts were swung like clubs and men whose weapons had been struck from their grasp hit out clawing at each other's faces with their bare hands. William, who had sorely missed his musket up to that point, was suddenly pleased to be holding a pike. He lay about him with it, carving into the French in front of him, feeling the judder as it slammed into bone, splintering and shattering ribs and limbs, leaving twitching bodies where there had once been men.

The 48th pushed forward over ground made still more uneven by the bodies of their dead. Yet, cruel as their losses were, the French were taking even more casualties. Gradually they fell back, step-by-step at first, and slowly, to cover the retreat of their wounded. Then, finally, they broke, fleeing back to the valley.

The French retreat was followed by a brief resumption of the artillery bombardment, but after a while the guns fell silent. Judging from the height of the sun above the horizon, William estimated it could be barely 9 o'clock and yet, already thousands of men must have lost their lives.

As if both armies were reeling back in shock from the intensity of the fighting, there seemed to be an unofficial truce.

With the guns silent, they could turn their attention to the wounded. To William's relief, Peters, though weak, was still alive and Lieutenant Sykes agreed that he could be carried back to where carts had come up from the town to carry those who might still be saved down to medical assistance. "Though," Sykes said, "we must be realistic. I have few hopes for his life." William privately agreed, but, the rest of the men being within earshot, he loudly assured Peters that he would be made well as soon as he reached Talavera. "We'll see you when we march back down after our victory," he said. "And we'll be sure to save a souvenir for you." The best souvenir, of course, would be a purse taken from the pocket of a dead French officer, but even a pair of dead man's boots would be better than nothing, for if Peters lived, he would never march again and his future prospects were unenticing.

The French seemed in no hurry to restart the fighting. They, too, wanted to collect their wounded and, as the fighting had been taking place at close quarters, French and English troops found themselves meeting on the battlefield. William watched the enemy

suspiciously, but they showed no signs of aggression. It was another hot day and the nearest water was a little brook that ran between the two sides and, after a while, French and English troops squatted opposite each other, drinking from the same stream. At first they kept their muskets close to hand, but gradually they relaxed. Soldiers on both sides reached across the stream to offer their hands and soon they were mingling together like old friends.

Although there was no active conflict during the morning the French were far from idle. William could see the regiments on the plain manoeuvring into new positions. At first he assumed that they were going to withdraw – either yielding the field completely or regrouping after two failed assaults. Gradually, though, it became clear that they were preparing to attack again, this time with men in position to move forward along the entire Allied line.

William wondered whether he should order his men back, ready once again to face the enemy, but French and English soldiers were still fraternising on the hillside. He saw an Englishman trade some of his tobacco for half a loaf the Frenchman was carrying in his pack. Damn the Spaniards and their lies about supplies. They gave more to the French, who demanded it at bayonet point, than they would ever provide for their ostensible allies.

Sykes approached him as he sat pondering the iniquity of all foreigners.

"I'm afraid Sergeant Collins is no longer with us, Brown. He died in the last attack, together with four of his section. That leaves sixteen men without a sergeant. I want to keep them together if we can. They've messed together for months and it's best not split them up now. With Peters gone, you're down to fifteen, so I'd like you to take them over. That will give you thirty-one. It's a good number, but from what I've seen, you're up to scratch for that."

William had hardly known Collins, but he had seemed a good man. As to the private soldiers in his section, William could not say. He had seen them formed up on his left but now… He looked, a little anxiously over the hillside below him.

"Sergeant Kemp is keeping an eye on them," said Sykes.

William looked in the direction that Sykes was pointing. Kemp was standing over sixteen men who sat on the ground, more in the

attitude of prisoners than of the victors in that morning's fight. His pike was held as if he might well be intending to use it.

Sykes coughed awkwardly. "They came close to breaking, Brown. You'll need to establish your authority. Sergeant Kemp tells me that you're good at that."

Thank you, Kemp, thought William. That would be that little display with Franklin. Well, they say no good deed goes unpunished.

William called down to Hardy: "Round up the others and bring them over to me." Then he turned to meet his new men.

* * *

It could have been worse, in his opinion.

The sixteen men he had inherited from the unfortunate Collins seemed stunned by what they had been through, rather than mutinous. Kemp had seen Collins fall and his men turn, but the threat of his pike had turned them back. "I wouldn't say they fired well," he told William, "but they kept firing after a fashion – except for Wilkins and I'm prepared to make allowances for him."

William, too, would make allowances for Wilkins, for the man had been shot in the thigh, but the wound had been crudely bandaged with fabric torn from a dead man's shirt and he could stand well enough now.

"Let's see your musket drill, Wilkins."

Wilkins looked to be about forty – older than most of the men, but still fit to fight, and his experience would be valuable. He started his drill: load; handle cartridge. "We'll not use the cartridge this time, Wilkins. We don't want to start a panic." Wilkins obediently mimed priming his weapon and ramming down the cartridge. "Shoulder arms." William counted the seconds. Wilkins was doing his best, but he was too slow. Too much of his mind was on the pain in his leg and the effort of balancing without putting too much weight on it.

In William's opinion, Wilkins wasn't fit for duty, but the Army obviously viewed things differently. The man could stand and he could fire and they were going to need as many men as they could

get. After today things would be different: he was in no fit state to march anyway. But, for today, he was needed.

It left William with a problem, though. Wilkins was clearly not going to be fast enough to volley with the rest of them.

"Put yourself on the end of the rear rank, Wilkins. Load as fast as you can and fire every second volley. Do you understand?"

"Yes, sir. Thank you, sir."

The other men had watched in uncomfortable silence. Now William turned to them. "I want to see how the rest of you do. Just go through the motions. No powder."

He formed them into two ranks and counted the time. Twenty two seconds. Too slow.

“Again.”

They stood in the heat while he drilled them. The fifteen he had come to think of as his own men drilled as best they could – even Franklin. They had stood together against that hellish fire and survived. For now, at least, they would respect their sergeant, even without the pike. For the men who had fought under Collins, it was different. William could feel their resentment. It was there in the set of their shoulders, the stiffness of their necks. But there was no help for it – it had to be done.

“Shoulder arms.”

Thirty one men moving as one, with Wilkins that bit slower.

“Make ready.”

The sound of thirty muskets being cocked and one that little bit later.

“Fire.”

Thirty hammers fell on empty priming pans.

“Reload.”

Other sections were beginning to form up on the top of the hill. Unlike the French, the 48th Foot could do little to improve their situation. All they could do was to hold their position near the top of the mountain and wait for the French to come again. A Spanish gun team lumbered past with a cannon, but it was a small calibre weapon and would make little difference to anything.

William knew that survival that afternoon depended on the line holding and maintaining its rate of fire. He would not allow Sergeant Collins’ men to be a weak point in that line.

“Shoulder arms.”

Despite the increased activity in both armies, some French and British soldiers were still fraternising on the slopes of the hill. Gradually, though, men drifted back to their units until, at around one, the enemy’s drums began to sound, and the French hurried back to their eagles.

William watched them go and stood his men down. “Take a breather, lads," he said. "I don't think it will be long now.”

* * *

That afternoon they stood again and took it. It seemed to William that this had come to define his life: standing while the shells burst overhead; standing while the French volleys took down the men around him. Thirty one men – two ranks of fifteen with Wilkins standing alone on the left. With thirty one men standing in their red coats, targets for the French, he could hardly expect his squad to survive the afternoon unscathed and they did not. Half an hour after the first attack started up the hill one of Collins’ men fell. William couldn’t even remember his name. He moved Hardy forward to fill the gap and dressed the second line with Wilkins now in line with the others. The man was firing well enough, despite an obvious limp whenever he moved.

Another of Collins men was hit. This one, he remembered was called Jackson. The ball had torn into his left arm, which now hung at his side.

“Get to the rear, Jackson." Wilkins could shoot with a damaged leg, but with his arm broken Jackson was useless as far as the fighting was concerned.

He dressed the line again, filling the gap. Still the French came, the musket balls whipped through the air and the men of the 48th fell around him.

In all the smoke and noise, William scarcely noticed the French cavalry moving on the plain and the confusion of horses and foot soldiers. The first he was aware of the enemy’s manoeuvres was when the hill to his right was covered in blue figures. The British centre – a Guards regiment, no less, – had broken.

His first thought was that this was the end. Trapped on the left of the line, the 48th had nowhere to retreat because of the steepness of the ground on the side away from where the French now controlled the ridge. They would fight on, of course, because they were British and soldiers of the King, but the end was surely inevitable – death or captivity or to be left lying wounded on the field at the mercy of the surgeons. On the whole, he would prefer death or captivity.

An officer was galloping through the chaos below them. He avoided the worst of the fighting, although the sun caught on his sword as once or twice he swung at a Frenchman who made towards him. On the whole, though, he was unmolested. The infantry had enough to worry about fighting each other without picking a quarrel with a rider who seemed not to want to pick a quarrel with them.

Sykes had seen him. "Despatch rider!"

William and his men held their position, but to his right a section wheeled to fire on any Frenchmen who might try to bring down the messenger from the General Staff.

One more flash of sunlight on his sabre and the rider was clear of the fighting and heading up toward the 48th. Officers were already riding to meet him and William took his attention from his section for a moment to see the cluster of horsemen gesticulating downhill before one broke away to pass the new orders to the men.

Ahead of him, William saw another of Collins' section fall. "A pace to your left! Dress the line." Even as the men adjusted to the new gap in their number, William had stepped forward to pull the man to the rear. There was no time for gentleness: he dragged him back by his legs and rolled him onto his back. One glance at the blood-soaked tunic showed the man was beyond help. The musket ball had driven straight into his gut, and, although he still breathed, there was no chance of his surviving to reach the surgeons. For a moment William considered finishing him off with his pike. It would be a kindness, but it was not a sight he would be comfortable for his men to see.

He was about to kneel beside him, to give him what comfort he could when Sykes appeared at his shoulder. "We're moving down the hill."

William gave one last glance at the figure at his feet. He'd be joining him soon enough, for to move down the hill was surely suicide. Below them was a mass of fleeing British troops and beyond them the French, now confident in victory, moving in ordered fashion in pursuit of their enemy.

Well, he would at least die doing his duty. The drums began to beat and as William and the other sergeants shouted and gestured and occasionally struck at the more recalcitrant men with their pikes, so the British wheeled right and started in line towards the end of the battle.

Nobody there ever knew how they had done it. As the 48th entered the melee, it seemed as if they must be carried away in the retreat of the Coldstream Guards. But the sergeants kept their sections together; the sections held in their companies. Though the companies had to break their ranks to allow the fugitive troops to pass through, as they emerged from the chaos they reformed in two lines marching steadily to the sound of their drums: thousands of feet tramping in unison as they descended on the French. Faced suddenly with a counter-attack at the moment that they were sure they had clinched victory, the French hesitated and, in that instant of hesitation, the momentum of the battle shifted. Over on his right, where there had been nothing but a disorganised mass of fleeing men, William was dimly conscious of some sort of order reasserting itself and then, while his men fired and fired again on the enemy, the Coldstream Guards, as if desperate to redeem their reputation, marched back into the fight.

William could not but admire the struggle the enemy put up. Exhausted from their climb, at the moment of apparent victory they found themselves attacked from the front and on the flank. The 48th and the Guards poured fire into the French column and, slowly, Napoleon's troops were forced back. Even then, they did not break, but withdrew in good order, covered by skirmishers and renewed fire from their artillery.

There was no question of pursuing them. The men had fought all day, beating off wave after wave of attacks with no proper food and limited supplies of water. Thousands were dead and, as the noise of battle faded, the cries of thousands more wounded could be heard across the field. William counted the men still standing in front of

him. There were twenty one. Rather to his surprise, Wilkins had survived, holding his place in the line, though he staggered with every step he took and occasionally reached for the arm of the man next to him for support.

Sykes was alive, though his face was covered in blood from a head wound. He beckoned William to him. "Congratulations, Brown. You appear to be the only sergeant I have left. Please convey my appreciation to the men."

The lieutenant turned away, looking out over the mass of dead and dying. William waited until he realised that Sykes had nothing more to say and he turned and left him with his thoughts.

His men had abandoned their line and were now sitting or lying in a disorderly group.

"Well, lads," William said, "we've won."

He slumped to the ground alongside them. Tomorrow, he supposed, it might feel like victory. When he was old, if he ever grew to be old, he would tell people about the glorious battle of Talavera.

He couldn't say it seemed glorious now.

Chapter 8: Flour Power

Bernadita's guerrillas had taken care to lie up in a remote part of a country. James and Christophe were riding for over two hours before they reached a village where they could stop to rest and water their horses. It was there that they first heard of what had happened at Talavera.

News of the French defeat had spread through the countryside. Napoleon's men, the villagers told them, were on the run. Some, anticipating a victory at Talavera, had been moving to cut Wellesley's line of retreat but now Wellesley had turned and was ready to crush them.

It did not take years of working in military intelligence to understand the implications. Christophe saw the peril immediately. "They don't know about Soult. They think they're going to hit a small demoralised force and they are going to find themselves facing Soult's entire army!"

Burke had been quizzing the villagers for anything they knew about the battle. Their accounts would, he knew, be unreliable, but it seemed clear that there had been a huge fight. In such a battle even the winning side must have taken enormous casualties. He doubted that Wellesley's army would be in any state to take on Soult's fifty thousand fresh troops.

"We need to move."

There was no more question of rest. They pushed their horses as hard as they could, following the road that William had taken ten days earlier.

Burke had always been a better rider than his sergeant and Christophe seemed a natural horseman. Knowing the danger that Wellesley was in, they rode their horses from dawn to dusk, resting only when the tired beasts could go no further. Burke considered trying to buy fresh horses from one of the villages along the way, but Bernadita had given them the best of the mounts the guerrillas had available and, tired as they were, they would probably be better than anything else the countryside would provide.

They were tempted to pause awhile at Talavera. The smell of death still lay over the ground to the north of the town and the streets were crowded with the walking wounded, while those less fortunate lay in rows on the ground, attended by a pitifully inadequate number of military doctors.

The place was in chaos. Burke could see bodies still unburied on the battlefield and several times they were stopped by soldiers begging for food, for Cuesta had still not delivered the promised supplies. There was no chance here of finding better horses or anybody with the authority to allow Burke to take them. There wasn't, it seemed, even the chance of finding a decent meal.

They rode on.

Four days they rode. Again it was evening when they finally caught up with Wellesley's men. Again they had to wait impatiently while a sceptical sentry summoned the officer of the day.

This time, General Hill greeted him like an old friend.

"Good to see you safe. You will be pleased to know your man, Brown, is safe too." It was typical of Hill, Burke thought, that he would have remembered Sergeant Brown and taken care to find out that he had survived Talavera.

"Anyway," – Hill looked relaxed and sounded almost jovial – "you've arrived just in time for some fun. Talavera was a close thing but we're just mopping up now. There's 15,000 of the Frogs who are lying on the road back to Portugal and when we hit them it will be a fine end to our campaign." Then he saw the expression on Burke's face and suddenly looked much less relaxed.

"You have news for me."

"I'm afraid I have, sir."

It was not the most comfortable interview of Burke's life, but at least Hill, being a fair man, did not blame the messenger. Even so, explaining to a general who thinks he's about to win a decisive victory that he would be much wiser beating a rapid retreat is never a pleasant experience. Hill listened carefully, asked a couple of questions to confirm that Burke had made a proper estimate of Soult's force and then quietly, but very definitely, sent him on his way.

"You will appreciate, major, that I am going to be rather occupied for the next few hours."

Burke did, indeed, appreciate that. He appreciated it even more the next morning when, smoothly and efficiently, as if it had always been the intention, the army swung south, crossing the Tagus and putting the river between themselves and the French forces they had come so close to attacking.

One of the first things Burke had done was to find the orderly who had taken charge of his uniform when he had set off in his priestly disguise. Fortunately, the man had survived Talavera and, even more fortunately, he had managed to retain Burke's uniform. For the next couple of hours Burke was able to enjoy riding in uniform alongside the troops of the British Army. This, after all, was how his life was supposed to have been – honest soldiering, not skulking around in enemy territory and cutting throats by moonlight.

By midday, though, he was beginning to realise that there was no role for him in Wellesley's army. Sergeant Brown might slip easily into a dead man's shoes, but nobody wanted a major who had arrived so late in the campaign and who might well, for all anybody knew, be off again at a moment's notice.

That afternoon he worked his way up the column to where Hill was riding with his Staff. Although the general must have had a thousand things on his mind, he received Burke politely, as if he didn't have a care in the world.

"If we are pulling back, sir, doesn't that leave the guerrillas rather exposed?"

Hill looked a little puzzled by the question. "Indeed – but no more exposed than they were before we got here."

"You did suggest that I should liaise with these people, sir. If we are changing our plans, would it not be best to let them know?"

Hill studied Burke face for a long moment before raising a sceptical eyebrow. "Do I take it, major, that you have a particular interest in maintaining our lines of communication with these people?"

Burke felt the beginning of a blush. "It could do no harm, sir."

Hill smiled. "Be off with you then, major. Let your friends know that the news you brought saved us from a dreadful error. They have the gratitude of a grateful nation and if we can ever offer them assistance, we will do so." The smile faded. "Though in the

circumstances I cannot see what practical aid we will be able to give for some time."

"Thank you, sir."

Burke turned to go, but Hill raised a hand to detain him. "Don't be gone too long, Major Burke. We've raised a hornets' nest with the French and the countryside won't be too healthy. I'm going to hold onto Sergeant Brown, because I'm told he's proved a useful man to have. You're a useful man to have as well. Try to get back in one piece."

Burke saluted and Hill gravely returned the salute.

Now he just had to find clothes he'd arrived in and make his way back to Bernadita.

* * *

Burke had no wish to try to explain himself to any French soldiers he might meet. His clothes, while respectable, were those of a regular working man, but his horse was that of a gentleman. Ideally he would have liked to get hold of better clothes and try to pass himself off as an official riding on business, but there was no chance of finding smart clothes in the middle of the Spanish countryside. He would have to trust to his horse being able to outpace any Frenchmen he couldn't avoid, though he carried a carbine in the holster on his saddle and a pistol in his belt as insurance.

He set off back the way they had come. He needed to be north of the Tagus and that meant heading back to the bridge at Arzobispo that he had crossed that afternoon with Hill's forces. He rode easily, saving his horse for hard riding if he was to need it.

He arrived at the bridge to find it still in Allied hands. Cuesta and the Spanish army had stayed north of the river, apparently believing that the French would stay in their position and not respond to the British Army's change of course. Burke, who had no doubt that the French had their own spies and scouts, was less sanguine, but at least the presence of Spanish troops meant he did not need to worry about the enemy yet.

Evening was coming, so Burke decided to take advantage of the security offered by the Spanish forces to stay the night in

Arzobispo. Finding a room proved difficult, for all the decent accommodation had been commandeered by Spanish officers, but a farmer's wife on the outskirts of the town took pity on him and let him sleep in their barn. He'd slept in worse, and the farmer shared his breakfast with him, so he set off the next morning feeling all was right with the world.

Now he had crossed the river, he headed back towards Talavera before striking north to the area where he had left Bernadita's guerrillas. There seemed unlikely to be any real danger from the French who, between Cuesta and Wellesley's retreating army had plenty to keep them occupied. He rode on, enjoying the peace of the countryside. It was easy to forget, here away from the armies, that this was a country at war.

He took lunch in a little village where he was able to buy a passable wine and a dish that he was fairly sure had some chicken in it somewhere. He rode on through the hour of siesta. He was allowing his horse to make its own pace and he had spent enough years in the saddle to be able to relax as well on horseback as most men could in an armchair. He was on his way back to Bernadita and all was right with the world.

The sound of a woman's screams brought him back to the reality of war-torn Spain in an instant.

It was late afternoon and the cries came from an olive grove, just to the south of the road. For a moment, he considered ignoring it. His whole plan had been to avoid any sort of trouble. But then she screamed again and, reluctantly, he turned his horse toward the sound.

There were three of them: two holding her down and the third standing over her, his trousers already round his ankles. They wore no uniforms. Perhaps they were French deserters, perhaps they were British. Most likely they were Spaniards, driven from their homes by the fighting and now wandering about the countryside taking advantage of the breakdown of law and order that goes hand in hand with civil war. Burke did not really care. He knew what he had to do and he decided to get it over with as quickly as possible.

He drew his carbine, which he had kept loaded, and an instant later the would-be rapist was dead. The two other men turned to run. Burke pushed his horse toward the nearer and, drawing his

sword, made an almost lazy sweep towards the man's neck which finished him. He was about to turn after the third man when he remembered his promise to avoid any trouble. Dismounting, he found the girl shaken and sobbing, but unhurt. Her clothes had been disarranged but no worse than that, and as soon as she had recovered her composure she arranged herself respectably and thanked Burke for his help.

She lived nearby, with her parents who, naturally enough in that part of the world, were farmers. As it was already beginning to get dark, she offered to express her gratitude by asking her parents to put him up for the night. Burke accepted enthusiastically. After his night in the barn, the idea of an actual bed appealed.

The girl's parents were, if anything, even more grateful than she was. It seemed a sad fact of life in this part of Spain, which had been fought over for so long, that no one seemed particularly shocked to hear of the assault. "The French," her father declared, "are scum, but Cuesta's men are almost as bad. And those men who call themselves guerrillas – some of them are the worst there are."

"El Jefe," his wife muttered and, at the sound of his name, the farmer leant toward the window and spat through it.

Burke explained that El Jefe was dead and that he had seen him hang. The news was received with a moment's stunned silence and then, still not speaking, the farmer rose from the table, taking with him the bottle of wine that was to accompany their meal, and replaced it with a bottle of brandy.

* * *

The next morning Burke was on his way with a surprisingly clear head, given the amount of drink that had been put away the night before. He was, perhaps, a little less cautious than he might have been, but he suspected that the chance of running into another renegade band was slim and that there were unlikely to be any French patrols to worry about as Soult was obviously concentrating his forces ready for the coming battle.

His optimism proved well founded and the day passed without incident. That night, he again slept in a barn, but he discovered that

when he brought news of El Jefe's death, he was guaranteed at least a decent meal before bed.

The first indication that there might be something wrong came on the fifth night of his ride. He had been taking it easy, but he was nearing the point where he would leave the road to ride across country to Bernadita's camp. He had, as on the last three nights, stopped at a farm and, while the family sat and ate together, he had told the story of the end of El Jefe.

Each time he told the tale, it had grown a little and now he talked about El Gato and her heroic band, though he may, perhaps, have played down the position he had been in when she rescued him. At El Gato's name, though, the mood of the family changed. There was an awkward silence and the farmer and his wife exchanged anxious looks. Finally the farmer spoke: had he not heard? El Gato had been taken.

No one seemed quite sure what had happened: the farmer, his wife and both of their sons had different versions of the event, but it seemed that El Gato and her band had left their hideout a few days after Burke. The attack on Soult's column had apparently created enough alarm for the French to devote some effort to capturing the guerrillas and when El Gato's men had taken the opportunity to attack a poorly guarded supply convoy, it turned out to be a trap. The trick was similar to that which Burke had used when he first arrived in Spain. The carts had been full of armed men. The civilian drivers were soldiers too. Many of the guerrillas had been killed but Bernadita had been taken alive. The French intended, apparently, to make an example of her, putting her on trial and executing her in Madrid.

"So they've taken her to the capital?"

No: all the family agreed that she had yet to be moved. "All the soldiers are moving west. They've left her here under guard until the fighting is over."

"Where are they holding her?"

"In the windmill near Gamonal."

At first Burke thought this was ridiculous, but the farmer explained the windmill made a very practical prison. It had only one entrance. The walls were made of solid stone and the small windows were high from the ground. It was also isolated from the

village, the only other buildings nearby being a couple of other windmills. By the nature of windmills, they were built on open ground, making it difficult to sneak up on them. “If you don't have a jail," the farmer concluded, "a windmill is a fair substitute.”

"And the windmill there is haunted," added his wife.

The children jeered this suggestion, but the farmer agreed with his wife. The mill was indeed haunted, a previous miller having hanged himself from the sails. “A lot of people say they have seen his ghost. Even Guillermo has seen it.”

Guillermo was obviously regarded as an authoritative figure in the area. Once his name was cited, the sons became noticeably less cynical and went so far as to admit that there were, indeed, many people who believed in the ghost.

Burke tried to pull the conversation back to practical realities. “Besides the ghost, how many people are on guard there?”

They were unsure. Why shouldn’t they be? There were guards in the windmill itself, which was easily enough defended. As well as that, some other troops had camped out in one of the other windmills. “They patrol round the area. Everybody has been ordered to stay away.”

Burke closed his eyes and imagined the situation that the farmer had described. The idea of imprisoning Bernadita in a windmill had seemed ridiculous, but he realised now that it was horribly efficient. The first problem anybody would have was getting near the place. Then inspiration struck.

"It's August. How are you going to grind your grain?"

The farmer shrugged. "It's early yet. There won’t be much ready to harvest for a while. Anyway I think they're allowing one of the windmills to carry on working.”

It was a slim chance, but it was the only one he had got. "How far is this windmill?"

“Not far. Five miles or so up the track.” The farmer gestured northwards.

Burke smiled. "How would you like to sell me some wheat?"

* * *

In the end, it took a couple of days to organise. The local farmers had no sympathy for the French and were happy to help El Gato to escape, but wheat had to be harvested and threshed and loaded onto a cart. Even with all the farmers in the neighbourhood helping, it wasn't until mid-morning three days later that the farmer drove a cart full of wheat slowly towards the windmills.

A French guard stopped them on the road a full half mile from the three mills that dominated the surrounding countryside. "Where are you going?" He spoke Spanish badly and with a French accent.

The farmer gestured at the wheat. “To the mill, of course. Where else would I be taking my wheat?"

“The mills are closed.”

"One isn't. I can see the sails turning.”

“That's as may be, but you can't use it.”

Burke and the farmer had prepared for this eventuality. The night before he had procured paper and pen. He'd spent some time asking neighbours for the best paper, for it was important it look respectable. He had then produced a requisition order for wheat to be delivered to produce flour for military use. It didn't really matter what he wrote, because he was reasonably confident that any guard they met would be illiterate, but he had whittled a stamp and coloured some candle wax to make a reasonable simulacrum of a seal. Flamboyantly signed and tied with a ribbon the farmer's wife had cut from one of her dresses it looked reasonably official.

"I'm here on government business." The farmer waved his paper at the guard, who took it and peered at it as if he could understand perfectly. There was a moment of hesitation.

"I better search your cart." He spoke with the sullen resentment of a man who had been bested by Authority – that letter and the power it represented.

Burke, lying in the wheat, a handkerchief over his face against the dust, could only hope the search was not a thorough one. He was not disappointed. Having delayed the cart and shown his own authority with a few thrusts of his bayonet into the cargo, the guard, honour satisfied, waved it through. Burke, who had felt the disturbance as the bayonet passed far too close to his head, allowed himself a small and dusty sigh of relief.

The cart creaked and groaned its way to the windmill where the presence of a guard at the door suggested Bernadita was being held. As it approached, the guard, who had been leaning idly against the wall, started waving frantically at them.

"Pas ici. Pas ici."

"No hablo frances."

The guard came over and the farmer stopped the cart. The two of them argued frantically in their respective languages while Burke slipped silently out and walked quietly and without any fuss into the mill.

He moved quickly away from the patch of light from the door. Out of sight of the guard, by then surely returning to his post beside the entrance, he stood motionless, waiting for his eyes to adapt to the dim light. Here at ground level was where the milled flour would be stored. Even though the mill was out of use, there was one open sack tied in place at the bottom of the chute that ran down from the millstones on the floor above. Some more filled sacks were stacked against the wall, but otherwise this floor was deserted. That made sense: there was no point in keeping the prisoner immediately next to the only door.

Bernadita must be on the next floor, where the millstones were, or on the floor above, where the wheat would be winched in through the one small window and stored ready to be fed into the stones. She could be on either of them. The advantage of putting her on the middle floor was that there was no window. On the floor above, though, the space would be smaller with no millstones for her to hide behind. And, of course, any rescuers would have that much higher to climb.

He edged around the wall, seeking for any clue as to where Bernadita or her guards might be. He kept his eyes on the ladder, his ears pricked for any sound from above.

With his attention so firmly fixed on what was happening elsewhere in the mill, it was hardly surprising that in the dim light he knocked against one of the sacks propped against the wall. It toppled with a dull thump, opening to cover him in flour. He froze, listening in case anyone had heard the sound and thought to investigate, but there was no response from the unseen guards.

He made to dust the flour from his clothes. He was covered in the stuff. He imagined he must look ridiculous.

No, not ridiculous. He must look like some spectral apparition. He remembered the story of the ghost that was supposed to haunt the mill and wondered if the guards had heard it too. Soldiers were a superstitious lot and likely to have picked up on any ghost story going. Perhaps that gave him the edge that he needed to get up the ladder.

He scooped some more flour from the sack and applied it liberally to his face. More drifted onto his clothes. Now he slipped across the floor almost silently, though leaving a trail of flour to mark his passage. He started up the first ladder.

The woodwork in the mill was solid. He supposed it had to be, to support the weight of the millstones and the gearing that connected them to the sails. He'd never thought about the mechanics of a mill before and he was not over-concerned with them now – only grateful that the solid construction meant that the steps did not creak.

He reached the top of the ladder and peeked carefully over. He was peering into a windowless chamber, the only light coming down from the floor above. He wondered for a moment why windmills were built with so few windows. He supposed that the grain would otherwise attract birds and other pests and that the millers took care not to have wind blowing where they were working with flour.

Even in the dim light, it was immediately obvious that there was nobody on this floor. At the top of the next ladder, then.

He looked down at his clothes, still white. He moved in a little cloud of white dust. He had a notion how he could make use of that dust. It was as close to a plan as he had had when he entered the mill, but for now he could do nothing about it. He must be just below Bernadita and any guard set on her. He moved with even more caution.

He took off his sword belt and laid it carefully on the floor. The sword was too likely to knock against the ladder and, in any case, he had decided that it had no part in the trick he was planning to play.

The second ladder was as solidly made as the first and he was able to climb it with scarcely a sound. Above him, the opening that gave passage to the floor above was filled with light. This floor, he knew, would have a window. There should be some sort of pulley arrangement so that sacks of wheat could be hauled from carts below, allowing the grain to be fed from above into the millstones.

He stopped with his head inches below the opening. He thought he could hear faint sounds of movement. He imagined Bernadita bound in the room above, a bored guard, shuffling perhaps as he moved to glance out of the window. He would have to take his chance.

He did not draw the pistol he had in his belt. He did slip the knife from his boot, but he kept it palmed, with the blade stretched up along his arm. As he stepped through the hatch, the guard would see an unarmed man. An unarmed man, a ghostly white, where no man should be, for the guard at the door should have stopped him. Burke hoped that the man had been looking out of the window, for if he had the figure before him would be that much harder to see, the inside being obviously much gloomier than the sun-baked landscape outside.

It worked out even better than he had hoped. As he emerged into the room, the guard was, indeed, staring out of the window. Something – the footstep, a flicker of movement on the edge of his vision – made him turn. He stared in disbelief at the white figure that was now moving silently towards him.

"*Mère de Dieu me protège! Le fantôme !* "

His musket was propped against the wall, but he made no move to reach for it. Nor did he draw his sword. Instead, with an expression of terror on his face, he crossed himself.

He couldn't have been that superstitious, Burke thought. In a few seconds, he would have recovered his senses and raised the alarm. But he didn't have a few seconds, for Burke had already crossed the distance between them and now the knife was in his hand and, at the moment that the guard realised that the man facing him was quite definitely alive, the knife twisted into his guts and he fell to the floor.

Burke turned to where Bernadita lay half propped against the wall.

"I would applaud, but they have tied my hands."

He knelt beside her and cut her bonds. She stayed sitting for a moment, massaging life back into her ankles.

"You took a terrible risk."

He took her hand and rubbed gently at the rope marks. "You were worth it."

She smiled a sad smile. "And now, where there was one of us trapped here, the French have us both. They were worried that my men might attack the mill to save me, so there are at least half a dozen more out there somewhere. You can't expect to persuade them all that you're the miller's ghost."

"I have an idea about that." He helped her to her feet. "Can you help me move some sacks of flour?"

Bernadita, understandably, looked puzzled. "The French haven't harmed me. I can move all the flour sacks you want. But I'm not sure that housekeeping is going to help."

"I'll explain later." Burke was looking at the window. Yes, there was a pulley mounted outside so that sacks of wheat could be hauled up. A rope ran over the pulley, the free end wrapped around a hook on the wall next to the window. There was no complicated mechanism – the miller just pulled the sacks up by hand. He picked up a length of the rope, judging its strength. He and Bernadita would weigh more than a sack of wheat, but it looked as if it should hold. It would have to. It was their only chance of getting out alive.

He led Bernadita to the steps and they tiptoed down to the ground floor. She brought her mouth to his ear. "We can't get out through the door, James. I've told you: it's too well guarded."

He whispered back. "We're not going out. We're moving the flour sacks onto the next floor."

The sacks were heavy and moving them up the ladder surprisingly hard work. Burke was worried that their efforts would be too noisy and that the guard outside might hear them, so he stopped when they had shifted just four sacks.

He took out his knife and slashed the canvas, filling the air with flour. Soon Bernadita was white as he was. "But this won't help us, James," she whispered. "You got away with it once in the dark. We can't both be ghosts."

“Do you know why there are no candles in this place?” Burke asked.

Bernadita wrinkled her nose. “What has that to do with anything?”

“You’ll find out. Now let’s go and move the corpse.”

Still puzzled, Bernadita followed him up to the top floor where they manhandled the dead guard down to the floor below.

Back upstairs again, Burke produced a flint from his pocket and, using a strip cut from the dead man's shirt, proceeded to kindle a small flame.

"From now on, we have to move very fast. Do exactly what I say and ask no questions."

For a moment Bernadita looked as if she was going to argue, but then seemed to decide that on this one occasion she would play the part of an obedient woman. From another pocket Burke removed a small pottery flask. “Olive oil,” he said.

“Are we planning a meal?"

Burke didn't reply, but leaving her by the window he ran down the stairs, making no particular effort to be quiet. Once he reached the body, he tipped it down the next ladder onto the ground floor. As he did so he shouted up to Bernadita. "Scream as loud as you can."

Bernadita screamed. Despite all that they had been through since he met her, he had never heard her scream before. It was an impressive sound. It certainly impressed the guard on the door who rushed in and stopped in shock as he saw the body lying on the ground.

Burke already had his pistol out. At that range, he really couldn't miss.

As soon as he had fired, he was running for the top floor and the window. Untying the rope he pushed the free end through his belt at the buckle, looped it over and pushed it through again. He hoped he had judged it right. He needed the rope to run through the belt, but not too fast.

He pulled it through until most was lying on the floor, with just a few feet stretching from him to the window, where the other end was firmly tied to a hook suspended from the pulley.

“This is our way out.”

Bernadita looked down from the window.

"James, you're mad!"

He ignored her, reaching out to grab the pulley. "Put your feet on that."

She stood on the hook that ended the rope, clinging to the rope. James felt the rope tauten and braced to hold it. Fortunately, Bernadita was not a heavy girl.

"Keep screaming."

Bernadita did as she was asked. As she hung onto the rope for dear life, Burke heard a genuine note of terror in her screams.

"James, the guards …"

The little garrison that was to guard Bernadita was housed in the second mill. Burke approved: that was where he would have put them. Their job was to guard the perimeter and make sure that the remains of the guerrilla band were not able to stage a rescue. They were not there to ensure the prisoner did not break out: they were there to ensure nobody else broke in. Now, though, they were running towards the mill, alerted to a problem by Bernadita's screams.

One of the men raised a musket but Burke heard the officer shout to him not to waste time. "Get inside and grab her!" That made sense. All they could see was a girl two floors up, clinging to a rope and screaming, she wasn't going anywhere. Below, he could hear the first of the soldiers inside the mill. Time was running out.

Still holding the rope, Burke crouched over the flame that had kept burning on the floor. He poured olive oil onto a second strip of rag and stuffed it into the flask. He lit the end and took two steps towards the stairs.

As soon as he had thrown the makeshift grenade through the hatch he turned back to the window. He stepped through, Bernadita dropping alarmingly as he allowed some slack in the rope. Then he, too, was clinging on above the hook, his arms wrapped round Bernadita as they started to drop to the ground. At first the rope offered no support at all and they seemed to be plunging to inevitable death, but as it tightened round his belt there was a sudden jerk and they began to fall more slowly.

Burke had no idea what alerted the soldier below but, for whatever reason, the last of the Frenchmen suddenly re-emerged.

"*Attention! Ici!*"

Even as he shouted a warning, he was levelling his musket towards them. Burke saw the spurt of flame from the muzzle as he fired, but he was not too concerned. He was a moving target and if he was hit, it would be by luck, not judgement. There was a crack as the ball knocked chips from the stone above him and somewhere to his left.

Another soldier emerged and, standing alongside his comrade just outside the doorway, he, too, raised his musket to fire.

That was when the explosion happened.

Both of the Frenchmen were blown off their feet by the blast that smashed through the doorway. The whole building shuddered as if struck by a giant hand. Stones, shaken loose from the walls, fell, bouncing down alongside the fugitives. Burke looked up to see the beam that supported the pulley tilt as more stones fell from the wall around the window.

"Hold tight!"

They were halfway to the ground, which seemed to be rushing towards them with dizzying speed. He looked up again. The beam was hanging at a crazy angle. Any moment now it would give way, leaving them plunging earthward with no support.

Still more stones fell and a creaking from above warned that the sails were no more secure than the rest of the building.

Smoke was pouring from the window and Burke thought he saw the flicker of flame.

He felt a lurch as the beam shifted and he braced himself for the fall to the ground. When it finally gave way, though, the rope swung them towards the sloping stone of the mills walls. The impact was bruising, but Burke knew that no bones were broken.

They were still falling, scraping against the rough stone of the wall. He saw the beam pass them bouncing off the stonework as they slid helplessly downwards. Above, the first of the sails was shaken from its mounts, the wood splintering as it, too, bounced down the stone, finally shattering on the ground beneath.

All this seemed to be happening so slowly, but only seconds had passed. They were almost at the end of their fall.

"Push away from the wall!"

He kicked desperately against the stone, spinning out into the empty air and finally rolling along the mercifully soft earth. He glanced up to see another of the sails fall free and crash towards him.

He staggered to his feet. At least he could walk. He felt blood on his face but there was none of the pain that meant a broken bone. Beside him, Bernadita lay groaning. He staggered to her and knelt sheltering her with his body.

"Can you get up?"

"I think so."

He helped her to her feet and supported her as they moved away from the ruins of the mill. More debris was falling and it was not safe to stay close by. Burke looked toward the two men who had been shooting at them. A block of stone was on the ground beside one, red with blood where it had struck his head. The other lay with his neck at an unnatural angle. Bernadita, following his gaze, crossed herself.

The last sails were falling now. Flames billowed from the building and the updraft caught one of them: it somersaulted elegantly in the air before succumbing to gravity and smashing alongside the others. From inside the mill they could hear the crashing of machinery, the crackling of fire and a sudden piercing scream. A figure appeared in the doorway. It was covered in flames and, though it walked upright, it seemed hardly human, jerking spasmodically before it fell to the ground barely a yard from the door and the screaming mercifully stopped.

They stood for a moment longer, watching the wreckage burn. Bernadita turned to him with the sort of expression Burke imagined people usually reserved for witches, warlocks and their ilk.

"What did you do?"

Burke brushed some of the blood from his cheek. “There are no candles in a mill, because flour dust burns. It burns very, very fast. So fast that if you fill a room with flour dust and then set light to it –

“It explodes,” Bernadita finished for him.

“Like gunpowder. It happens more often than you’d think. Mills are more dangerous than they look.”

There was another loud crash from within the building.

"That will be the mill stones falling."

Bernadita looked away. "We'd better be moving. It's a long walk."

"Not necessarily." He gestured toward the track where a cloud of dust was being kicked up by horses galloping up from the village.

"The French!" gasped Bernadita. "You're right. We don't need to walk – we need to run."

Burke did not move. Already the horses were coming close enough to see that the men riding were not in uniform. Minutes later two of Burke's new friends from the village pulled their mounts up alongside him.

They stared at the devastation and seemed not to hear Burke as he spoke to them. He had to repeat his question.

"The sentry gave you no trouble?"

"Sebastián shot him as soon as we heard the mill blow up." The farmer's son turned to Bernadita and bowed. "I think Sebastián will be volunteering to serve with El Gato."

Burke looked at Bernadita and then turned to the mill where they had both come so close to death. "I'm not sure," he said to Sebastián, "that El Gato will be returning to the guerrilla life."

Bernadita placed her hand on his arm, gently, but firmly, moving him to one side. "Major Burke is a most gallant gentleman, and I owe him my life, but he cannot speak for me. I love my country, and so long as one French soldier remains on its soil, I shall fight for its freedom. Major Burke, I know, will return to General Wellesley's army to do his duty, and I shall return to those of my men who have survived. We will be joined by those like Sebastián, who are, even now, taking up arms against our oppressors. One day, we will be free. Until that day, I fight. *¡Por dios, rey y patria!*"

The two men from the village raised their fists. "*¡Por dios, rey y patria!*"

They handed the reins of their horses to Burke and Bernadita, who mounted and set off down the path together.

Bernadita moved her mount across the path until she was riding knee to knee with Burke.

"Don't look so sad, James. You always knew, I think, that I would stay here, fighting for Spain. I have learned a lot from you. You pretend that you do not care that much for your work, but you

always return to it. You are a soldier. You have to believe in the war you fight. And I have become a soldier too. I believe in the war I fight and I must fight it until we win or until I die."

They rode in silence, back through the village and along the road west. Burke knew he would not be able to cross the bridge at Arzobispo again: the French would hold it now. He would have to make his way towards Portugal on the north bank of the Tagus, but he would find a crossing point eventually and rejoin the army, as Bernadita had said he would.

It was Bernadita who broke the silence. "I must turn off the road soon, James. And it is best, I think, that, as we must part, we part there. But ..." She gestured to a convenient olive grove.

Burke said nothing, but turned off the road and into the trees. Neither spoke as he unsaddled his horse and lay the saddle blanket on the ground. He watched as she undressed, drinking in her beauty, marvelling that he had known her. And then they lay down on the ground. She wrinkled her nose at the blanket. "I shall stink of horse."

Then she laughed and he laughed and they held each other and it was good.

Afterwards, he watched her ride away. She did not turn or wave.

At last he mounted his horse and set off to the west.

Chapter 9: Farewell and adieu to you, Spanish ladies

Sergeant William Brown was tired, but he was damned if he would show it. He had somehow managed to keep his section together, even as other sergeants had given up on men who, after weeks of retreat, were simply refusing to march any further. A quarter of the troops who had engaged the French at Talavera had died on the field or been too badly wounded to march with those who were now making their way as best they could back towards Portugal. Wellesley had found wagons – God alone knew how – to carry two thousand with them. Brown and his men avoided the wagons if they could, not just from a superstitious dread of marching with dying men, but from a natural aversion from the piteous cries of the wounded, jolting in unsprung carts, every rut in the road another source of agony. Thousands more had been left behind in the hospitals when the British withdrew. The Spanish had promised to protect the English wounded but had withdrawn themselves without a fight, abandoning the English to become prisoners of the French. No official announcement of this disaster had been made but, as is always the way with such news, it had percolated down from the Staff to the field officers to the NCOs. Wilkins and Peters would both have been among those taken prisoner and Sergeant Brown's section felt the loss personally.

By now every man in the army knew that they could expect no succour from the Spaniards they were ostensibly defending. Their resentment showed in their weary tread and the number of men claiming exhaustion and quietly falling out of the ranks. Normally Brown would have dismissed such men as malingerers at best and deserters at worst, but the frequent stops to bury those who had died on the march demonstrated that some, at least, could really go no further.

It was not helped by the fact that the men were constantly hungry. Any pretence that the Spaniards would supply the promised provisions had evaporated as the army began its long retreat. The

only meat they saw was a quarter of a pound of goat's flesh twice a week and, for an army that was known for its enthusiasm for roast beef, this seemed little better than starvation. To add insult to injury, the goats arrived alive and the slaughter and butchering was added to the duties of the troops. One of those ordered to assist with the slaughtering was one of the men Brown had inherited from Sergeant Collins. His name was Taylor, but he had no skill with needle and thread. Before joining the Army he had started an apprenticeship with a butcher, so he was better suited to the task than most. "In any case," he boasted, "I get to keep the guts."

The traditional right of soldier slaughtermen to keep the offal of the animals they killed was usually just a token acknowledgement of their efforts, but such was the hunger gripping Wellesley's men that goat offal could be sold for about double the usual price of the whole animal. Taylor's sudden affluence was not resented in the section, though, for he always kept some back and was happy to share it with his comrades. It meant that, while Sergeant Brown's men were hungry, none was actually starving.

"Keep your line, damn you."

He sounded fierce and swore and waved his pike, but he knew, and his men knew, that the fierceness was motivated simply by the need to keep them moving. They had to stay together, forcing themselves to keep step. "Don't walk, you idle bastards. March!" The alternative was to fall out of the line and face an uncertain future in a foreign country – and the French, they knew, were close behind.

William Brown had enjoyed being a regular soldier again. Despite the blood and the horror, he was already beginning to look back at Talavera as something he was glad to have lived through. He had followed the flag; he had served his country. He had fought in his red coat and done his duty. That had been proper soldiering. Not this, though: herding a dwindling flock of tired and hungry men to some sort of safety far to the west, where the French might hesitate to follow. There was no glory here – and as the Spanish still failed to provision them, and the bandits raided the baggage train in the night, he could not be sure why they were there at all. It couldn't be to fight. They were in no condition to fight anyone, and such ammunition as they had was being given to the Spanish, for

they needed the munitions carts to carry their sick. There were whispers of dysentery and William feared for the consequences if any disease were to take hold amongst men already so weakened.

He heard a horse trotting up the column. In more usual conditions, that would have been an everyday occurrence, but the horses were dying every day for want of food and all but the most senior officers walked, resting their mounts as much as they could.

The figure approaching was smartly dressed in the uniform of the Queen's Royal Regiment and the horse seemed well-fed and smartly turned out.

"You're supposed to salute, Sergeant Brown."

"You're supposed to be with the guerrillas, major."

Burke slipped from the saddle and fell into line with Brown's men. "I just got back. Changed into my uniform and came to find you." He looked over at the section who were carefully facing eyes front. "You've had a rough time, I understand."

"Nothing my men can't handle, sir."

Burke nodded. "So I see. Fine bunch of men, sergeant. They should make you proud."

"They do, sir."

He looked at them, forcing a swagger into their step because they saw their sergeant being given a hard time by an officer. He was proud of them. They had fought and they had suffered.

"And they've come through." Burke had finished the sentence Williams had started in his head. They had been together for years, but he was still astonished at how well the major knew him.

"We're not home yet, sir."

Burke smiled. "Actually, I bring news about that. I've been with General Hill. He tells me that we're two days off Merida. There are proper provisions there and the army will rest and resupply. The word will be coming down officially later today, but I thought you'd like to know."

At first William said nothing. He looked at his men, exhausted and shabby, but marching doggedly on and then at Burke, smart in his uniform, looking as if he had arrived back from an afternoon riding out with hounds. There was a still unhealed cut on his forehead, but otherwise he seemed untouched by the war.

Burke gave an almost imperceptible nod at William.

"Thank you," said William.

"I imagine there will be new orders for us when we get to Merida."

"So long as I see the men safe there."

"Absolutely," said Burke. "Absolutely. I'll walk with you a while on the way, if that's all right with you, sergeant."

"You'd be very welcome, sir."

They continued on their way to Merida. Twenty men and their sergeant in dusty tunics that were once red. A stranger might look askance at the sight of an officer in immaculate uniform falling into step alongside them.

Sergeant William Brown and Major James Burke didn't think it odd at all.

HISTORICAL NOTE

James Burke (as far as we know) never served in the Peninsula. His adventures here are based on those of another spy: Sir John Waters. Captain Gronow, in the unfailingly entertaining *Reminiscences of Captain Gronow* says, "He could assume the character of Spaniards of every degree and station, so as to deceive the most acute of those whom he delighted to imitate." His detailed knowledge of religious matters is particularly commented on ("He would converse with the friar upon the number of Ave Marias and Pater-nosters which could lay a ghost,") although Captain Gronow doesn't mention his disguising himself as a priest. Burke's disguise as a ghost is taken directly from what is claimed to be a true story about Sir John.

I've put in a reference to Burke sailing on *HMS Statira*. I can't say that she ever sailed from Tilbury to Lisbon (she probably didn't), but she certainly escorted convoys from Guernsey to Portugal. Captain Boys was a distant ancestor of my wife's best friend at school and I am grateful to Deborah Boys for sight of his letters home. Sadly, most of the detail was edited out. (The bane of historical novelists is that you can't keep in your wonderful research findings that don't move the plot forward.) It was still the kind of background detail that can make this period come alive for me.

The details of Wellesley's march and the battle of Talavera are taken from Sir William Napier's *History of the War in the Peninsula*. Looking at the map (and checking against other accounts of travelling that route) the Army seems to have travelled exceptionally fast, but Napier should know what he was talking about. I have used Napier's spellings for town names: this is often slightly different from what appears on a modern atlas.

I am very grateful to Rob Griffith (who has also, entirely coincidentally, written fiction based on James Burke) for correcting some details of life in battle. He's a re-enactor and, like many re-enactors, knows an incredible amount of detail about the drill of the period.

Another expert in the Peninsular Wars explained that I could not have a padre discussing theology with Burke as Hill's command had no padres. It's the sort of detail I love, however much rewriting it generated. Very many thanks to Gareth Rennie for that gem and all the other advice and information he helped me with.

Thanks also to Robert Pocock of 'Campaigns and Culture' who organised my trip to visit Spain and Portugal, which has given some insight into the realities of campaigning there. He has also corrected some of my worst geographical errors, though I am sure that plenty remain. I was famously unable to find my way from the town of Talavera to the battlefield, so it would be unwise to rely overmuch on my book for route planning (though it's a lovely part of the world to get lost in).

I'm sure there are still errors in my military details and I can say with confidence that they are all mine.

The guerrillas are usually represented as heroes. Charles Esdaile's revisionist history, *Fighting Napoleon*, suggests that for every El Gato there were several El Jefe's. El Gato's exploits are entirely fictional.

William's opinion of the condition of footwear in the British Army and the importance of cobblers is very much in line with the experience of Rifleman Harris, a soldier-cobbler of the Napoleonic Wars whose memoirs were published as *The Recollections of Rifleman Harris*. I recommend that book to anyone interested in the experiences of the fighting man of the time.

The account of the Spanish flight the night before Talavera is accurate. Some French light cavalry had been reconnoitring the Allied lines and come across some of Cuesta's troops. Rather than just turn back with the news, they had fired their pistols at them. They were probably as surprised as anyone when the Spaniards, most of whom were well out of range, all returned fire with their muskets. Most of the Spanish army can have had no idea what they were even firing at but, hearing what they thought to be the noise of conflict all round them, they had panicked and broken. Ten thousand infantry and all the artillery fled to the rear. The artillerymen carried off their horses, the infantry threw away their arms and the adjutant general was supposed to have been one of the foremost of the fugitives. Even Cuesta had started to retreat and the

situation was saved only when General Wellesley, who was fortunately at that end of the line, pulled British troops into the gap, holding back the French long enough for the Spanish to recover and make some sort of defence. The French, who can never have expected the success they achieved, were content to ride away. Events such as this and the failure of the Spanish to provide the promised supplies to British troops (the food shortages I describe are, if anything, an understatement) go some way to explaining the contempt in which many British soldiers held their Spanish allies.

Flour dust is, indeed, highly explosive. My son, Captain Michael Williams, has studied explosives in his role with the Royal Logistic Corps and it was his account of the 1981 Bird's custard factory explosion that gave me the idea. I made the original explosion much less impressive and he told me that I needed to write it up, not for dramatic effect but because my blast was unrealistically small. He showed me a selection of photographs that he had seen during his studies which convinced me that the explosion I have described is, if anything, on the small side.

The account of the retreat after Talavera fairly represents the condition of the Army at the time. It is ironic that Wellington was made a Viscount (Viscount Wellington of Talavera) as a reward for this battle. It could reasonably be claimed as a victory on the day, because the French were forced to yield the field, and the government desperately needed a victory for political purposes. Strategically, though, the battle is more realistically viewed as a defeat. The ground was ceded to the French as the Anglo Portuguese army retreated and the Spanish army under Cuesto was in no condition to hold it. British losses in men, horses and materiel were substantial.

I am very grateful to Jane Jackson, the author of several historical novels herself, for her comments on the book, which has been vastly improved as a result. It would probably have been even better if I'd listened to more of them.

Finally, very many thanks to Marcus Cribb for stopping me from putting the wrong period uniform on the cover and to the 3/95th Living History Society for providing photographs of the right ones.

Burke will be back …

I hope you have enjoyed *Burke in the Peninsula*. This is the first book I've written about James Burke for a while. The original three have just been republished: I hope you will have a look at them if you haven't already. They haven't been written in chronological order, so this one actually starts off directly after the events of the first book, *Burke in the Land of Silver*. The next one, due out later this year, takes us back to Burke's very first foray into the world of espionage in Ireland in the run-up to the Irish Rebellion of 1798.

If you want to learn more about the books and the world that James Burke lived in, I recommend that you have a look at my website: http://tomwilliamsauthor.co.uk where you can sign up to my newsletter and be the first to hear about new books. You can also follow me on Facebook (https://www.facebook.com/AuthorTomWilliams) and Twitter (https://twitter.com/TomCW99).

I'm sure you've seen notes from authors before asking that you review their books on Amazon, but it really makes a huge difference. Without a big marketing budget (and hardly any authors are given those), Amazon reviews are crucial to getting books to an audience. If you have enjoyed *Burke in the Peninsula* and would like other people to have a chance to enjoy it too, it would be so helpful if you could write a few words on Amazon. Just a sentence or two saying that you liked it and you think others might is all it takes – we're not talking about the Times Literary Supplement here. I do read all my reviews (writers who say they don't are almost certainly fibbing) and I love getting them.

Thank you again for reading.

OTHER BOOKS BY TOM WILLIAMS

James Burke, spy

Burke in the Land of Silver

Burke and the Bedouin

Burke at Waterloo

The Williamson Papers
(Adventures in the age of Empire)

The White Rajah

Cawnpore

Back Home

Contemporary Urban Fantasy

Dark Magic